DAUGHTERS OF SILENCE

DAUGHTERS OF SILENCE

A NOVEL

Rebecca Fisseha

Edited by Bethany Gibson.
Excerpt from "Käthe Kollwitz" in *The Collected Poems of Muriel Rukeyser,*
copyright © 2005 by Muriel Rukeyser. Reprinted by permission of ICM Partners.
Cover design by Julie Scriver with images from Light Field Studios,
iStock.com (figure); dmitrlch, Adobestock.com (wall texture);
and valeriya_sh, Shutterstock.com (pattern).
Page design by Julie Scriver.
Printed in Canada.
10 9 8 7 6 5 4 3 2 1

Library and Archives Canada Cataloguing in Publication

Title: Daughters of silence : a novel / Rebecca Fisseha.
Names: Fisseha, Rebecca, 1980- author.
Identifiers: Canadiana (print) 20190090928 | Canadiana (ebook) 20190090944 |
ISBN 9781773101026 (softcover) | ISBN 9781773101033 (EPUB) |
ISBN 9781773101040 (Kindle)
Classification: LCC PS8611.I8525 D38 2019 | DDC C813/.6—dc23

Goose Lane acknowledges the generous support of the Government of Canada, the Canada Council for the Arts, and the Government of New Brunswick.

Goose Lane Editions
500 Beaverbrook Court, Suite 330
Fredericton, New Brunswick
CANADA E3B 5X4
www.gooselane.com

For Zeni,

Mimi,

and all who survive.

What would happen if one woman told the truth about
her life?
The world would split open

—Muriel Rukeyser, “Käthe Kollwitz”

ONE

The announcement comes during down time, after duty free, and before the last meal service. I am preparing a tray of plastic cups for my turn to walk the cabin with the hourly offering of water. Our in-flight manager hangs up the interphone, looking none too pleased.

"We're diverting to Addis Ababa. Vienna airport is closed," she says. She explains to us, the crew in the galley, that ash from the eruption of a volcanic mountain with some unpronounceable name in Iceland has blocked the whole jet stream.

"Why wasn't this mentioned during pre-flight briefing in Johannesburg?" I say. An act of God was not what I had in mind when I wished for an extended absence from Toronto, relief from Le'ul's relentless brotherly love.

"I'm sure we'll be in and out in no time. Hey, you're originally from there, right Dessie?" she says, reading my name tag and pronouncing it "DC," instead of calling me what I go by at work, D.

I smile, picking at the label of the water bottle. "Well Barb, you know the expression. You can take the girl out of..."

"Ethiopia?" she says, helpfully, and waits for me to deliver the punchline, if that's what it is. When I don't, she supplies it. "But you can't take Ethiopia out of the girl, eh?"

The flight attendants laugh. I join. That's what we do: smile, laugh. The cabin is our living room, the air suffused with cheer, the passengers our personal guests. For days after a trip, I can't wipe that smile off my face. Even after I do, the lines remain.

The captain broadcasts the news via the PA system. As soon as she signs off, Barb dispatches us into the twin aisles of the widebody, armed with smiles as bright as the midday sun, to soothe passengers' anxious concerns.

So many planes are on approach to make unscheduled landings at Addis Ababa Bole International Airport that we have to stay in a holding pattern over the city for what seems a long time, but is not long enough for me. Eventually we land. While we wait for further instructions, I look out the window. Seeing the word የኢትዮጲያ on the bodies of the green-yellow-red-tailed planes suckling at the gates on home soil, I feel stirred, as if I'd come across a favourite childhood toy.

We are going to either resume our journey or disembark and wait it out in the terminal. The scenario no one wants—least of all me—is an overnight stay. I console myself that if it's the latter, at least I will be with my crew, probably at the Hilton. There won't be time to do anything other than sleep, eat, wash, and fly right back out.

The captain informs Barb that we will disembark. In the commotion of gathering in the terminal, no one else notices the tourism posters advertising *Dessie: Heart of Ethiopia*. I wonder why a city, which seems to offer nothing but a lake and wildlife, has been elevated to the rank of Axum, Gonder, Lalibela, the standard tourist attractions. If anyone asked me about my namesake, I would share the only two facts I know about it: my mother spent time there when she was young, and she never forgot the bone-shattering cold there during kiremt.

"Well, at least for you, you can see your people now," Barb says. Then, she remembers, and turns sombre. "Especially at this time of mourning for your mother."

What a lucky coincidence, the crew all agree, patting my shoulder. I nod and smile. Yes, it will be such a wonderful surprise. They mean well. Though we might not get scheduled to fly together again for months, even years, when we're out on a trip, crew are family. But I know that my mother's death, a little over a month ago, is the least of their concerns. With each development in the diversion of the flight, their mood has fallen. Who the fuck wants to be stuck in Addis Ababa? Not me either, I want to shout at them.

"Just keep your phone near you. I'll call you the minute we get the all clear," Barb says. I watch the Hilton shuttle drive away with the crew in it while I stand between my suitcase and tote. I want the van to reverse up the ramp from the terminal, come back for me. But the van descends into the parking lot and disappears around a corner.

I am in Ethiopia again, all of a sudden, as an adult, on my own. I feel panicky, as if there's a bowl of liquid trembling inside me, threatening to spill over. Am I now to just show up at my grandfather's house nineteen years after I told him that I would be gone only for four? Worse, let him believe that I am here intentionally, to grieve Ema with him, as would a good granddaughter?

I look up. Kiremt is not for a couple more months, so the mid-April sky is cloudless. Even if we were in the middle of the rainy season, the skies ominous with clouds, who would believe that hail could happen here unless they saw it? Ice pellets the size of marbles really do drop from this equatorial sky. How I used to wish they would smash through our rooftop and force a stop to what was happening inside my house.

I amble down the ramp like an exotic red bird, rolling my suitcase and tote amidst disoriented, frustrated passengers clutching hotel coupons. I follow the first man who says he has a taxi for me. This should be a dream, because I am not supposed to be here. But I'm not asleep against the window seat in the back row of an airplane cabin. I am wide awake, in the back of a yellow-and-green taxi sedan. Kidist Mariam, the bestower of kisses, is watching me from her sticker on the top right corner of the windshield.

The taxi driver wants to know where to. I open my mouth to tell him to go to the post office, the main landmark of my grandfather's neighbourhood. I trust that I will remember the rest of the route to Babbaye's house once we're in that area, which is one of the few parts of Addis Ababa I know by heart. My only grandparent is eighty-seven now. Last time Ema came here to see him, almost two years ago, I had wondered if she ever feared that one day soon she would be going to Ethiopia to bury, not visit, her father. So much for that.

But I'm not ready for Babbaye. I need to gather myself first, before I go to his house where I'll be met with tears, where I will face his double sorrow over Ema's death and the place of her burial. Whether for hours or a day, spending time with Babbaye—also the person who had refused me the one time I did want to come back to Ethiopia—is going to be hard work.

Taking my pause to mean I didn't understand him, the driver asks me again, in English, where to. In Amharic, I instruct him to take me to the Ghion Hotel, where Ema used to stay when she came for work. Maybe I will be lucky enough to get room 521. The room Ema always booked. In Toronto, I've continued my new routine of tracing her footsteps, going where she would have gone, seeking out places where I might still feel her presence.

Even if I'm not able to get 521, I'll stand outside her door, as if I were again a little girl whose mother, wanting some peace and quiet, has banished her child from the room. I will wait for her outside her door. When I imagine she's come out, I will follow her downstairs. We'll have a glass of red wine at the bar, a sunset stroll in the garden. We'll sit on the edge of the pool, swirling the water with our feet while she has a cigarette, careful to keep the smoke away from children, rubbing the ash into the stone.

I sigh, sink further into the back seat, and lift my heels out of my shoes. From my purse, I pull out Ema's pack of Djarums to sniff them, like an ex-smoker managing her cravings. The driver glances at me in the rear-view. I suspect he's thinking, She's habesha, yes, but in that blood-red uniform, not an Ethiopian Airlines girl. No, I'm not one of those girls who wears forest green, as if they had sprouted out of this lush land.

•••

Babbaye had interrogated me about this land at the farewell party for my family, the day before we left Ethiopia. I was eight years old. The party had to be at his house because our own house was empty, ready for tenants. He called me over to where he sat, pinned my arms at my sides so that I stood as rigid as a proper Little Patriot, and asked me the second impossible question of my life.

"My child, tinishwa arbegna, how do you feel about leaving this land?"

Land, I knew, meant the whole of Ethiopia, which I'd only ever seen on a paper map, but which Babbaye had walked across. Or so it seemed to me. My head was full of the stories my father had told me about Babbaye's valour as an arbegna during the five years of resistance to the Talyan—as my grandfather says "Italian"—occupation in the thirties. During those years, Aba said the Patriots became known for possessing a spirit of bloodthirsty, come-what-may defiance toward foreign interference. They let their hair grow into unkempt Afros because they had vowed to cut it only when Ethiopia was deloused. They had developed a lion's palate for raw meat because to make fire was to betray their location in the bush and mountain hideouts from which they launched attacks on the Talyans, making them regret the day they dared to pursue empire.

Babbaye had called me his little arbegna since I was five years old, but my Ethiopia was much smaller than his. My Ethiopia was made up of the patches of land on which stood his house, our house, my school, my parents' workplaces, the Bole airport park and observation deck, the Ghion pool, and Sodere Resort. To these places, I had none of the deep attachment I knew Babbaye had to his Ethiopia. I was attached to him. *He* was my land. About leaving him, I felt heavy with the weight of emptiness, like the rooms in our house.

But that was no kind of answer. Because in those days the adults, Babbaye more than anyone, cared deeply about the actual land. Just four months before the party, on the twentieth of Ginbot, Babbaye's enemy's enemy had at last conquered Addis Ababa and sent the dictator—the face of the Terror—running. It was a new time, a fresh start that began with the decision to sift the land for what was left of the dead. Diggers clawed splintered bones and tattered cloth out of the disturbed soil. Babbaye was melancholy. The hopes, whispered by his friends and relations, that the remains of his six sons would be among the exhumed had so far remained just that: whispered hopes. Now his youngest, my mother, his only child not disappeared by the Terror, was leaving with her family.

So, in answer to Babbaye's question of how I felt about leaving this land, I repeated the promise Ema and Aba had been saying to everyone since our departure was announced.

"We will be back after four years, Babbaye."

He asked the question again.

"I'll come back."

He shook his head slowly, like a long-suffering but infinitely patient teacher. I opened my mouth to say, I want to stay, but started crying instead. The festivities continued. Crying was expected. Someone sitting next to Babbaye said even a bride should weep on her wedding day.

I wished Babbaye and I were really how we must have looked: an old man and a little girl, the last of his bloodline, struggling to say goodbye. Rather than a girl forced to keep giving her favourite adult the wrong answer because he didn't know how to ask her the right question. All the talk in those days of new freedom was about the dead, known and unknown. I wished Babbaye would recognize me as one of his unknown dead. But the three years of my terror were never on the news and my breathing body was there for all to see.

When I started bawling, Babbaye seemed satisfied. My crumpled face and wet cheeks gave him the answer he wanted. He pulled me close and rested my head on his shoulder, wiping away my tears.

•••

The taxi driver warns me that we're almost at Ghion Hotel, probably remembering my earlier indecision. He's read me well. If I were to go to Ghion now, at some point between walking to the front desk, getting a room, and making my way to the elevator, I feel sure that someone in that perfumed, glittering lobby would recognize me. Instantly they would know that I am doing the unthinkable: I have arrived in my birth country, my mother laid to rest in outside-country, and I have not gone to my grandfather's house. Someone will know whose grandchild I am, and will call Babbaye's house to tell on me. They won't say anything to me directly, of course. That's not how it works.

I lean forward and redirect the driver to the old post office, near Babbaye's area. I must sound unsure of that destination too, because the man asks me to call my people. I refuse. He insists. "Use my phone. That way, you'll have my number."

I try to sound certain. "Once we are by the post office, I'll remember the way." I sit back, my heart pounding. I am going to Babbaye's.

"And can you slow down when you pass Foreign Affairs?" I say. I want to catch a glimpse of Ema's office, at least. Former office.

"I can't slow there. Only stop to drop off or pick up."

When we drive past, I understand why. Flimsy gates that used to be wide open have been replaced by solid black iron ones stencilled with the yellow star of the Ethiopian flag. In front of them are concrete guardrails reinforced with barbed wire. In front of all that, cold-eyed soldiers in blue fatigues stand, hands gripping their rifles. Only the vine, flowing thickly down the high walls and gate pillars, is free. Of the four floors of the honeycomb-shaped ministry building, the topmost windows are visible, but not Ema's, where I had stuck that torn scrap of my letter to my second grade pen pal.

Ema wasn't supposed to have ended up at Foreign Affairs. She was all set for a career in academia alongside my father at Addis Ababa University. But Babbaye's enemy informed her that she was welcome to serve in the ministry as a junior legal advisor. She grew to love the work, but in those days, when the tension and paranoia of the Terror was still a reality, receiving the message of "welcome" was really an order to report for duty, which she had to obey.

•••

Once I see the post office, I guide the driver to Babbaye's easily, warming up my Amharic by saying the directions in my head first. He parks beside a turnoff onto a rocky unpaved road, and searches his pockets.

"Not a bad ride. Some Adisaba roads make you do the eskista," he says, doing a little dance like a Harlem shake.

"And not a sheep in sight," I say, remembering Isak's tirades about what ferenjoch chose to write about on returning to the West after they'd visited here. *You'd think they were on a mission to locate farm animals.*

"We ate them all for Fasika," the driver says, laughing. "If you had come three weeks earlier you would have been fighting them for a taxi." He holds out a battered business card over his shoulder: *Wondwossen (Wondu). Driver. Anytime Day or Night.*

"Thanks," I say, reaching for it.

"No, add my number in your contacts."

It takes me a moment to catch on. Maybe he can't afford to give these out willy-nilly. Could be his last one. I do as he says, grateful for the chance to dally here.

"Nice slogan."

"Ya, our kind we don't sleep much!"

I pay him in American dollars, with tip. He insists on carrying my bags and escorting me to Babbaye's gate. We pick our way down the rocky, muddy road, along Babbaye's cinder block wall that is topped by broken glass embedded in cement. Babbaye's red metal gate, and the pedestrian door built-in on its right side, are closed.

"Go back, Wondu. You're not parked well," I say.

"No trouble." He puts down my bags, and bangs loudly on the door. We wait, studying what's left of the peeling paint, a pattern resembling the map of some unknown planet with red continents and metallic grey oceans.

A tall housemaid opens the small door in the gate. She is dressed all in black. An inverted netela is draped over her shoulders. She looks irritated, as though this is her house and we're bothering her. As soon as she sees me, she flings the door wide.

"Dyesiye!" she exclaims joyfully, like she'd been on the brink of giving up hope that I'd ever come. Her rural accent adds a third syllable, making my name sound like the Amharic word for "my happiness." She steps over the threshold, throws her arms around me. I have no idea who she is.

She releases me and falls at my feet, nearly pushing me off balance. From the ground, she wails at the stones, slams herself against them, questioning God's judgment, calling out Ema's name. "Why, why, why did Igziabher do this? Where is she? Zimita!"

Wondu calmly intervenes, trying to raise her up. She slips out of his grip and back into her dramatics, pounding her chest on each word. I am not sure which is heartfelt, her happiness in the first seconds of seeing me or this outburst immediately after. Wondu alternates between consoling, commanding her to stand up, then pulling her when she won't. Their movements look almost choreographed. I hope he's not copping a feel.

"Say her name," the woman intones, slapping the backs of her hands on the ground with each phrase. "Call to her. She won't answer you. Try. She won't respond. Where is she? Is she here? Is she with you? Igizabher should have taken me. Why spare me? Show her to me. Such a mother, such a daughter she was, such a daughter you are. I know she is with you. I know you have brought her."

"Get up. Stop it. Enough," Wondu says.

This woman is everything I've wished I could be from the moment I heard my mother "didn't make it." So this is where my words and my body have been. But what right has she to so much sorrow? It's as if she's using this occasion to shed tears stored up for somebody else.

Passersby stop. They cover their mouths, or hold hands over their hearts while mumbling phrases of condolence. Nefs yimar, nefs yimar, beseeching God's mercy for my mother's soul, then move on as abruptly as they stopped. Some add salt to the wound by naming Ema's brothers, who preceded their sister to the Creator. One man says nothing. He steps around us to enter the courtyard. Following his cue, I pick up my tote and step over the wailing housemaid. That shuts her up.

Wondu walks in behind me with my suitcase. The woman follows us, sniffling, dabbing her eyes with the black edge of her netela. We walk single file down a flagstone pathway, through a leafy courtyard lined by coffee, banana, and lemon trees. The pathway splits in two in front of the stone steps that lead up to the porch running the length of Babbaye's house, which is built on a high stone foundation. A second branch of the pathway, passing in front of Babbaye's mefakiya bushes, leads around the right side of the house. On lower ground, to the left of Babbaye's house, there is a row of attached homes, their entrances obscured behind enormous hydrangea plants.

I put down my tote at the foot of the porch steps. Wondu, his work of delivering me safely completed, does the same with my suitcase, glances at the housemaid, and jogs back to the gate. The woman stands back, looking star-struck, as if I'm a legendary person whom her friends will never believe she actually met. She regards me with her whole body, the way you stare only if you know the person doesn't know you're staring. Except I do, and she's not in the least deterred.

"Who are you?" I ask, in case she is another distant "cousin" from what's left of Aba's side, way out in Harrar in the east—none of whom I've ever met—which might explain why she is so devastated by Ema's death.

"I am a worker of this house."

"Since how much time?"

"Some years."

She must know me from photos that Babbaye has on his living-room shelves. The top row was photos of the departed—his six sons, his wife. The one below was just for photos of me, one taken at my baptism, another at my kindergarten graduation. My parents must have sent him more recent ones. I am touched that he may have kept me up there all these years.

"And your name is what?"

A smile precedes her answer. "Gela."

She clearly enjoys saying her own name, as if she picked it herself. At the gate, Wondu is having trouble with the latch. "Please don't stand here. Go inside," she says to me, as she goes to open the gate for Wondu.

I am impressed by a name at once so basic—simply meaning *body*—yet sensual. Wondu looks impressed too, as much by Gela's profile as by her door-opening abilities.

Gela returns. She picks up my tote. I climb the steps to the orange-tiled porch. The once-white ceiling is now rust-coloured and sagging. I stop and turn to Gela.

"Do you do crying or shouting to everyone who visits?"

"What can I do?"

"You shouldn't give people fright."

She is older than me, but she doesn't challenge this scolding from her junior, because I am family, and that gives me the right.

Hanging on the stained beige porch wall, above the door, is a black frame with an eight-by-ten of Ema's most recent official picture, taken seven years ago in 2003, when she became consul general in Toronto. Around her neck in a loose side knot she wears her silk print of Afewerk Tekle's painting *King Solomon Meets the Queen of Sheba.* Her look is one of grim resignation. A half-inch frown line sits boldly between her plucked and pencilled eyebrows, confirmation of a hunch, which shows only faintly in her wedding portrait, that life would turn out to be no laughing matter.

The double doors leading from the porch directly into the living room are open. Below me, Gela sighs broken-heartedly, looking at my tote as if it is a baby that has finally dropped off to sleep. Her forehead and chin are scarred where there once were tattoos, typical markers of a rural Christian. She endured having crucifixes needled in, then removed when she came to the city. By heat or blade, who knows. I think of the daisy that I carved on my inner wrist with the tip of a compass when I was ten. That mark is so faded only I know it is there.

I am grateful that, unlike this woman, Ema's scars from her surgeries were all out of sight. She had, however, developed an unconscious habit of lightly scratching the back of her thigh over her clothes, where the first irregularly shaped mole was removed. Her gesture was a constant reminder of the unseen scar.

"She is here now. Igziabher yimesgen," Gela says, praising God while looking up at my mother's picture, then at me. I hurry into the living room before she begins another round of her hysterics.

TWO

The living room is bare, just a dizzying expanse of zigzag parquet. Stiff-backed chairs line the walls. There is one side table, at which four old men sit huddled, pens in hand, marking up papers. Babbaye sits alone at the spot of my interrogation nineteen years ago. I hurry to him and hide my face in his old neck, what I have wanted to do since the day I rode away from that red gate for the last time. He lets me cry my longing for what is empty to be filled, for what is missing to be replaced. When he's deemed that I have wept enough for now, he puts his hands on my cheeks, his lips between my eyes, and kisses me.

Babbaye trembles with the effort of maintaining a proud bearing. His uncombed hair, his beard, are as full as that of young arbegna. He still wears his green khaki suit with the rigid brown leather belt, and his extendable metal cane with the foam handle is, as ever, hooked on the armrest of his chair. His skin is the same deep, etched brown of a rifle stock, his smell the clean earthiness of Ethiopia.

There's the business of living, and then there's this, coming face-to-face with your origin, which makes everything go quiet, as if the years you've been apart never happened, or they mean nothing.

"Where is my child?"

"I'm here, Babbaye."

"Where is Tobya?"

I break eye contact. So brilliant is his grief, it's like looking directly at the sun. I've never heard anyone refer to Ema by what I know is her old name, Tobya, the folk way of saying "Ethiopia."

On the far wall of the long, wide living room, next to the back door, there is a huge colour photograph hanging in a frame as big as the black void of the fireplace beneath. A single white candle burns on the mantelpiece. Tobya is the young woman in that picture: Ema while she still had a gap between her top front teeth, rocking a seventies blowout, large hoop earrings, and a wide-lapel floral shirt. Only because of that picture can I be sure that my mother was once a carefree girl.

"Haven't you brought my Tobya?"

Oh no, not this again. When Aba, Le'ul, and I were packing Ema's belongings at the residence, about three weeks ago, Aba had told us how Babbaye hadn't asked *if* we were bringing Ema's body back, but *when*.

Under a chair in a corner, I see our old blue rotary phone, the thing I've heard Babbaye's voice through for nearly two decades. I could just call Aba on it now, have him tell Babbaye what Ema wanted for her burial, what she *actually* said.

The four old men pause in their writing to listen for my answer. These, Babbaye's oldest friends, must have been the ones Aba said had come here to Babbaye's house, at dawn, the day after Ema died, to tell Babbaye the merdo of Ema's death.

There is no sign of the photos of Ema's grave at Scarborough Bluffs Cemetery. I had emailed them to Aba for

Le'ul to doctor, before they were sent to Babbaye. Aba must not have sent them. One should have been tucked into the corner of Tobya's breezy portrait, to complete her story.

Where Ema rests now, it is utterly dark, in a box deep inside the Earth. Though in my mind I see her in there clearly, as if she's asleep under a spotlight, intact, despite what I'm told happens to flesh and skin after death.

Haven't you brought my Tobya? is not what I wish it was: a grieving father posing the same question again and again, knowing the answer will never change, because he can't *not* ask. No, it is a real question with only one right answer.

Yes I have.

But I haven't. I don't have the right answer for Babbaye. I have brought only myself. My useless self. Although I'm welcome, I'm not who is wanted. I look down, wishing I were not here, wishing that on the day I heard the merdo from Aba, I hadn't taken it for granted that we would return Ema to Babbaye, that she would be picked up by a funeral director at Bole, and buried in her own land with her own people. I want to punch myself for having been so oblivious, and then so compliant.

I should re-enact Gela's theatrics at the gate, demonstrate my sorrow in the proper way. The room has been emptied out for such a show, after all. Not just to reflect the starkness of loss, which is how it seemed to me at first glance. It is a stage for interpreting grief. For women to howl, spin, fall, keen. To beat their chests, pound clutched fists the size of their hearts hard enough to splinter the flat bone, punish their flesh for powerlessness against death, and their unworthy hearts for the audacity to keep on beating.

But I don't feel any impulse to move or make a sound. My fists are clenched but my arms stay limp, in a half-formed cultural instinct. I am not going to risk falling on my knees and hurting myself. Barb might call at any moment. I will my phone to ring and for it to be her, telling me that the jet stream is clear of ash. It's time to go. It was never time to come. Ghion Hotel never seemed so appealing, so much of a haven, as now.

Gela enters, carrying my bags, from the porch. She puts them in the larger of two adjacent rooms across from us, the bedroom where all Babbaye's children slept until, after the Terror, Ema slept alone.

Gela exits through the back door, which connects the living and dining area to the alleyway between the main house and the service quarters. Babbaye's gaze leaves me, as do his hands. The men pick up their Bics and resume their work, understanding that the Shaleqa will not get what he wants. *Yet,* their postures seem to warn. To everyone else my grandfather will always be the Shaleqa. By the time of his retirement from the Ethiopian army, Babbaye had risen to the rank of Commander of a Thousand. Only Ema called him Abbaye—father. What I call him, Babbaye, is a childhood mispronunciation, which stuck.

I try to see the papers the men are scribbling on. Based on what the cover page says, it is a memorial program in the making, for Ema's Forty Day. So the tezkar is a real thing. Not another tradition Aba made up so he could get Le'ul and me together.

Today is day thirty-six since Ema's ireft. Rest, the Amharic euphemism for death. As if it is really a rest between this life and whatever comes after, a stopover where the dead decide if they want to travel on or turn back.

The portrait on the cover page is the same one of Tobya on the wall. Below it, *Consul General Zimita Tessema Gedlu.* The

Ethiopian calendar dates are written first: *Miyazia 27, 1951–Megabit 5, 2003 (May 5, 1958–March 14, 2010).*

Noting my interest, one of the old men gives me some of the pages to read. I remember him. He's the professor Aba was TA for at Addis Ababa University, the one who got Aba the gig tutoring Ema when she returned to Addis Ababa from Dessie. She had fallen behind in her studies, having been away in Dessie to hide from the Terror. If not for this old prof, I would never have come into this world.

On the program's inside front cover, the same portrait of Tobya appears again in black and white. Her official photo is on the inside back cover. Her beginning and end. There are more captioned photos on the pages in between. *Zimita Tessema Gedlu and Mesfin Endale Getachew in front of the Institute of Ethiopian Studies at Addis Ababa University 1973 (1980). Wedding portrait 1975 (1982).*

An *embassy function in Vienna 1995* shows Ema in a strapless ball gown; Aba looks more like her dad than her husband in his rented tuxedo. I'm amused to see *Zimita Tessema in front of the Axum Obelisk in Rome 1996.* There are many photos of Ema moving from the edges to the centre of grouped dignitaries as she rose through the diplomatic ranks—at the *UN General Assembly at the United Nations Headquarters in New York City 1998*; *presenting her credentials to Canada's Governor General 2003.*

The back cover is a family picture, the only recent one, taken on Ema's birthday in 1995 on the lawn of our Vienna apartment building, days before the move to Rome. Sun, cake, tray of champagne. I wear a Disney princess smile, displaying the exact opposite of the terror I feel inside. Le'ul is scowling darkly. Between us, our parents look content.

In none of the photos is the woman I know as Ema.

The rest of the pages are text, in Amharic and English. The prof explains that Ema's programs are to be given as keepsakes to guests at the memorial gathering on the Forty, and sent by post to mourners abroad. He is glad that I can still speak Amharic, save for the occasional fumbled syntax or mispronounced word. As for reading, I admit that I can get through a passage if I really have to.

He understands. "We spend too long to get to the point," he says. "Very often the reading hasn't been worth the trouble of enduring paragraph-long sentences."

"So I should just skip to the end?" I ask, to see if he remembers our old joke. When Aba used to take me to campus to show me off, this man loved to ask me to recite my ABCs, knowing I would skip right to Z, just for a laugh.

"I recommend it!" he says. I interpret this as permission to ignore the Amharic text altogether. The English translations are formal messages of condolence to the family from colleagues, the university, diplomats, and the ministry.

Along the bottom of every page is a Bible quote in Amharic that I don't read so much as recognize—Ema's epitaph, which will be engraved on her tombstone in both languages. It's not just the dates there are two versions of apparently, because I see there's a discrepancy between the Amharic and English versions of the epitaph. The one word Aba had worried over, sitting on the bench beside me at Scarborough Bluffs Cemetery, the day we had gone there to photograph Ema's grave for Babbaye. *Charity* versus *love.* We had chosen *charity*; here the translation says *love.* But I am not going to be the one to point out the difference to the scribes when I don't know if it's intentional or not.

Aba's poem of lament, which Uncle A B Z tells me my

father co-wrote with him via email, spans three pages. Since Uncle A B Z is the one who introduced Ema and Aba, Aba wanted his input, in case he was forgetting crucial details of their early days. Dear Aba, always making sure his references were impeccable. When did he find the time to write all this, I wonder, while failing to send the photos and sidestepping Babbaye's requests for Ema's body?

The poem, depressing even in English, ends with Aba confessing that he married the much younger Ema because he felt confident that he'd never have to endure a world without her in it. Like Tilahun's slow jam played at practically every habesha wedding, where the singer basically implores his beloved to outlive him.

I'm caught off guard to see my own name, Dessie Mesfin Endale, at the bottom of one short poem.

"I wrote this?"

"No," Uncle A B Z says. "Usually, the funeral service supplies fixed poems into which the names of the departed are inserted. But yours, the Shaleqa himself composed."

I muscle through the heightened Amharic of the poem. Once I absorb, on the umpteenth rereading, the sentiments Babbaye has expressed for me, I find the metaphors, even the rhythms, are apt. If I thought grand thoughts like he does, had I never left Ethiopia, I would have come up with no better. I hear the voice of my parallel self, the one Babbaye could have made real if he'd taken me in when I wanted to return. That daughter could have written this.

Uncle A B Z says, "Are there parts of it you desire to change? It is not too late to write your own words."

"I can't say it better." I give the pages back to him. What I would add are resentful thoughts I am not supposed to have toward my own mother anyway, now that she is among the irreproachable departed, about her burial forcing me to stay in a place I don't want to be.

I feel new tears coming on, the kind I cry just for Ema. I can accept black-framed photos of other people's mothers hung over a doorframe or above a lit candle on a mantelpiece or printed on a tezkar program. Names of other people's mothers can be wailed to the sky. But I can't accept any of it happening for my mother.

To calm myself, and because I don't trust Babbaye has any more hugs left for me, I escape to Ema's bedroom. In there, the smaller pieces of furniture and the decorations from the living room are piled in a high mess on the bed frame. The mattress is on the floor. Ema is everywhere in between; she has perfumed the air with her tizita. I wade through the memory of her to the open window, which overlooks the courtyard and Babbaye's mefakiya garden directly beneath. I open my phone. There's nothing from Barb.

But, there is a text from Isak.

Was your flight diverted too? Where are you?

A firework of hot joy explodes in my chest. He's been keeping track of me. I text back.

In Addis!

I watch my phone until the text confirms as sent. I know better than to stand waiting for it to show as read. This is how it goes between Isak and me when I am in places with bad networks. How it used to go. The simplest conversations took us hours to complete.

I scroll up to the last message I had sent him.

I need a break.

I delete it.

I never dreamed I would be the one to end us. With every word I typed of that last text, I hated Le'ul more than ever, as if he were controlling my fingers. Isak hadn't replied. I hope he didn't believe that I wanted to break up, and was giving me space to realize that in my own time. I would have said yes if Isak had asked me to marry him that day we rode the ferry. I would have had with him the children it had never occurred to me to want before my mother died.

Still no reply from Isak. He was just being nice, not declaring his enduring love.

This room has a bathroom en suite now. I don't have to walk all the way to the end of the back alley, to the last room in the service quarters, to pee. When I was little, that room had been too dark and cavernous for me. I refused to go in there even with two adults standing guard, one with me and the other outside the door. So a dull red potty was kept in this bedroom just for when I visited, and whisked away by the maid after I used it. The new bathroom—a renovation financed by my parents, I'm sure—is tiny but has all the necessities: toilet, sink, shower.

I return to the living room with a spring in my step, as if that little crumb from Isak was all the food I needed, and reclaim my spot beside Babbaye. Clustered nearest the porch door are half a dozen new visitors, soft and round elderly women wearing black head wraps over which they have draped inverted netelas, spread out to cover their dark dresses. Babbaye introduces me to the women as the child of the departed Tobya and her husband, Mesfin. Having my parents referred to by their first names is a jarring reminder that to the rest of the world they are regular people, not two ends of the axis on which my world spins. Spun.

"Hi!" I say, automatically slipping into my chipper in-flight persona. I want to slap myself for my inappropriate greeting. I give a small wordless bow meant for the whole.

"Ah, the only blood," one woman says. They must know about Le'ul, the adoptee, of course, but to them blood is what counts, especially now that Ema is gone. They can choose to ignore the fact of Le'ul's existence.

"Yes, the only," Babbaye says. His only surviving child's only child. I feel the crushing weight of my responsibility to continue a lineage.

"We remember how you cried at the farewell," the woman says. I don't know how I'm supposed to respond. Should I cry again for them, the new arrivals? We don't call condolence visits leqso without reason. One goes to "a cry" to, well, cry.

Other than that, there's no mention of how I have grown or changed since I was eight. My adult self, what I've made of my life, even the fact that I'm wearing blazing red when everyone looks as if they walked out of a black-and-white movie, is irrelevant when held up against my basic identity: Child of Zimita. I am distilled to my essence, my daughter-ness.

There is some curiosity behind the women's eyes though; I know they are sizing me up against Ema. Has the Little Patriot who cried so hard when she left Ethiopia turned out to be worthy of her mother's legacy? Do I carry her well enough that they can set down their burden of grief? They throw pleased glances at my short hair. No one asks what I do for a living, but if they did maybe they'd agree with me that as a flight attendant, my scarf always tied to the side of my neck like my mother used to do, I am also representing a nation.

We sit in a grim mood punctuated only by Babbaye's

sporadic mutterings. "My child. My Tobya. So you decided, you have had enough of this life? I say your name. Please answer."

Clearly, Babbaye has a long and shared history with all those gathered. They are still coming to sit with him, so long after Ema was buried in Toronto. But none correct him when he continues to speak of my mother as Tobya, the name she was given at birth. He changed it to Zimita, *silence,* after the end of the Terror, when she was a young woman. In death Ema has become Tobya to him again. It makes no sense that the picture mounted for all to see is of plain Tobya, the young nobody, and not of distinguished Zimita, the pride of her country. But maybe sense is too much to expect from a man who has outlived all his children.

I want to touch, comfort Babbaye, but my hand stops at his cane. I reposition it this way and that, lean it against the wall, though it was leaning against the armrest just fine before I moved it. I push my nails into the dense foam handle, to watch the impressions fade.

"And your father is here also for the Forty?" another woman asks me.

"No, he hasn't come," I say. Maybe he would have, Le'ul in tow, as usual. They come to Ethiopia once a year, pay their respects to Babbaye first, then go exploring in rural areas. But Babbaye's constant long-distance grumbling about Ema's burial place had to have scared them off. Why go in the direction of trouble you can avoid? Unless you're me, of course.

I'm even the only stray female sitting among the men. I miss Aba terribly, remembering how he loathes when genders segregate at social gatherings, as if a mixed group couldn't possibly have anything in common. He would have introduced the women to me too, believing that I had as much right to know who they are.

The time is long past lunch, too early for dinner, but a meal is about to be served because it is nefs yimar food that the women have brought. A couple of maids in their twenties enter behind Gela through the back door, from the kitchen across the alley. They have towels draped over their forearms, and carry urns full of hand-washing water, with bowls to catch the runoff. In their long patterned dresses worn over leggings, with mismatched tops, shawls draped about their shoulders and heads, they remind me of the maids and nannies who had a hand in raising me. One after another, they would fall short of Ema's exacting standards and there'd be a brutal scene of her firing them. Until their faces faded from my memory, I would look for each of them in the faces of the country girls—bent under clay water jars or bundled lengths of eucalyptus branches as long as their bodies—whom we drove past in the tourism bus every kiremt, on the way to Sodere Resort.

Gela does the honours for Babbaye first. There's a wordless synchronicity to their movements. She knows just when to stop pouring the water so he can lather his hands, and just when to start again so he can rinse.

After the hand-washing, the maids return to the kitchen then come back, one carrying a stack of plates, the other following her with a tray of rolled injera. I am so hungry, I could probably eat two whole injera by myself. But I feel too much shame to binge on this occasion. So I take only one roll, which is a quarter of one injera. The maids leave and come back again, behind Gela, each carrying one bowl of shiro, gomen, or misir wot. As before, they make their way around the room, pausing for each person to put a spoonful, just one, of each stew on their plates. Easter has just passed so fasting is over. It's not Wednesday or Friday either. So I guess it's just my luck that we're making do with split peas, greens, lentils—made with oil, not butter, and barely salted. To give myself more energy, I pick a Coke when the girls return with bottled drinks resting on their sides on trays.

The conversation is peppered with Vienna, just as it was at our farewell party. When we were leaving Ethiopia, everyone was talking about where we were going: Vienna. Now, everyone is talking about the place from which we never returned: Vienna. Everywhere else my family has travelled to or lived since, together and apart—for work, for love, for pleasure, for escape—becomes collapsed into one word, *Vienna*, which summarizes what matters: we went away and stayed away.

That evening, after everyone has left, I hover by the door to Babbaye's bedroom. Babbaye sits on the edge of his bed. I'm unsure whether he needs help getting ready to sleep, and if so whether I am the person to help him or if that, too, is Gela's department.

In contrast to the clutter-packed bedroom on the other side of the wall, this room is sparse, furnished only with bed, dresser, wicker basket, and a blue wooden chest at the foot of the bed. That blue chest used to hold clues to a life before I existed. Babbaye's metal helmet, his chest plate of medals, my grandmother's rolls of hand-spun cotton thread, ancient family photos in plastic bags. What else, there must be so much else. The chest is so big and deep.

"My Tobya hasn't come," Babbaye says.

I feel myself start to lose my patience with him, just a bit. My heart aches for him, too, though. He will need a long time, probably all his remaining days, to accept that his daughter's body is staying buried in the Canadian earth, no matter how many times he calls and writes for her to be brought home. There's nothing he or I can do about it.

Ema hid her cancer from her father throughout her life. He deserved to know what was happening to his one child. He still does, for what it's worth. I can't tell him anything about her last day, her final moment, because I wasn't there. But I can share the withheld part of her story.

I part my dry lips, peeling a strip of skin. "Many years ago," I start, gently, "when I was a little girl, a bad spot was erased from Ema's skin at Tikur Anbessa hospital. Do you remember that's where I was born, Babbaye?"

Having a regular conversation in Amharic is one thing, but explaining a medical condition, especially Ema's as I understand it, is like trying to untie shoelaces wearing mittens. The back of my neck seizes up. I barely recognize my voice, and I feel myself hunching over.

"The bad spot was a false kiss of Mariam," I say. "You know she had lots of them naturally. But that one the doctors erased was unnatural." A kiss of Satan, I suppose. "That spot was not on her skin from birth. It was dangerous so they cut it out, from the back of her leg."

Babbaye frowns. He either understands me well, or not at all. I press on. "But they had not cut away all of it, as they had thought. A piece was left behind."

All those years, here and in Europe, Ema's doctors and Aba had regularly checked her skin for new moles. That had been pointless because the leftover speck from the original was deeper within her, beyond detection.

"That piece, it grew, became . . ." I am at a loss for the Amharic word for cancer, then it comes. "She had nikisat."

"Nekersa?"

"Yes." Nikisat is tattoo. Idiot. What Gela used to have on her face. What my grandmother used to have on her neck. What I once drew on my wrist without ink.

I give up on further details of the surgeries that Ema had in Canada every time Dr. Hoggs discovered that the melanoma had spread into a new organ, and all the treatments Ema had in between surgeries to keep it at bay.

"It was her wish to rest there?" Babbaye says. He doesn't want to rehash what took his daughter, when there is the harder to stomach issue of where she is now.

"Yes. Aba said."

"A thousand fighting men used to obey me, but in my own family I am refused. My wish is not important."

"Isn't hers?"

"Did you hear her, with your own ears, utter the words that she wanted to be received by the earth of strangers? When she spoke this, were you present?"

I can't bring myself to tell a simple lie: *Yes, she did say so, I heard her.* I'm kind of on a roll with the truth. I repeat verbatim what Aba said she had said.

"She wanted to be where all her children are."

Babbaye tilts his head, his mouth curves into a wry, tired smile. "Is that so?"

He braces his hands on his knees as if to rise. I straighten up as if to complete the movement for him.

"There is no such place." He bends to remove his shoes. The conversation is over because clearly I haven't proved myself capable of it. Fine then.

"If my work calls me I'll have to go. I'm not sure if I can stay," I say. Now a lie comes easy. "But I came anyway because I had to be here for the Forty."

Babbaye unties his shoelaces, so slowly, with one hand,

the other cupping his knee. He couldn't care less about me being here, alive. Why get precious over a woman's body unless she's dead?

•••

In the larger bedroom next door, where I am to sleep, Gela finishes putting sheets on the mattress. As should a proper mourner, I will be camping out on the floor. I close and lock the wooden exterior shutters, which I couldn't reach as a child.

"What else do you need?" Gela asks me, straightening up.

"Nothing."

But I do wish for life to rewind back to when it was simple, measured in snacks, naps, play, a time when I could do no wrong because, as a child, I was a constant miracle.

I unfold a pillowcase and turn it inside out. My arms inserted into the pillowcase, one hand in each corner, I gesture for the pillow. "Can I ask, what is the Forty about?"

Gela hands the pillow to me, watching me curiously. I grab it by the tips.

"Tezkar is when the spirit of Etye Zimita leaves this earth, to rejoin Igziabher."

"Oh."

She is so casual with my mother's name, even adding the affectionate possessive of sister. Sister Silence.

"Only after that day is she completely gone," she says.

With one flick of my arms and a few shakes, the pillowcase slips over the pillow. I toss the pillow on the mattress.

"So where do the knowers say her spirit is, in the meantime?"

"With you."

"Just me?"

"With all who she loved and who loved her."

"She is still loved. So, if the tezkar is about the spirit, what does it matter where her body is? When even Igziabher doesn't care about that?"

Her eyes widen, she's stunned. "The grounds are pretty," she says, gathering herself. "I have seen the pictures of the resting place that were sent."

Aba did send the pictures I took, then. They are in this house somewhere. "Yes, it is a beautiful resting place. When her monument is finished, you'll see how it's even more pleasant."

I step out of my shoes, and undo the hook of my skirt zipper. I start to unbutton my blouse from the top. Still she doesn't leave. "But," she says, "can *there* replace *here*, Ethiopia, with all her kin? Is she not alone in that land?"

"Loneliness is not so bad. Besides, you just said she is everywhere with all her beloveds. I'm confused. What is the part of us that feels, Gela? Our spirit or our dead body?"

She bends and smooths wrinkles on the bedsheet. "You being at the Shaleqa's side for Etye Zimita's Forty Day is what is important."

Classic habesha deflection. I can't blame her. I've just done to her what I hate when passengers do to me, getting too personal precisely because soon they'll never see me again.

"Am I safe under all that? It's like a mini Ras Dashen," I say, baptizing the towering mess on the bed frame in the name of Ethiopia's tallest mountain.

"After the Forty Day, all will be put back in its original place," she says. She bids me good night and shuts my door after her. I unzip my skirt and pull up my blouse. The wrinkled bottom half of Ema's slip comes out, dark green silk with black lace trim, my favourite one. As a child, I was so fascinated by these pretty, flimsy dresses, beautiful secrets women wore underneath their clothes. Such a treat it was to slip my hand under the hem of Ema's dress to feel the slippery fabric. But I also couldn't wait to grow up so I, too, could wear a secret of my own.

I drape my neatly folded uniform on the extended handle of my upright suitcase, my purse on the top, and my shoes beside my tote—the way I do at home prior to a trip.

In the bathroom, I turn the shower on as hot as it will go and sit on the toilet lid, resting my elbows on the sink. The floor quickly becomes wet with water spattering out from under the too-short shower curtain. Steam blurs my face in the mirror. I wipe it away to reveal only my nose, jawline, and lips, the parts of my reflection that are identical to Ema.

I take off Ema's slip and drape it over the shower rod. Under the uneven, weak waterfall, I unfold a washcloth and scrub myself without soap, enjoying how thin black curls of dead skin fall away from me, flecking the white shower floor. Then I wash the slip as best I can. When wet, the green silk turns almost black. I rinse every inch of the fabric, believing I am bathing Ema's body, as I should have done. Dripping with water, the slip weighs as much as a newborn. When I wring it out, it becomes almost weightless, a shifting mystery.

I step out of the shower, towel off, and lay the slip flat on the toilet lid. With my travel blow dryer, I run a stream of heat over it, imagining the feel of rippling hot silk is as soothing for Ema as it is for me. I slide the clean, dry slip back on my clean, dry body, loving how the warmth of the silk mingles with my heat.

In the bedroom, I layer one of Ema's plain white, loose-fitting cotton hager libs over my slip, and another one over the bedsheet for extra warmth. I plug my phone in to charge, turning the ringer up to the loudest setting. I pop a melatonin, turn the light off, wriggle under the covers, then lie staring at the distant ceiling, swallowing repeatedly to get the sleep-adjusting tablet down my throat.

The looming heap of objects on the bed frame above me creeps me out. I think of the mountain in Iceland that caused the air travel havoc, a volcano quiet for almost two hundred years then blowing up, hurling a scalding blast of shattered rock up into the jet stream. I turn my phone flashlight on again and pass it over this mountain, trying to discern if this cluster—decorative ornaments, wall hangings, plastic flowers, a radio, a VHS player, sofa cushions, drawers, lamps, and even a tank shell casing the size of a child's leg—is stable.

I see a book in the pile. I crawl over and extract it.

The mountain trembles, then resettles.

The Art of Forgiveness, Lovingkindness, and Peace.

The edges of the pages are still crisp, flush. I trace my finger over the cover, a forest of purple bamboo bordered by green diamonds. Ema didn't even start this book. I tuck it under my pillow, like the *Metshaf Kidus, Mezmure Dawit,* or *Wudase Mariam* prayer books that habesha parents store under their children's mattresses, to protect them from evil spirits.

THREE

"There's a book I want you to get for me," Ema had said to me almost exactly two years earlier. "I need something to read when I'm in Adisaba."

She was going to Ethiopia again in a month, at the end of April. Her almost-Excellency, my mother, was in high demand. Really, she was wasted on Toronto.

We were as alone as two could ever be in the residence wing of the consulate on St. Clair Avenue West. She was sitting in front of her gilded triple-mirror bathroom vanity, parting the wet hair at the back of her head in a perfect grid with a pintail comb. The front half of her hair was already set. I had her pink hair rollers beside me on the wide edge of the Jacuzzi, organized into neat regiments, along with securing clips and pins, just as I used to do when I was little and insisted on being her helper. She had let me, even though I slowed her down.

I responded to her in English. "As if you don't have enough reading material, Ema."

"I'm not going for work. You still have family there."

"Just Babbaye."

She dropped her hand and gave me a look that said *who have I raised?* Her Djarum, tucked into the groove of the turquoise stone ashtray on the countertop, scented the bathroom with clove. "Hab Dahlak" played softly on her phone. I handed her a roller. She took it and pushed her phone toward me, then dragged deeply from her Djarum. The smoke she exhaled was as diaphanous as her hager libs, the only thing she ever wore at home.

I paused the song on her phone. I would give her the benefit of the doubt. Maybe just this once, the book actually was for her, and not something she wanted me to read with the hope that it would crack my unforgiving stone of a heart.

I opened her browser window. Just as I thought. I slid the phone back on the counter.

"Order it online."

She held out her hand for a pin. "It's private."

"Then have your secretary pick it up."

"Dessie. I want you to buy this book."

"Even if you start reading it, we both know you're not going to finish it."

She waited for me to give her a pin. I didn't move. I didn't trust myself to not press the pointed tip into her flesh, break her skin, sink it in as deep as love and hate will go. She scooted over and took a pin herself, knocking the advance guard of a regiment into the tub in the process. She secured the roller in her hair, parted the next section. I concentrated on not getting up and walking away. I pressed my palms flat on the skirt of my uniform. Stay put, D.

The one thing that I had wanted Ema to read, a simple one-page letter I wrote in an eight-year-old's beginner English, she might as well never have read, for all the difference it made.

Ema reached for another roller. I quickly passed one to her, and rescued the fallen rollers from the abyss of the tub. I reunited them with their comrades in the formation. Ema pulled her sectioned hair taut in the roller's teeth, raising the flesh on her scalp.

This was one of those rare times I had my mother all to myself. I could stay as long as I wanted. Aba was out on one of his "thinking drives." He would be back by midnight at the latest. If I slept over I would see him, too, for a bit. The important thing was that Le'ul was not here. He'd locked up his room and gone to his latest assignment somewhere in Asia.

"You look like a clown with your hair like that," I said.

Ema started coughing, a sound I dreaded, being an undeniable reminder that my mother's body was invaded by disease. I unrolled a Ricola from a bowl on the counter, one of the many such bowls she kept all over the residence. She abandoned the section of hair to receive the cough drop from me. I then took over her hair, but I tangled it in the roller because I couldn't make myself pull it tight.

I cupped her chin, turned her cheek up, and kissed her, as if I were the mother, she the child. "I have an early flight tomorrow. You can handle the rest of this without me."

I shoved all the pins, clips, rollers into her mother's mesob. I placed it on her lap. One woven basket, where my grandmother used to keep her raw cotton with spindle, was the only thing Ema had kept of her mother.

Ema grabbed my hand and kissed my palm, wordlessly thanking me for spending my time with her, as if she wasn't worthy. I slipped my hand out of hers and left the residence by the back way, through the French windows to the garden, so I wouldn't have to chit-chat with Tiru or the other staff.

I wished Aba had been at the residence. We three could have had a perfectly nice visit pretending that I am their only child. Ema wouldn't have tried to send me on yet another errand to buy a book or a poster or a ticket to a talk about forgiveness, which she pretended to need for herself, when I knew it was just her latest way to prod me toward Le'ul. Mostly, she sent me to look for books. So far, my admittedly weak countermove had been to deliver what I was asked, no comment, then fly away on a work trip, or hole up in my condo by Kipling Station.

My God, I thought, even "Hab Dahlak" defers reconciliation until the next generation, who will hopefully have less baggage, more love. During the war between Ethiopia and Eritrea in the late nineties, while her own cancer returned and spread undetected, Ema had shuttled between three continents to broker a peace that had held about as well as the bond between two incompatibly damaged people. "Hab Dahlak" came out after all that, in 2005. Ema had three years, hundreds of listens, to hear what it was telling her. Leave things be. To my thinking, Ema's cancer was all the more reason to leave things between Le'ul and me as they had been for the past twelve years. To her, it was exactly why she must tamper with the carefully drawn borders between her children. She was not about to give up. Hers was the long game of a diplomat.

I didn't care what absolution, what relief, it would be for Ema if I forgave Le'ul. I wouldn't, ever. If I could, I wouldn't have chosen to live alone in Vienna, when they all went off to Rome, and then moved to Canada, the farthest place I could think of. When Ema, Aba, and Le'ul followed me to Toronto five years ago, I almost quit my job and left. I wasn't about to hesitate, even when Aba told me that Ema had declined the greater promotion of ambassador to the US in New York, to be with me in Toronto. *She would have been Her Excellency by now; she chose you instead.*

What trapped me was the progress of Ema's cancer, detected the same month they arrived. I couldn't abandon my sick mother a second time. But the only way I could bear to stay was by leaving as often as possible. What was supposed to have been just a gap year of flight attending—before I started something real—became a lifeline.

•••

Three weeks after Ema asked me to buy the book, I found myself in Book City on the Danforth. To buy only magazines. A girl who travels for a living can never have too many magazines.

A man stood too close to me in front of the rack I was browsing. Tall, slim. Jeans and T-shirt worn with casual care. Cloth bag. Beard. Shambhala beads. Vaguely habesha. He glanced my way once. He stared at the magazines but didn't pull any out. My instinct for identifying weirdos, making sure I have a clear pathway to the exit—learned in childhood and honed at CanAir—compelled me to move away. Without making my escape obvious, I walked through cards, notebooks, New Arrivals. The man kept reappearing, apparently indifferent to me, like the love interest in a habesha music clip.

From the remainders stack I'd barricaded myself behind, the stranger picked up a book, and flipped through it. The title jumped out at me.

The Art of Forgiveness, Lovingkindness, and Peace.

He lined up at the cash register with the book. I stood in line behind him. I bought something too, though I forgot what the moment the clerk handed me the shopping bag. Outside, I saw the man ahead of me on Bloor Street, walking toward Broadview Station. We got on the westbound train. We got off at Bathurst. We stopped at the bakery. Then I saw him getting on the No. 7 Steeles bus, munching on a spicy beef patty, which I knew by the red dot. I boarded the idling bus. He opened the book. I walked over to where he sat by the window and clutched a support pole, towering over the empty seat next to him.

If I were a habesha dude I would have opened with their signature line, *Don't I know you?* In English, I said, "Have you met me?"

He allowed five seconds to lapse, the universally accepted length of time that weirdos should be ignored so that they will move on and bother somebody else. I stayed. He lifted his attention from the acknowledgements page to look steadily at me.

"Are you habesha?" he said, in Amharic.

I could have answered yes or no. I am, and am not, Ethiopian. Whichever answer I chose would be half true, like a broken clock that is correct twice a day.

I turned away. "Excuse me."

"No problem," he said, in English. "Or who you are depends on who's asking?"

English it was. I sat across the aisle. "I just sensed you wanted to speak to me."

"Only if you're habesha." He winked. "I am, by the way. But mixed. Italian."

"Talyan?" I said, with Babbaye's inflection. "That's rare."

He noted my sarcasm with a single clap. Talyans, Babbaye's first enemy, had been making love *and* war either in Ethiopia or Eritrea for over a century. In such moments, I sent a quiet thank you to Aba for imparting to me the fun facts of our history, like the twenty dollar bills he stuffed into my hand whenever I saw him, just in case. *A queen for my princess.*

"I wouldn't be your grandfather's favourite person," Talyan man said.

"Once invaded, forever wounded, as the saying goes."

The bus let out an airy fart, lurched out of the station. We swayed in time. Talyan man introduced himself as Isak. I switched to the seat next to him, took *The Art of Forgiveness* out of his hands, and brandished it in his face as if it was my passport to his company for the ride.

"I was in the same bookshop. You didn't see me?"

"What did you buy?"

I patted the shopping bag, trying to remember what was inside. "Same." I opened his book. "You're a Buddhist?"

"Are you?"

"Me?"

"Why do you say *me*?"

"I've never met any Ethiopian Buddhists."

"Now you have." He pointed his index finger up to emphasize himself. His nails were long, clean ovals. He levelled the finger at me. "And you at least seem interested in Buddhism."

"I'm raised to be Orthodox Christian."

"Faiths—not that I think Buddhism is one—aren't mutually exclusive. It's all one."

Listening to him intellectualize religion, I felt I was encountering Aba as he might have been when he was young. Isak watched me less like a man, more like a friend. I wanted to keep talking.

"True."

"Oh, come on," he said, "fight me on it more."

"I'm not confrontational."

"You must be an only child."

"I resent the implication, but yes I am."

"I have five sisters."

"Wow. I would envy you one. That is all I ever wanted. Older. But five is unfair."

"You can have one of mine."

"How nice of you."

"But they're all in Adisaba so you'd have to move back."

Pass, I almost said, but stopped my tongue just in time. I didn't have a great history with born-and-bred habesha chicks. I'd never met any as an adult, in fact, until I started at the University of Toronto.

When I came to Canada, I didn't know a single person. I had fantasies of reconnecting with Anja, my grade two pen pal from when I lived in Ethiopia, who I'd long ago lost touch with. At the time, there were no habesha students in the psychology or art departments where I'd enrolled to become an art therapist. But midway through my freshman year, I saw a bunch of habesha students in the food court, at a table with a sign that said *Africa Is Not a Country.* They were battling Student Affairs for denying their application to start a habesha student association since there was already an African Students' Association on campus. One of the women, Sara, asked my name and added it to the petition. Before I knew it, I had dozens of sisters. For life, I thought.

"Let me see how it goes with you first," I said to Isak.

"Do you want to let me know what you thought of the book, when you finish?"

I couldn't tell if he knew I had lied. He took out a pen from his canvas bag and poised it over the inside flap of his book, intending to write my phone number.

"Oh don't spoil a brand new thing." I repositioned his hand over my inner wrist, where my skin was so warm, it took to his ink on the first stroke.

I didn't recognize the area code. He told me he lived in Massachusetts. He was a graduate student in geology at Yale. "If the Canadians had offered me a full scholarship, the University of Toronto would have been my first choice," he said.

"We could have met before now."

"Your stalking indicated as much."

"You were following *me*."

"All I know is we're both on this bus, and neither of us is checking for a stop."

I failed to think of a retort, in the same way I always lost when I accused Ema of looking at me intently for no reason. She would say, *How could you know I was watching you, unless you were watching me, too?*

Isak changed the subject by telling me about the job waiting for him with the Geological Survey of Ethiopia, and his plan to one day head his own gemstone enterprise. We ended up back at Bathurst station. He stayed on the bus, I got off, thus settling the matter of who was following whom. He pops into Toronto on long weekends, he said, leaning out of the bus like a prince in his chariot. Next one was Memorial Day weekend. "Call me in the meantime."

I promised to, then rode the eastbound train, back to Book City, where I bought the book Ema had wanted. I waited one more week, until the day she was to leave for Ethiopia, to give it to her. Her departure time was an hour after I returned from a flight, so we met at her gate. I got there with minutes left before she boarded, so there was only enough time to hand over the book.

Walking Aba to their car afterwards, I almost asked him how he met Ema—though I know the facts: it was at Addis Ababa University, quite the scandal what with him not just her personal tutor but also fifteen years her senior. What I wanted to know was how they had felt and talked the first time. If they had needed the excuse of a book to set up a proper date. I wanted to know when was the very first time Aba teasingly called Ema *my leopard* on account of all her birthmarks, and when did she craft her rejoinder, *The leopard and the elephant. What a sight.*

But Aba spoiled my mood by indirectly bringing up Le'ul. "Am I spending Fasika this weekend alone?" he said.

That was code to let me know Le'ul was back from an assignment. If I said yes, Aba would make plans with Le'ul. If I said no, Aba and I would celebrate Ethiopian Easter at my place, or most likely at the smaller Lalibela restaurant.

"Yes," I said, just to punish Aba for ruining the moment.

The conversation should have ended there, but Aba asked, "You have a trip?" I nodded, lying, and taken aback that he even asked. My parents had stopped tracking my flights long ago, perhaps when they realized that sometimes I say I'm away when I'm not.

"To . . . ?"

Right then, I decided I didn't want to wait until Memorial Day weekend to see Isak.

"New Haven."

•••

Two days later, a little over a week after I met him in Book City, Isak welcomed me at Boston Logan. We went to Peet's in the airport for a drink before we took the train to Yale. Without discussing it, we gravitated to a corner nook in the café, the kind of prime spot people hogged for hours.

As we shuffled in from opposite ends of the booth toward the centre, he commented, "That's one way to get in."

"That's what she said," I replied.

He stopped inches from me. "So, I've never belonged to a book club."

I hadn't even taken the book out of the shopping bag, much less cracked it open, so I redirected, fast. "Are you enjoying yourself out here?"

"Not at first. There was the condescension of the Americans. Subtle, as it has to be within vaunted Ivy League halls. But detectable still, in the difference between what they explained to me versus what they assumed an African would already know. I've learned to take it in stride."

"Good. Keep your eyes on the prize."

"Except sometimes one needs to put them in their place. My roommate"—up went his index finger with the exquisite oval nail—"on day one nicknamed me his 'starving Ethiopian' as a kind of ironic endearment. Mind you, he was the one who looked as if he'd missed one too many meals. *That* kind of brazenness does raise my ire."

"Any other part of you it raises?" My face grew hot. Damn. As if to meet a man a second time required me to be seductive. "I've been there, though," I said, scrambling for normal. "People making assumptions about you."

He excused himself to get us drinks. He returned, set down the mugs. "You need to know, if we're going to go further with this," he said, starting what I already recognized as his typical preamble to an important point, "and I think we are going to, or at least I think we can... I am celibate."

My eyebrows shot up. I couldn't believe my luck. "Forever?"

He laughed. "Well, I usually don't plan that far ahead."

I collected myself. This was where some would say he was too good to be true. But he was better than true. He was perfect for me. I nudged him playfully, now that I knew he wouldn't interpret touch as an invitation to pounce on me.

"It's okay," I said, as if I had not come plucked, shaved, and moisturized, ready for the inevitable.

He stirred his coffee too long, watching me as if I was the one who had made the revelation. I watched him back. "What?"

"I'm looking at the first woman on either side of the Atlantic whose immediate question hasn't been *why*."

"Congratulations to me, then." I took his stir stick. "May I? I assume we can share this, since you brought only one." I sucked on it. Pure sugar. "Maybe I think sex is overrated, so I forgive you."

"On the contrary, sex is misunderstood. Between having and not having sex, there's a field of erotic potentiality wide as the space Moses parted for the Israelites to cross the Red Sea."

I blew on my tea. "Lord have mercy."

"Sex is, in fact, everywhere, when one learns to awaken to it in the everyday. Once one does, one enters a constant state of meditative arousal. For instance, have you ever peeled an orange? I mean, *really* peeled an orange?"

"I'm a cutter."

"There would still be peel on the cut sections."

"I pull the flesh with my teeth."

"All right, say there's no knife."

"Then the orange lives another day."

"You're messing with me."

In truth, I was already on cloud nine. In my twenty-five years, I'd never felt more relaxed with a man, a new relationship—if any of the all-inclusive resort flings, layover one-night stands, and Toronto-based situationships could be so defined. I have never actually *wanted* to have sex. I looked at sex as a required activity that I co-operated in, with convincing enthusiasm, in exchange for the good stuff, all that there was to life besides bumping fuzzies: snuggles, nature hikes, mojitos, thrift store shopping, bad movies, good theatre, sushi, sleeping. *Sleeping.*

That weekend with Isak, I *slept* the best sleep of my life with a man in the same bed. Nothing was expected of me. I lingered in bed long after I woke up. Later, I peeled, and ate, an orange.

•••

Two weeks later, when Ema had returned from Ethiopia, I went to see her and Aba. Their Toyota was in the garage, but I couldn't find them anywhere in the residence. I figured they were either in the office wing, or gone for a walk, so I waited in the bedroom on the second floor, flipping through television channels, texting with Isak. I called Ema, no answer. I called Aba. I heard his church drum ringtone nearby. I found him on the stairs to the uppermost third floor, stretched out in his tracksuit as if he was on the living-room recliner, reading his novel for this year, *The Brothers Karamazov.*

"Aba what is going on?"

He pointed his thumb over his shoulder, at the closed door to the third-floor landing.

"Your mother is up there."

"I don't... what?"

He closed his book and sat up. "This is as far as she'll let anyone go."

The third floor of the residence wing was guest quarters,

almost never used. I climbed up to the door. Locked. I knocked. No answer. I knocked again. I sat on the stairs, one step up from Aba so I could be eye level with him. "Why?"

"She has decided, from now on, whenever she comes home after the hospital, she will quarantine herself for twenty-four hours."

"*Quarantine*?"

"Until the chemicals, or as she calls them the poisons, have left her system." Aba gave me a *you and me both* look that let me know we had to let Ema have her way.

"Maybe it's just as well, for everyone's sake," I whispered conspiratorially.

Ema's moods had become increasingly unpredictable and atrocious since her cancer recurred. She yelled horrible accusations. *All these false alarms, you must wish me dead already.* In such instances, only Aba could calm me with a look that was like a hand firmly pressed on my sternum. Once, when I had to deal with Ema's woe-is-me all by myself, I had snapped back at her, *If you want to go, then go!* I stormed out, fearing this was going to be the shape of our days from now on: I drop by for a visit—when Le'ul is gone and I know it's safe—with the best intentions, end up saying something vile to Ema, then having to leave.

I apologized first thing, the next time I saw her. She brushed off the incident as if it was nothing. Show-off, I thought. She might as well have said, *See how easy it is to forgive?*

Aba's phone rang. Ema, I thought. The screen said LE'UL. Aba declined the call. Thankful, I lay my head on his shoulder.

We sat, a pair of self-appointed sentinels hopelessly in love with our charge. Then Aba stacked his phone over his book and stood up. "Are you coming?"

"Let me stay here a bit with her."

He went on to their bedroom. I listened as he turned off the TV I'd left on, then went to the ground floor. I twitched my ear to the third floor. Still nothing. There were noises from the kitchen below. At the residence, my hearing became attuned, like prey in the wild.

The housekeeper, Tiru, appeared at the bottom of the stairs, holding a tray with a bowl of soup and a plate of sliced bread. She excused herself as she went up past me, as if she was doing nothing more extraordinary than vacuuming around my feet. She left the tray on the landing for Ema.

On her way back down, she said, "Your place setting is at your mother's spot for today. You'll also want to look at the garden while you eat?"

I wasn't hungry, but I stood up, "I guess I shouldn't let my father eat alone."

"Oh you know men, they started without you," she said as she left.

I froze, and slowly drew my foot back from the step below.

The men?

Just knowing that on Aba's phone Le'ul's name was right next to mine had made my skin crawl, much less that at this very moment he was feeding in this house. I sat down, trying to absorb what was happening: Ema's soup on the landing, her deathly silence behind the locked door, Aba's carelessness—he had said, *Are you coming*, knowing what he was leading me into—were warnings. Life was changing. Either Ema had won Aba over to her quest for some kind of spontaneous reconciliation between me and Le'ul, or Aba had made himself her deputy. Or, once again, my needs had simply been shoved aside.

I left through the basement. Since I couldn't trust Ema and Aba's cues anymore, I stopped going to the residence. What was the point, if I couldn't even be sure that Her Excellency would be available to see me? After a couple of months, I suggested Ema and Aba come over for dinner and to watch *Fool's Gold*. It had been a while since we watched a bad movie just to laugh at how bad it is. I missed that. They couldn't come, because apparently Ema didn't have the health anymore to go farther than her office or the hospital. So I went to her office. She looked fine. My distrust grew, but there were only so many appointments I could make with my own mother, only so many times I could casually ask Tiru whether Le'ul was travelling, before people started to talk.

I steeled myself and started visiting Ema at the residence again. Every time I input the gate access code, as the painfully slow mechanical gates opened—Le'ul perhaps watching me on the CCTV at that moment—I felt raw, bone-tired, edgy, weepy. It became harder to keep a tight smile on and curtly shake my head in response to the deceptively innocent question my parents kept pushing on me. *Will you eat with us?*

If Ema happened to be in quarantine, and Aba was out or breaking bread with his son, I foraged from Ema's meal tray. She would have been furious if she had caught me. I dare your poisons to do their worst, Ema, I thought. This is not the first time I've purposely swallowed something that could kill me.

FOUR

My cellphone rings. I snap awake and sit bolt upright on the floor mattress, ready to fly. Yes, it's Barb. No, we're not flying out today, nor any time soon by the looks of it. The ash is thick. We're caught up in the worst global flight interruption in aviation history since the Second World War. The crew, resigned to their impromptu East African holiday, is browsing the day trips on offer through the Hilton. Their thoughts are with me, is all Barb says. Had the circumstances been different, I think they might have fished for an invitation to Babbaye's house. Or I would have lured them with a promise of the authentic local experience of meeting the last of the arbegna.

I have an email from Le'ul. About Ema's headstone. He has attached a photo of the one we'd picked from the funeral home's catalogue.

We went to see it in the mason's workshop. Aba got Stanley to tell him where he has them made. Can you believe Aba tried to lift it? He must think he has the strength of Samson. You should be here for the dedication on tezkar day.

Le'ul has never messaged me. Not email, not text. Not even so much as a sticky note. Ema must have given him my email address. Am I supposed to respond? I won't. I do want to know how Aba is doing, but asking Le'ul about Aba feels overly familiar, an encouragement toward a relationship I don't want. Since I was five, I've only ever obeyed then avoided Le'ul. What are the rules of a world without Ema?

The partial gold engraving of Ema's epitaph in Ethiopic script trails the bumpy surface of the marble boulder. How unique the stone will look in Scarborough Bluffs Cemetery, I think, where the headstones are neat slabs like miniature doors.

I get up, resolved to follow the example of my crew and make the best of this unplanned, indefinite layover. They don't call what I do emotional labour for nothing. Stay cool, smile, avert disaster. If disaster happens, save others first.

I have a hunch Ema's hager libs won't be the right outfit for today. Everything else I have packed is sundresses, sandals, and light blazers, for early spring in Johannesburg and Vienna. Over my slip, I wear the darkest things I have: black jeans, a grey blouse with white polka dots. Footwear will have to be my old white Converse. I wrap one of Ema's netela over my head and shoulders, completing my hybrid look.

I find Babbaye on the porch, sunning himself in a chair, while brushing his teeth with a mefakiya twig from his garden. I sit on the topmost porch step, my back to him, and lean against the wood railing.

In my mind, I skip down the flagstone pathway ahead of me, between the trees, and out the open gate. Beside it, there is one small house, which I didn't notice yesterday. Like Babbaye's main house, the others in the compound are also old-fashioned wattle-and-daub construction, from when Addis Ababa was a town. My great-great-grandmother, who was blood related to some royal, brought this land into her marriage. She intended these homes for the generations. Of her two daughters, one was barren. The other—my grandmother—had seven children. Of those, only my mother survived the Terror. But I suspect I'm not the only remaining descendant. Maybe my barren great-aunt's husband had illegitimate children. Babbaye's sisters, who dispersed during the occupation and with whom Babbaye never reunited, must have had kids too. Cousins once removed, who I'll never meet.

Had Ema lived to inherit all this, she probably would have sold it. My parents sold our old house in Bole years ago. They had accumulated a stack of brochures with artists' renderings of neat communities, intending to buy a pre-construction condo on the new edge of Addis Ababa.

"Who's been living in these homes?" I ask.

"Tenants," Babbaye says. His tone does not invite further questions. The man who walked in past us when I arrived yesterday must have been one of them.

I wish, instead of spending the day sitting in a room full of long faces again, Babbaye and I could just go for a long walk. Maybe to my old neighbourhood, for old times' sake. Babbaye used to regularly walk from this house to ours—about a forty-minute drive—which would cost him the better part of a morning. One of my earliest memories is of waiting by our gate, to hear the *crunch-tap-crunch* of his boots and cane on the gravel outside. As soon as I saw his boots in the gap between the bottom of the gate and the ground, I'd start yelling hello so loudly that the maid, all the way in the back kitchen, would know to rush out and open the door. If she took so long that he had to ring the bell of his own daughter's house, God help her.

She would bring a chair out to the garden for Babbaye. He would lean his cane against the side of the chair, direct me to sit by his feet at the spot where he could easily pat my head, and we would commune with the sun at exactly the blazing time of day everyone else avoided it. I imagined we were arbegna on lookout, though only stray cats sauntered past, oblivious to us. If I fell asleep on the grass, Babbaye would wake me when it was time for a snack, fruit from the young koshim hedge that was our fence. He'd push his hand right through thorns as long as my little finger to get the wild peaches for us to feast on. Afterwards, he would brush his teeth with a twig. I remember once, after much nagging over many afternoons, I finally persuaded him to make a twig toothbrush for me. I scrubbed away happily until bitter saliva mixed with the juice of the branch began to collect in my mouth.

"Can I swallow the juice?" I mumbled.

"Only by experience can one know what kills," Babbaye said, calmly scraping under his nails with a koshim thorn.

Terrified, I gulped, accidentally swallowing the strange fluid. Babbaye thought I'd called his bluff. He stopped wiping the tip of the thorn on his palm mid-motion. I squeezed my eyes shut, hoping death didn't hurt. Babbaye laughed. I opened my eyes.

He was saluting me. "Tinishwa arbegna!" he said. Little Patriot. "You have earned a dagger. Here!" He gave me his thorn. My bony chest expanded with pride. I knew my parents would take away my prize if they saw it, so I stuck it straight down deep in the soil under the yellow hibiscus. When I went back for it another day, it was gone. I only found the slimy body of another frog that Le'ul had beat to death with a bat.

Now I reach through the slats of the railing to tug at a branch of a mefakiya bush in Babbaye's garden. The plant surrenders a branch with a shiver. I dig my fingernail around the bark at the tip, peel it. Between my back teeth, I grind the lime-green stem into a fine brush. It's splintery and shockingly bitter but I brush vigorously anyway, slipping and stabbing my gum. I can feel Babbaye watching me.

"What you have broken is gesho," Babbaye says, behind me. "For making tella. To brush with gesho is to make yourself cry from the bitterness. Mefakiya is the plant next to it."

The plant next to it looks the same. Same leaves. Okay, maybe fatter, smaller leaves.

"Ask me to prepare a brush for you."

I shake my head. I made my twig, I will brush with it. Bloody saliva and sour breath are nothing to a warrior.

I can't. I drop my hand and turn aside to spit, repeatedly. Babbaye doesn't comment. I rub my tongue on my sleeve. Female voices, wailing loud enough to wake the neighbourhood, start to make themselves heard from the other side of the compound wall.

"Shouldn't loud crying have stopped by now?" I say.

"They will stop when Tobya comes."

I hear the scrape of the chair as he gets up to go inside. I follow him, before the mourners let themselves in and I have to face them alone. One by one, Uncle A B Z and the other three old men arrive, accompanied by the same women from yesterday, who I decide are the wives. There is another group, younger people who may or may not be their grown children. Again, the introductions are one-way.

One of the maids brings a tray of pre-filled cups with coffee and tea. The other brings breakfast, a basket of home-made bread cut into cubes. No sign of Gela. Throughout the morning, a steady stream of mourners arrive. The women's loud, demonstrative grief tapers off into low-voiced small talk— once they have drifted off into the gender zones, settled into a chair, and moaned at the parquet for a respectable length of time. Then, with fresh wails from up the road, the restored calm is shattered, and the cycle starts all over again.

I hope to fade into the background but I feel assessed, today by the younger folk, like an imported doll fresh out of her packaging. Even the simple, dark outfit I have chosen feels extravagant, as if Ema's lacy green slip underneath glows neon through it. The damn netela keeps slipping off my head. Every move I make, or fail to, confirms or throws into doubt everything they believe they know about diaspora—a catch-all name for us who live abroad, I learn, as if we are a sub-species or divergent strain of habesha people.

These young visitors openly ask me questions about life in the outside-country, but don't really listen to my answers because they already have their fixed ideas about "outside-country" and those of us who live in it. The questions are merely an excuse to stare at me, absorb all my features, mannerisms, to compare them against their assumptions.

They have their fixed ideas specifically about me, I know, whom fortune has smiled on apparently. My family's departure was a voluntary, government-endorsed migration, not a life-or-death escape carried out under the cover of night, with forged documents, or none at all. "Oh, who taught you to clean?" One of them asks, when I moisten a tissue from my pocket with a drop of mineral water and use it to sop up breadcrumbs from a side table. I surprise not only them but myself with a clever comeback, bristling inwardly while my face betrays nothing.

"Dirt."

•••

Sara and some of the habesha posse from university had paid me a condolence visit in Toronto. Five days after Ema died, they showed up at my place. My concierge called me while I was at the cemetery. I told him to let them into my condo. When I returned, I found six women and five men I hadn't seen in nearly eight years crowding my tiny living room. They used to bemoan how people in our community don't travel to see each other—across town or across the ocean—until someone dies. I myself had gone along on condolence visits to the homes of habesha people I barely knew.

They declined my offer of refreshments. I went to my kitchen to get bottled water anyway. On my way back, I overheard Asrat, former shepherd now mathematics PhD, who never let his permanent freshie accent stop him from using English idioms, say, "So this is how the other half lives."

I passed out the water bottles in a silence as loud as the constant hum of a plane engine mid-flight.

"I guess you can't cut your hair," Azmara, the only person there who was new to me, finally said in her sing-song Amharic. Habesha bereaved should wear black, which I was not, and the women should cut their hair, which I had not. The men would stop shaving their beards.

"Because of your job?" she asked, seeing my blank expression.

I gave her a long look, unsure whether it was an innocent question. "Yes."

"Those jobs don't come easy," she said, cracking her bottle open. Not an innocent question, then. Her comment cranked up the awkwardness even more. I suspected Azmara was Sara's latest disciple, wounding on her queen's behalf. While Sara, who knew the group called her bandira behind her back because she wore such heavy makeup she looked bright as a flag, sat next to me on the couch, daintily sipping her water.

At the end of our fourth year at university, I had given Sara money for an outfit to wear to a mass interview for CanAir flight attendant jobs, and had gone with her to the Convention Centre on the day of, to calm her nerves. Somehow, despite my jeans and raggedy Converse slip-ons, I ended up getting invited into the interview room, and landing the job. I guess the best way to ace an interview is to not give a shit about getting hired. I am also tall, and speak two European languages, or claimed I did. So I became one of fifteen new hires out of seven hundred applicants. I figured I might as well enjoy a year of travelling for free before starting a real career. But according to Sara, one of those spots had her name on it. It was an open secret at the time that CanAir was starting its first Africa route, to Johannesburg, and that some spots were reserved for blacks.

Sara poisoned the group against me. They shut me out as fast as they had welcomed me in, four years earlier, during their kerfuffle with Student Affairs. I knew they felt that out of all of them, I least deserved this dream job. Little girls of our generation grew up coveting the life of a flight attendant. Hostesses, as they were called back then. I was not one of those little girls. My fantasy was to one day outrun the airplanes. I used to sprint on the observation veranda at Bole airport, racing the planes as they sped up for takeoff.

Even before the CanAir job drama, the group had already deemed me guilty of the good life. They saw me as spoiled since they had learned who my mother was from a photo of Ema in my dorm room. To me, she was just Ema. I didn't think I had to tell them what she did for a living any more than they declared the jobs of their family members.

But to their way of thinking, Ema was synonymous with the Ethiopian government, the source of all their problems, the reason for their exile.

For almost four years I endured innuendo and jokes suggesting that I enjoyed the good life at their oppressed expense. Privately I laughed at them for their naïveté, to think a person could get rich through a career in the Ethiopian government. They had no idea it was actually my father who brought in real money, with his frequent invitations to guest lecture, be a visiting professor, or consult on research projects and design doctorate programs at universities all over the world. Regardless, when I "stole" a job that would have changed Sara's life, with which she could have supported her entire family back home, I became the permanent unforgiven.

Despite my alleged betrayal, Sara kept in touch. I knew I was just a contact for her by then, useful if the airline issued another cattle call, maybe started flying to Addis Ababa. When that didn't happen, I finally became dead to her. Until then, I went along with the charade. What did I know about how sisterhood works?

•••

Every time I think I have felt my phone vibrate in my pocket, I go to Ema's room to see if it is a call from Barb. But it always turns out to be a false alarm. Then, after lunch, I receive another email from Le'ul.

Aba wants you here for the dedication. In our culture it's a big deal you know, when the monument is dedicated to the departed on the Forty. Exactly when did you say you'd return? Be well. We're eager to see you soon.

Attached is a photo of him and Aba next to the headstone, also from the workshop. The engraving is complete. *And now remain these three, faith, hope, charity.* እምነት ተስፋ ፍቅር እነዚህ ሦስቱ ጸንተው ይኖራሉ. Because Le'ul and Aba are standing on either side of the stone, the words seem to refer to the three of them—the stone standing in for Ema. Le'ul has his hands locked behind him. He squints, probably counting down the auto-timer under his breath. Aba slouches, gazing out of the frame, directly at me. He has one hand on the knobbly top of the stone. He holds a flat object in the other. I zoom in. The object is a framed photo of me.

I return to the living room, gather some empty beer bottles by their necks, two in each hand, and leave through the back door. In the kitchen, the maids are scandalized. They vehemently reject any more help from me, as if I will break a bone from carrying empties. I get it. Protocol. Everyone has their role; I can't wreak havoc on their system simply because I don't want to play mine of sitting to be stared at, served, and judged. If I insist on playing the help, they say I have to get permission from their boss, Gela.

So I go searching for her, starting with the other rooms in the service quarters, all of which open onto the back alley—two maids' bedrooms currently holding the larger furniture from the living room, a storage room full of blue plastic barrels, lastly the frightening bathroom. I backtrack, passing the kitchen again, and the mitad bet next to it for baking injera, and turn the corner past a clothes washstand. I follow the alley alongside the house, past Babbaye's bedroom window and under clotheslines, which end in the courtyard.

Parting my way through hanging laundry, I hear a snatch of song—haunting lyrics I've heard hundreds of times on Ema's phone—playing at such low volume that had the breeze changed direction a second earlier, I would have missed it. I reach the source, the lone house to the right of the gate.

The door is ajar. I try to push it open further, but it sticks on something on the other side. I enter sideways, snagging my netela on the rough wood.

Gela, dressed all in black as she was yesterday, sits on a cushion-less settee against the wall opposite the door. She appears entranced by the music coming out of the rickety boom box on top of a coffee table, on which she has one foot propped. The only other place to sit is a bunk bed, the top of which is piled with suitcases. I stand in front of a massive wardrobe by the door. The singer, Teddy, promises that he is bound by oath to not betray his beloved, from whom he has been forcibly separated by unnamed powers.

The song repeats. Gela turns down the volume. "I hope you don't mind a visitor," I say. Gela waits, the expression on her face saying, *What now?* I know that look. It's the same one I give passengers when they act the diva, forgetting they are in coach.

"The kitchen women won't let me help."

I hadn't meant to sound so whiny.

"Lomi and Aberash are day-workers, hired for this mourning period. The Shaleqa will not end it until he buries Etye Zimita."

"So my grandfather has informed me. Well I am here for this period, too, not to sit idle. I'm not a princess. I can work."

"Tell them I said, 'Let her do whatever she wants.' Between your work and theirs, there is no difference. The Shaleqa told me how you earn your bread."

I don't appreciate her acting as if she's doing me a favour.

"Babbaye never talked so much."

"He has been poor for hearers."

If I have one pet peeve it's people underestimating my job. No matter how it may look, I, the granddaughter of a Patriot, the daughter of a professor and a diplomat, did not end up a maid. “Actually,” I say, “there is a difference between your work and mine. In my work, my responsibility is to save lives. Serving, cleaning is—”

“To pass the time until someone dies? I saw in the news a few months ago how much lifesaving you can do,” she says, referring to Ethiopian Airlines Flight 409, which crashed into the Mediterranean shortly after takeoff from Beirut this January.

“We do our best, but we’re not Igziabher,” I say.

“There were thirty-one habesha on that journey. Twenty-three domestics like me, eight lifesavers like you. All thirty-one bodies were brought from the ocean home to Ethiopia. For their grave, there is a monument in Selassie Cathedral. It was commemorated on their tezkar. Yesterday, you asked about the Forty. I answered you, but not fully. The Forty is also when the monument for the departed would be revealed. And there would be a celebration.”

“I’m aware.”

“The Shaleqa, as you know, has no grave for his daughter to dedicate a monument on, yet. But still he wants a celebration on the Forty. Don’t ask me why.”

“I didn’t.” I mean to fold my arms but end up semi-hugging myself. “You shouldn’t play music during mourning.”

“This is not music.”

I quote Aba at her. “All politics, but you can still dance to it.”

“This is a song of mourning.”

“For my mother?”

“For anybody separated from their love by a force greater than either of them.”

“Who are you supposed to be separated from?”

"Does it matter?"

I pull at the snagged thread on my netela, tug it back over my head, ashamed of myself for being so small-minded. I look away. Through the open gate, I see a soccer ball bouncing down the lane. She stops the music and gets up. I back out of her way then follow her toward the service quarters behind the house. As we walk, she reties her head wrap over hair that, despite her show of grief yesterday, has not met with scissors.

In the kitchen, the day-worker who Gela introduces as Lomi is cutting cubes from a flat, round homemade loaf of bread dotted with black seeds. The other woman, Aberash, is at the sink, washing the dishes from the lunch service. She steps aside to let Gela rinse dozens of tiny, handleless sini. Gela signals for her to give a tray to me. I've got my green light.

I hold the tray out as Gela lines the wet sini on it in concentric circles. From the stove, she picks up an enormous stainless-steel coffee kettle. She fills each cup to the brim with the dark potion, raising the stream high without interrupting the flow between cups, unbothered by the splash or spill-over, as if that is part of the appeal. I hold the tray steady but squint against the coffee spatter leaping into the air between us. Gela catches me doing this, and smiles. I feel at once so glad that she may like me after all, and surprised at how much I care.

"Tell me you hate these tiny sini as much as I do," I say.

"Why?"

"They're not even traditional. They're made in China."

"What isn't? One day even you and I may be made in China."

"I've been there," I say, then reflexively brace for one of Sara's scathing *of course you have* looks. But they're just interested in what I have to say. "In one small-town bus station, they rubbed my skin to see if the brown comes off." All three of them gasp in shock. I finally feel let in. "Sini are unfair for buna," I say. "Why aren't we allowed to have buna all at once in a big cup, why do we have to drink it in tiny amounts that get weaker as the ceremony goes on?"

"It's not a law. Drink from any size cup you want," Gela says. Lomi and Aberash agree.

"Back home I drink the whole jebena in one mug," I blurt out. The atmosphere cools a fraction. Shit. I don't know which part of what I said was wrong.

"Enough talk," Gela says, "go serve these before they cool."

Transporting a tray of full sini from the kitchen to the living room is a delicate operation with many obstacles: the raised threshold from the kitchen to the alley—over which I almost stumble—the dip in the centre of the alley, the two low steps to the threshold of the main house, and the blind landing before the living room entrance.

I manage the first trip just fine, even with Lomi breathing down my neck as she follows with the basket of bread. On my second trip I have to wait in the corner of the living room with the tray while a new visitor finishes her erratic display of grief in the middle of the floor. I've come to understand that a little wailing, some moderate tossing of the body, is just how one announces oneself to this house of perpetual mourning, even if it means the coffee gets lukewarm. So much for *Love and coffee are best when hot,* a favourite saying of Aba's whenever he had to wait too long for Ema to get dressed and come down for breakfast.

Shuttling sini, rinsing and putting them face down on the drainer, ready for the next round, making sure people are drinking tea, soft drinks, or beer in the interim, become tasks reserved for me. Gela, Lomi, and Aberash seamlessly manage the bread, the chairs, the ice, returning empties for new drinks, doing the dishes, reheating the food that women bring for the next meal, maintaining the logbook of who brought what, warming water for hand-washing, buying new hand soap, laundering hand towels, keeping the scary bathroom at the end of the alley clean and stocked with toilet paper, and—no one's favourite task—indulging the occasional mother or aunt so-and-so who comes into the kitchen to play lady of the house.

Lomi and Aberash are impressed by my industriousness. Gela was right, I think. Take away my uniform, I am really mostly a maid who occasionally gets stopped for questioning, as happens in flight. I accumulate a large collection of bottle caps on my tray. As I dump them all into a Tupperware container, Lomi says to Gela, "The caps are not returned with the bottles, does she know?"

"I know," I answer. True to her name, Lomi's acidic like a lemon. She has insisted on treating me as if I don't know Amharic since I mis-conjugated one verb, one time.

"She's teasing you," Gela says to me, playing peacemaker.

"In that case, later we can play Pepsi," I say to Lomi. She titters, covering her mouth. Pepsi was not what I used the bottle caps for when I was little. The game can't be played except with a group of girls. I didn't have a group of girls to play with. I only had Le'ul. His game was hammering the bottle caps flat with a rock, which he needed me for because my right index fingernail was not damaged like his was, so I could dig out the plastic under the caps. He had to save them. I was happy that I could do one thing better than my big brother. With rocks he hammered the bottle caps in the car shed, which annoyed the maids no end. I think, flattening bottle caps must have been part of the process of making some kind of village toy Le'ul remembered from before he came to Addis Ababa and Ema and Aba adopted him.

This memory of my and Le'ul's before-time is one of many such fragments that have begun to surface after Ema's death. Some are memories of things I believe really happened. Some, I know I'm imagining based on childhood photos of us. Some are as singular as a dream. But I cherish each one, like a child does her precious collection of odds and ends. I like to relive them now, when I so miss having a true brother, with whom I could grieve.

FIVE

On a day that Ema wasn't quarantining herself on the third floor of the residence, I found her lying flat on her bed, eyes closed, hands on her belly. I kissed her awake. She said she was cold, one of those phantom breezes only she feels. I went into her walk-in closet to get her a gabi, maybe the newest addition to her collection from her last trip to Ethiopia. In recent years, I'd developed the habit of counting her gabi and hager libs, for reassurance, ever since I heard Aba ask her when she was going to stop buying new ones, and her response, *When I die.* The taller the stack, the more life she expected.

But the first thing that met me in the closet was a childhood photo of Le'ul and me, intentionally placed on top of a stack of hager libs.

I just got here, I thought, I literally just got here and the pressure has already started. Ema was ready for me with her latest tactic in her forgiveness project: this picture, from back when our lawn was so new that the koshim hedge was mere saplings along a chicken wire fence, through which the unpaved neighbourhood road was visible. Le'ul and I are dressed in our Sunday finest, for a family excursion to Bole airport park, where families went to stroll, take photos, enjoy the café, admire the pilots and hostesses, and wonder at the planes from the observation deck. I am about three, mid-giggle, holding on for dear life to Le'ul's hand, as if my joy is too much. He faces the camera head on, looking stern as an eleven-year-old who has sworn on his life to protect his sister.

I yanked out a gabi from the bottom of a stack, toppling it. Forget counting, I was so mad I could have watched all that cotton go up in flame, set the fire myself. I stepped on the mess on my way out of the closet, and threw the gabi at Ema. It unfurled midair, and landed partly on the floor. "I know what you're doing," I hissed. "Maybe all those politicians you negotiate for, they don't see you coming, maybe they have no idea how you get them to do what you want them to do. But I know what you're doing."

She pulled the gabi over herself. "Forgive him."

I felt my heart seize. "What about me?"

"I *am* thinking about you."

"Really?"

"I've had to forgive worse."

"What could possibly be worse?"

"He didn't know what he was doing."

"Were you there?"

"He's suffered. You haven't seen because you stayed behind in Vienna. In Rome—"

"In Rome you three lived nicely without my presence."

"In Rome he almost died."

My stomach plunged. The image that came to mind was my little boy brother Le'ul in the photo, not the adult monster. I waited for her to explain if he hurt himself or if someone, something, hurt him.

"Is that all you've got? Well I've got news for you, too. We are all almost dying, every moment. You should learn how the human body works."

She was so shocked that she lifted herself up onto her elbows. We stared at each other, dumbstruck that I, normally such a good-natured daughter, could be so cruel.

"What?" I huffed, with shaky bravado. "You're the only one allowed to keep saying mean things?" The more I felt pressured, the quicker my boarding school self emerged, the vicious twelve-year-old who I didn't like any more than Ema did.

"Please, my sweet, obey me," she said, getting herself tangled in the gabi as she crawled up to kneeling. "Say yes. Grant me more life. Don't shorten my life."

She reached for me. I swung my arm out of her grasp. "You give me too much credit, Ema." I staggered back and tore out of the room.

Just as I barged into the foyer downstairs, I saw the handle of the front door being lowered. I retreated to the living room, to listen for signs of Le'ul. But the gentle closing of the front door, the scratch of Velcro, finally Aba's long exhalation as he lowered himself on the bench and removed his walking shoes assured me it was safe to step into view.

Aba's face broke into sorrow the moment he saw me. He shook his head. "Oh why did she tell you? We had agreed between us, there was no use in you knowing."

I guessed he meant Ema's latest prognosis. I waited for details, afraid if I asked, I wouldn't get them. Aba was too stricken to continue, and the most exposed part of the house was the last place I wanted to stay, so I spoke first.

"She can't help what she says anymore, Aba."

"Dr. Hoggs advised me privately after her appointment. He said he won't discourage the families of his patients from believing their loved ones have less time than they actually do. Why can't these doctors talk plainly?"

I stared at the pattern of stylized lions and doves on the wool rug until the meaning came to me.

"Ema will live."

Aba relaxed. He held out his arms to me. I walked into them and got a grateful kiss on each cheek. My translation had given him peace. If only he knew it was my refusal, not the cancer, that was single-handedly robbing Ema of time.

From then on, I decided the best thing I could do for Ema's health was to not see her. When I knew she was in for treatments, I sat on a bench in front of the cardiac centre, opposite her hospital. When she was at home, I gave her strength by doing for her what she used to enjoy but claimed she could no longer do. I walked to the waterfront on her favourite route. I watched the movies she'd have loved-hated. I shopped for her style of simple black clothes. Sometimes Aba was with me. He understood. Other times, Isak was. He didn't ask, just got used to eating a lot of mille-feuille, Ema's favourite dessert.

•••

For our first anniversary gift, while we were cooking a pasta dinner at my place, Isak gave me a rock. The stone looked dull. So did my face; I couldn't hide my disappointment.

"It's not any rock," he explained. "It is an uncut Ethiopian opal, from deposits newly discovered in Gonder. In water it changes colour, but will crack if dried too quickly."

He droned on about the opal's properties. Then he stopped. Normally, he had no problem with the sound of his own voice. He loved to read his papers aloud. That day, my undisguised inattention, added to my failure to at least pretend to be pleased, "raised his ire."

"So, you are not beyond all that after all," he said.

"Beyond what?"

"The trappings of what can be got out here in outside-country for lots of money."

Despite his stylishness and unaccented English, I found him most charming when he had his fresh-off-the-boat slip-ups, like using the Amharic expression wuch-hager, to mean anywhere not Ethiopia.

"I thought you were the type of person who appreciates something of her own."

"I do. I thought it was just a rock at first," I said.

"So what if it was? The fact of it originating from your own country makes this rock more meaningful than all the jewellery you can get out here in the so-called better life." He spread uncooked pasta on the countertop and aligned the pieces in a straight row. "I for one am not impressed by the West. People sacrificing even their offspring for it, fragmenting their children..."

We hadn't discussed marriage, much less children. I ignored the implication that sex would happen someday after all, along with the sadness that welled up in me at the prospect.

"Who are you calling fragmented?"

"I'm not calling you anything," he said, picking out the broken sticks of pasta and throwing them into the sink. My job was to stir the sauce, boil water, and clean up. "But have you not told me how conflicted things became between you and your mother the moment you moved to Venice?"

I smiled.

"What?" he said. By then he could tell which were my real smiles, and which were irritation, annoyance, or fury pulling up the corners of my mouth.

"We're good now."

"But you said things got so bad you were sent to boarding school? Maybe if they'd sent you back home instead—"

"I didn't get *sent* anywhere. Boarding school in *Vienna* was my choice."

"The point is—"

"And I turned out okay." I flourished the sauce-coated spoon in the white kitchen.

"That kind of rupture can be avoided. If not avoided, reversed."

"You want people to move back when they start a family? Never mind there are hundreds of thousands of habesha abroad. Where would you store us all?"

"Taking a child out of its native environment creates problems, sooner or later."

"Everything is hunky-dory in Ethiopia? Must be the holy water."

"Don't worry about getting the hang of things back home. My sisters are there."

"Why? Where are you going to be?"

"I'm sure I will have some work-related travel."

"*You* will have work-related travel? Have you *met* me?"

"How long do you see yourself as a hostess?"

"Flight crew."

"Whatever is decided, I'm sure everyone will adapt," he backtracked. The air buzzed with the question, *How did it never occur to us to talk about this?* He upturned his right palm and held it out to me. "Come."

I was supposed to put my left palm over his while we talked it out. It was some sort of woo-woo couples' activity he read about. The person who has their hand on top was supposed to feel a much-needed sense of control.

"Fuck off." I wet a paper towel to clean up the pasta sauce I'd spattered on the kitchen walls, imagining Babbaye stabbing Isak's Talyan grandfather to death on the battlefield. That was my gratifying go-to fantasy whenever I saw what lay dormant in Isak, beneath his hipster New Age façade and vintage Ray-Ban tortoise-shell frames: his habesha core, a bone-deep patriarchal authoritarianism that claimed final say.

Isak's version of our future was clear. Isak's career, a real one, driven by passion and talent, would take priority over the one I'd stumbled into: a waitress of the sky. Forget the one I have given up on, so much that he didn't even know about it, art therapist. We would become a continuation of my parents. Except Isak would be Ema, the high-profile spouse doing big things in big places. I would be his faithful follower, allowed to pursue my interests but with the understanding that I can drop it any time, and pick it up wherever.

Such an arrangement worked for my parents. After Ema became a diplomat, Aba finally had the freedom to write his books on the most obscure Ethiopian topics. What would I do, following Isak around? Raise kids? I couldn't see myself embodying the image that always came to my mind when I thought of motherhood: Afewerk Tekle's painting *Mother Ethiopia*. This eternal habesha mother seated in a pose evocative of the shape of Ethiopia, against a blue background, cradling an infant in the folds of her thick, white yards of gabi. Incidentally, that was the only one of the maître artist's works of which Ema didn't own a silk print scarf.

Yet, on balance, Isak was a rare find. Not just a significantly evolved habesha guy but also someone who felt familiar the first time I met him. I'd been steered to him in Book City by the girl I used to be. If she'd had a chance to grow up, she would have picked Isak too. She knows precious from common.

•••

I had become used to having superficial, brief conversations with Ema on the phone, so I didn't realize right away that she wasn't making sense and her pauses were abnormally long. Then Aba told me they had upped her morphine. When she was in again at Princess Margaret Hospital, I waited until after visiting hours and went there purposely in uniform so I could talk my way in explaining that my job made it impossible for me to visit at any other time. At the reception desk, the nurse confiscated the bouquet I had brought for Ema, grabbing the stems in a chokehold and shaking them until pollen dusted our wrists, to show me why, as if I didn't speak English.

So I stood empty-handed beside Ema's hospital bed. Half of Ema's face was covered by a breathing mask. Her hair was dishevelled. Her eyes were deliriously blank. I waited for her to recognize me, play our game like we used to when I was little and followed her everywhere at home, in the billowing wake of her green velvet dressing gown. She'd suddenly stop, whirl around, and act baffled to find me behind her. *Hey! Where did you come from? Whose are you?* she would exclaim. For the split second it took for her velvet robe to swirl around her body, I'd be a deer in headlights. Her question sounded so genuine every time, for a second I really felt like a stray. Then I'd remember to say: *Yours!* She'd laugh at her silly mistake.

Of course, my sweet! she'd say, and continue striding long and sure, while I hurried to keep up.

I slipped my palm under Ema's inert hand connected to the IV. What new game is this, I wondered, my heart descending the length of my body like an empty elevator. Ema was the one looking up at me, unable to ask me the important question. And I could barely breathe, much less remind that tall goddess in green velvet that I am hers.

SIX

On the morning of my second day in Addis Ababa, Barb has no new news. I am weary of keeping a smile pasted to my face. Babbaye tolerates me. He doesn't pay me any more or less mind than he does anyone else. Mostly, he sits pensive, murmuring his sorrow when moved to speak, or his response to the words of consolation from his visitors.

Gela gives me one more responsibility: to make sure that the rock, used to keep the gate open, stays in place. She suspects one of the tenants, specifically that man who stepped over her yesterday, keeps removing it in a silent protest against their landlord's unending mourning period, which has people coming and going all day. So, I step out regularly to check on a rock. As a reward, on every trip back to the house I get a crash course on what life can do to a face—when I catch a fleeting simultaneous glimpse of my mother's two portraits above the porch door and the fireplace.

Late in the day, as I reopen the gate, two women arrive. One is a tiny, yellow-robed old nun who smells heavenly of church incense. Her raisin face is topped by a skullcap. She holds a double-headed wood cane in one hand, amber prayer beads in the other. She shuffles over the threshold, assisted by the other woman at her elbow, a novice so demure she might have been a virgin plucked out of choir practice in the Garden of Eden.

In the living room, the novice sits next to the nun, and focuses on the parquet as if it were inscribed with sacred texts. In a rare show of deference, Babbaye walks to the nun, intercepting me while I am asking visitors about refills. I follow him, an empty glass in each of my hands.

He seats me between him and the nun. He says, "Listen to this woman. She is your relation. She is your grand-aunt, your grandmother's only sister."

The barren one, who late in life had apparently taken vows to become one of the Ethiopian Orthodox post-menopausal nuns. A widow who took her vows after many years of husband-minding, renouncing the world before it renounces her.

"This is the daughter of Zimita," Babbaye says.

"Selam, Emmahoy," I greet her, proud of myself for remembering her title.

"I knew," Our Mother squawks, clicking her beads, launching into a speech, "I knew this would happen. My child, listen. I saw it in a dream."

My guard goes up. What's *this? It?* That my mother would die? Or I would come?

"Your grandmother came to me in a dream, to this house, through those doors. I sat here, as I sit now." I look at the porch doors, expecting a woman I have never met, then back at her, a woman I have just met. "The wife of the Shaleqa wears the whitest hager libs. Her hair is plaited back from her forehead in thin rows and gathered at the back like a black cloud. Her netela is open at her neck showing her nikisat."

She has just described the portrait which has been on the first row of Babbaye's shelf since the dawn of time. The tattoos were seven green rings around her neck. Her cause of death was grief, when she accepted that the Terror would never return her sons, alive or dead.

Instinct tells me I'm not going to care for where this line of dream-telling ends up. I tip the glasses in my hands until they are horizontal, testing the rims with the dregs of Fanta and St. George beer, daring them to spill over the imperceptible lip.

"Your grandmother is as beautiful as Fasika day. I say, *Sister, why have you come after so long away?* She answers, *I have come to fetch someone.*" Emmahoy taps a gnarled fingernail on my knee for effect. "Have come to fetch someone."

All that's expected from me is to submissively accept Emmahoy's enigmatic testimony. Or riddle it out quietly like the enkokilish Aba used to distract me with when I got restless in restaurants as a child. He'd introduce a session by calling, *Enkokilish!*

I would give the response, *Min awkilih! What should I know?*

What feeds you like a mother, but punishes you like a stepmother?

A honeybee.

What I should do now is hold my peace. Shut up and breathe through my nose. These nuns, Aba has told me, don't want their pronouncements questioned any more than the monks and priests for whom they cook and clean.

"Fetch who?" I say.

Emmahoy is surprised. "Your mother. She had come to fetch your mother."

"Did she say that?"

Emmahoy's eyes, gleaming furiously, flick to my grandfather. I believe Emmahoy had this dream, but not what she and Babbaye say it means. Why would my grandmother be so interested in a daughter she didn't want to live for? She came to her sister, in her husband's house. Obviously she came to "fetch" one of *them.* I spill the Fanta, suddenly frightened by even half a chance of Babbaye's imminent death.

I don't know what's taking Gela so long. Usually she comes in within moments of a new guest arriving to offer an assortment of refreshments on a tray carried by Aberash, just like the lead hostess in business class.

"Let me bring you some water, Emmahoy." I can't imagine what else a nun would drink. I escape from between these co-conspirators.

The kitchen is empty. I know Aberash has gone out to return empties. I grab a plate, heap misir wot from some so-and-so's house, and wolf it down with bread. With each bite, I feel myself calm down. Babbaye is so determined to get Ema back, he has even recruited an ally from the brink of the afterlife to present a compelling argument for his case. Like the Axum Obelisk, he won't stop until he's accomplished his mission. For Babbaye, the one silver lining in Ema's two-term posting to Rome was his belief that she was using her position to keep alive the obelisk repatriation issue. Ema and Aba used to joke about how Babbaye behaved as if the Talyans had looted the stone from his own backyard, in the late thirties when he was a sixteen-year-old resistance fighter. For sixty-eight years, he kept up pressure for the stone's homecoming. He sat on every repatriation committee. He signed every petition. Two years ago, in 2008, the tall rock, repatriated from Rome, was finally reinstalled in Axum, in its original hole.

I finish my food and gargle my mouth with the last bottle of mineral water in the kitchen. I go to the side alley to spit.

A tomcat observes me from the roof of the main house, then hops soundlessly to the roof of the service quarters. His landing on the corrugated iron creates a delicate rumble that fades as he saunters away.

Pacified, I go to the storage room to get bottled water for Emmahoy. I walk into a dense fume of fermentation. Gela and Lomi stand over one of the blue plastic barrels. Lomi pours water into the barrel from a deep pail. Gela stirs it in with a wooden stick.

"Stay back," Gela says. I go closer and peer at our distorted reflections in a well of dark brown liquid. "It's tella for the guests on the Forty."

"All this?"

"Not only for them," Lomi says. The twinkle in her eyes tells me plenty about her relationship to the ale.

After they have diluted the liquid and closed the lid, they start to seal the barrel with mud from a shallow tub. I unhesitatingly plunge my hands in. The women don't protest. They have stopped trying to anticipate or fathom my impulses. I miss them already, delighted that now I, too, have people about whom I can exclaim, the way older habesha folks do about their age mates, *Oh so-and-so? We came up mashing earth together, you know!*

Soil. All this pressure about Ema's burial comes down to which soil is best. To Babbaye, there has never been a question of what soil is best. Even me, if anyone had asked me when I was very little, I would have said Ethiopian soil is best, too. Especially after the rain, when the soft lumps slid down my throat like butter.

In the before-time, I spent so many afternoons making mud people that I would even get it in my eyes. I remember

Le'ul holding my face up to the light, and using a corner of Ema's clean pressed handkerchief to scoop out the dirt. He once tore out a blank page from the back of one of Aba's books for me to make my mud people on, so he could carry them inside for me. That was how I stopped having a big leqso every time the cats destroyed my creations while they dried in the sun.

SEVEN

I was at Union Station, waiting for Isak and whatever he'd excavated to gift to me for our second anniversary, when Aba left me a voicemail. He said it was about Ema. I should come home when I landed. Since the day the nurse took away Ema's flowers, I hadn't been able to bring myself to visit my mother. I tried to remember the last thing I had said to her on the phone, or she to me. Something about time. Yes, before we ended our lethargic conversation, she had said, *Never rush.* That was how I knew, before being told. Ema was gone. I noted the present date and time on my phone: 2:15 p.m. March 14, 2010.

When Isak arrived, I wanted to go to Centre Island. He reminded me it was off-season. Let's ride the ferry anyway, I said, just for the view. He pried out of me why I was being so strange. I told him of Aba's call and my hunch of what it was about. He said I had to go home immediately.

"I should come with you..." he added.

There was an unspoken *but* at the end of his offer. We knew that with habesha families, the only significant other you bring home is the one you intend to marry. You don't subject your parents to round after round of cancelled futures every time you split up with a lover.

"Is this your idea of a proposal?" I laughed. Isak didn't. I turned away. "What's the point? Hurrying back will not change anything."

I was too ashamed to go home yet, because the next thought that had come to my mind after I memorized the date and time was, *I can finally leave Toronto. You finally got what you wanted, Ema. No more false alarms. You can go home for good now, and I will never have to be near Le'ul again for as long as I live.*

I was on the cusp of a whole new after-time. After Ema died. I wanted one last lull of normalcy before I faced the consequences of my failure as a daughter.

Isak refused to ride to the island with me. He agreed only when he saw how determined I was. I would go with or without him. Aba thought I was away, so it was very important to me that I really did go away, even if it was for thirty minutes, and came back. Isak sat inside the ferry for the trip. Then he took my condo key, to wait for me there, while I went to the residence.

Aba ushered me into the foyer like a guest of honour at a reception. A rush of mourners came out from the living room. He pulled me into a tight hug, as if to protect me from them, but really I knew he didn't want to have to look at me when he whispered, so closely in my ear that at first I didn't understand, "She didn't make it."

As if dying was a failure on her part, when really the failure was mine, to motivate her to stay another day.

I become rooted to the carpet, petrified by the snarling lion at my feet. Knowing the news in my gut and actually hearing it were very different things. My body wouldn't move. It believed that being still could stop time, make the fact of Ema's death untrue.

A man parted his way through the mourners. Aba pushed me toward him. I fell into the person's chest. It felt like home, gave me comfort, until I saw the nail of the index finger, withered by a boyhood infection.

I was crying on Le'ul.

My impulse was to shove him away, scrub myself clean, change clothes, run. But the more calculating part of my brain told me to stay put, receive Le'ul's hug, sob dryly against his lean frame, allow his sweet cologne into my lungs. I would only have to do it this once. Everyone was watching. Hugging was what a grief-stricken brother and sister should do. I deserved the flashbacks that this contact brought me. This revolting embrace was punishment I must sustain for being a disgrace of a daughter who was already looking forward to burying her mother in Ethiopia so she could be free of Toronto, of Le'ul, at last.

Once I had calmed down, the mourners returned to the living room. Le'ul squeezed my puny hand in his muscular paw, grinding my bones, and told me to go upstairs and see what he and Aba had chosen for Ema to wear tomorrow.

Ema's black Max Mara suit, pink micro-pleated blouse, silk print scarf of Afewerk's Africa Hall painting, black purse, and heels were laid out on the bed. I swept everything to the floor. This was unacceptable, all wrong. Ema used to remove this kind of outfit off her body as soon as she got home from work. She couldn't wait to get back into her hager libs, what she dreamed of wearing every day for the rest of her life after retirement, when she would be back in her country permanently. If I knew nothing else about my mother, I knew that. She was always trying to feel as if she was in Ethiopia.

I spread out several layers of her hager libs and netela,

what she had worn for rest. I folded them perfectly and carried them downstairs. In the living room, Tiru directed me to sit on a sofa between Aba and Le'ul. She tried to take the clothes but I wouldn't let go.

From the gathered mourners sitting on every available surface, and leaning against the walls, I recognized only the consulate staff and their family members. I was surprised, a little jealous even, at how wide my parents' circle of friends in Toronto seemed to be. Then it struck me that some of these might be Le'ul's people. I still hadn't looked at him directly, nor he at me. But I was aware of his high-boned, snakelike profile, wiry goatee, of his side pressing into mine, his hairy arms coming out of his rolled up shirtsleeves.

After hours of sitting in state, as if we were the dead ones, Le'ul drove Aba and me to the funeral home. I gave the clothes I'd chosen for Ema to Stanley Chan, the funeral director, explaining that she would be happy with any of them, but she wore the set embroidered in orange thread most. I wanted to dress her myself, but I knew she wouldn't want me to see all her scars, not at the same time. I also gave Stanley one rose from her garden, for her to hold. Stanley said she would be ready for viewing tomorrow. He gave us the codes to enter the building after hours, a shared code for the main door and a private code for the room she would be in.

Back at the residence, I felt the mourners watching my every move. They watched Le'ul, too. Though we did nothing except sit next to each other. We didn't talk, but I was sure they would think that was just from shock. Aba alternated between long spells of silence, moaning, mundane conversation, and bursts of anecdotes about himself and Ema.

When dinner was served, I sat next to Le'ul because it was expected. He spooned rice onto my plate. I imagined Ema's ghost pleased to see us so familial. After dinner, the mourners got to leave but I had to stay overnight because that, too, was expected by the staff. Once Tiru had turned in for the night, I locked the basement door behind me and slept on a couch in the den. I remembered Isak, and texted him to go home.

The second day passed. I sat between Le'ul and Aba again, allowing myself to be looked at with pity, spoken to consolingly.

In the afternoon, we went to the funeral home to see Ema, accompanied by an entourage of mourners who gathered around to watch Aba and me cry over her, kiss her cold lips, squeeze her rigid feet. Le'ul stood aside, as stoic as a bodyguard. I overheard approving comments about Ema's outfit. I felt vindicated. Finally, I had done one thing right by Ema.

In the middle of the second night, I woke and found Le'ul curled asleep on the floor beside the couch. I'd been in such a daze I forgot to lock the basement door. I sat up and swung my legs over as if to get up. My bare foot, lit by the moon, hovered over his neck. I contemplated how, if I completed the motion and stood, I could swiftly crush his delicate throat under my heel. But I felt Ema's sadness. Ema, alone at Stanley's with only the rush of traffic outside for company, her gauze-thin netela and her hager libs useless against the cold.

In my parents' bedroom on the second floor, I found Aba lying awake on top of the bedcovers on Ema's side of the bed, talking to himself. I said we had to take Ema a gabi. When I spoke, I realized how crazy I sounded. But Aba was up and in her closet, in complete agreement, angry with us for not having instructed Stanley to dress Ema in all the hager libs.

"What are we keeping the rest of them for?!" he said, messing up her stacks.

I hurried him out of the house and drove away quickly before he noticed Le'ul wasn't with us. We found Ema just as we had left her. I tried hard to detect any difference, to prove that she was fooling us, that she had changed her mind about dying as casually as she used to change her flights. She hadn't. Her mouth was still closed over her fallen jaw. The rose was still trapped under her rigid, overlapped palms. She looked more emaciated than ever. Her Mariam kisses blended into her darkened skin. I covered her with the gabi we had brought, leaving only her face exposed, but her chill seeped through the fabric. She would never be warm enough.

"Had she been in Ethiopia," Aba said, "we could not have had this pleasure, her all to ourselves. She would have been at the church overnight. Her face never revealed."

"When are we flying her home?"

I'd heard of other habesha sending bodies back to Ethiopia. I'd donated money for families I didn't know when they were raising funds for repatriation. I'd worked many flights where I knew which passengers were escorting the remains of their loved ones in the cargo hold. But I never paid attention to the details of how it was done. I never expected I'd need to know.

"Does Babbaye know we are bringing Ema soon?" Babbaye had wanted Ema back since 1991, when we left Ethiopia. How bittersweet this would be for him. Aba didn't answer. He seemed so brittle. He had aged decades in days. He had new grey hairs. His skin looked smeared with ash. I feared that if Aba had to think about one more thing he would disintegrate. I let the question be.

Aba started to chant, in Ge'ez, the psalter that he had known since he was a little boy training to become a priest at the one church in Harrar. I had never heard him recite from

Mezmure Dawit, but I knew the things of childhood never really leave you.

I sat on the floor with my back against the wall, listening, drifting at the edge of consciousness, where the guttural sounds of the ancient language seemed to belong.

Early on the third day, accompanied by double yesterday's entourage, we escorted Ema from the funeral home to an Ethiopian Orthodox church I didn't even know existed in Toronto, on Eglinton West. Ema's coffin was draped in embroidered red velvet and placed in front of the altar. Aba and Le'ul were in the front pew of the men's side. I sat nearest the aisle in the front pew on the women's side, with Tiru, who that morning had pulled me into the powder room and urged me, *Don't let your father see you cry.*

During the hours-long service, through the fog of incense and chanting, I didn't have to see all the sad faces behind me to know none of them felt a fraction of my grief, not even Tiru, who stood for the entire service instead of sitting for the sitting parts, weeping enough for the both of us. For all that show, and notwithstanding the numbness I'd been moving through the past two days, I knew nobody would ever love or miss me the way I loved, missed Ema.

Everything that had ever been between us landed on me in one solid mass of sorrow and regret over words said and unsaid, actions taken and abandoned—but at the core, unscathed, constant, was a simple, timeless kernel of love that obliterated the petty clutter of our history. I burst into tears, suddenly walloped by a desire for a daughter of my own. I cried for a child who might never exist. I needed to create a *her* who would love me as only a daughter can love a mother, whether she told me all the time, or never. I loved Isak, but I truly understood love only after Ema was gone. Even Aba's grief was pitiful in comparison to mine. Sure, he knew her longer, but what was romance compared to being one flesh, one blood?

Even at his best, Isak never would give me the love of my own child. Even she might not be able to fully comprehend her own feelings. I'd learned, in the seconds it took for Aba to whisper in my ear, *She didn't make it*, as if it was a dirty little family secret, how impossible it is to love a mother as absolutely as she deserves to be loved until after she is gone. What better company for the departed than the aura of a child's pure adoration?

In the car after church, I fell asleep on Aba's chest in the back seat, as if knocked out by the realization that hit me during the service. When I awoke, we were driving into a place called Scarborough Bluffs Cemetery.

"Why are we here?" I said. "Aba?"

He patted my shoulder, to strengthen me for what was about to happen. "She wanted to be where all her children are."

We were not going to the airport, as I had assumed. We were not taking Ema to Ethiopia. We were burying her here in Toronto.

As my mother's coffin was lowered into the ground under a rain of soil and roses, a blue butterfly darted under it and never came back out. No one else saw, only me. I feared the butterfly was crushed. I walked away, in search of that dash of blue. I roamed the grounds all the way to the perimeter fence, a few feet in from the edge of the bluffs that rose above the lake, and then turned around. At first, I thought my butterfly had turned into a person. A human being whose shape, height, colour I knew, who wore the suit and sunglasses of the man I love. I looked away. My mind was tricking me. Isak shouldn't be here, so it couldn't be him. Again, I looked. Yes, Isak.

Isak stood next to Ema's grave, hands in pockets, patiently waiting for me. He didn't see the one person walking against the flow of mourners, coming up behind him. Le'ul. But he felt Le'ul's touch, a comradely slap on Isak's shoulder. Isak turned, already offering his hand in greeting. They chatted, facing each other, perfectly aligned. One person with two heads.

Isak had to return to New Haven right after the burial. I saw him off at Union Station. I flinched away from his goodbye embrace. Because of grief, he probably thought. I couldn't erase from my mind Le'ul's hand on his shoulder, the memory of breath passing between them.

"I will call you from the train. I will call you again when I get to Grand Central. You can call me any time. Call me every minute."

I nodded, knowing I wouldn't. There was puzzlement in in his eyes—*you told me you were an only child*—but he left without asking. I knew I had to explain, sooner or later.

When I was halfway home, Isak texted me. He'd accidentally taken my condo key with him. I had left my spare with Ema. I went back to the residence to get it. I couldn't find it anywhere upstairs. I was too nervous to go to the third floor, where Ema never wanted any of us to be, as though she might still be up there and yell at me to go away. I gave up and returned downstairs, figuring my concierge would let me in. I crossed the empty formal dining room toward the French windows that open onto the garden, in the same moment that Le'ul entered from there.

I became still, stared at the floor. The watchful, trapped-animal feeling of my childhood sprang back. Only the length of the sideboard was between us.

"Where were you?" This was only the second time he'd spoken to me in the last three days, again in Amharic which made me feel grabbed by the neck and yanked to the past.

I spoke in a small voice, in Amharic, afraid that if I responded in English Le'ul would think I was defying him. "At Union Station."

"Your friend is gone."

"Yes."

Le'ul took a digital camera out of his jacket pocket. "I was getting this for you from the car." The camera was brand new; I remembered Aba gave it to Ema last Christmas. I received it, warm from his body heat. I slipped the handle around my wrist.

"It should be in your bag. Handle it with care. That's an expensive camera."

I obeyed. On the sideboard, there was a bowl of Ricola cough drops. He plucked one out and tossed it to me. It fell. "You don't want one," he said.

"It's the last batch Ema bought."

"She would want us to enjoy them."

I stooped to pick up the Ricola. I unrolled the wrapping as slowly as Ema used to, the weaker she got. Le'ul watched, like this was essential medicine I must swallow, until the lozenge disappeared between my lips.

When he was gone, I spit it out into my palm. Yet, as I shut the garden doors behind me, I couldn't bear to let go of anything of Ema's. I put the sticky, warm thing back in my mouth.

Isak offered to FedEx me my condo key so I wouldn't have to wait until he returned on the weekend. I wanted my key, but I wished he'd not visit me again so soon. Rather than say so, I told him I could wait, and booked off two days right after the end of my four bereavement days, so that I would be working at least part of the time Isak was here. I spent the days at home, going out only once, in the morning, to see Ema.

Every time I went to Scarborough Bluffs Cemetery, I felt I was going there to confirm that Ema would be in Toronto forever now, and so would I. How could I ever work up the willpower to abandon Ema, after not even saying goodbye to her, knowing she chose me over New York, over becoming *Her Excellency*, over resting with her ancestors in Ethiopia? She chose me. I had to choose her.

The mound of soft soil was all but covered by heaps of flowers. A wooden cross stuck in the earth like an explorer's stake in *terra incognita* proclaimed her full name, *Zimita Tessema Gedlu*. This was my mother now, I thought, this collection of objects, which I'd seen countless times in other contexts but never expected to see in relation to my own flesh and blood.

Alone with her for the first time since my last visit to Princess Margaret Hospital, when she didn't even recognize me, I felt shy. I was with an intimidating stranger. Even if I could think of something to say, what was I supposed to address? The approximate location of her head, the air, the soil, the cross, the lake, the flowers?

"Do you like your flowers?"

No answer. Silence. True to her name.

"You have yellow, white lilies, sunflowers, red, white roses, pink gerberas, white daisies, a spray of purple somethings." I hoped she liked them. "You would have loved them."

The past few days had been unseasonably sunny and dry for early spring. The flowers were drooping. I wished I had a way of saving their beauty, before they rotted in the compost bin by the gates. Something, maybe her, reminded me the camera was still in my purse. I first deleted the few pictures from the memory card, mistake shots that Aba or Ema took of unidentifiable things while figuring out how the camera worked. They never did well with technology. Then I photographed Ema's flowers. Over the next two days, as the flowers wilted further, I took many more pictures, relieved to have a purpose.

After my so-called friends, Sara and her posse, paid a condolence visit on my last day off, I cut my hair in my bathroom. Later, I got it corrected at a salon. Just as I had hoped, I got my first shift back at work the day Isak was arriving on his visit. Only a quick run to Halifax, though. My crew, who were informed of my bereavement, found it easier to cheer me up by complimenting me on my new look, as if it was a fashion choice, than by directly telling me they were sorry about my mother's death. I hated the feel of my exposed neck, when I stood chiming greetings at the open door of a turboprop. The air coming through the gap between the plane and the gangway felt like the unwanted touch of a man. I had to make a conscious effort to keep the grin pasted to my face, welcoming people to a space where there are no sharp edges and anger is officially taboo.

When I got back to my place, Isak buzzed me up. He didn't get up from the couch as I hung my purse on the same hook where he'd hung my key. "Is it because he's adopted?" he asked. I had barely kicked off my shoes. "You don't consider him your real sibling?"

"Only technically he is family."

"Not technically. He *is* your family."

"He's Aba's very distant cousin-by-marriage. He was raised by a single mother in some village near Harrar, then orphaned at eight. People in the village saw him on the street, asked around, and sent him to us in Adisaba. He literally turned up outside our gate one day. That's what I've been told. My parents adopted him. No one consulted me. He and I were never close. Even actual siblings sometimes have completely separate lives, you know."

"But they acknowledge each other's existence."

"What do you want me to say? Now you know. I have a..." I refused to use the word *brother.* I got so tired of agonizing over *adopted* brother or *step*-brother. Ema thought it would help if I said *not-flesh* brother. Le'ul was all and none of those. He was someone I couldn't shake off any more than I could step out of my own skin. I was trying to grant myself permission to not speak of him.

"Brother." Isak finished the sentence for me.

"Adopted brother."

"Big deal. He's still your brother."

If Isak said that word one more time, I was sure I would stab him.

He wasn't done lecturing. "You need to let go of this bad habesha mentality of adoption as something to be ashamed of. We're happy enough to give away our children to whites, but can't claim them ourselves?"

"Did he call me his sister?"

"Who else would he say you are?"

"Why didn't you go home last week? How did you find out where the funeral was?" My turn to interrogate. "What'd you do, ask around at Ossington and Bloor? Can't throw a rock in that area without hitting a big habesha forehead."

"No," he said, dignified. "I called the consulate and expressed a wish to pay my respects. The death of a diplomatic representative touches their community. It is not a street gossip topic."

"Could have fooled me."

From the turnout, it was clear that Ema's funeral was the social event of the year for the broader community, right up there with a Teddy concert. The ambassador and his wife came from Ottawa. People came to gawk as much as mourn, I was sure of it, to capitalize on at least the first floor of the residence being opened to the public. *See how the other half lives.* Once a year, on the twentieth of Ginbot, the anniversary of the day Addis Ababa was liberated by Babbaye's enemy's enemy, all embassies threw a reception that was by invitation only, for dignitaries and prominent members of the habesha community. For Ema's funeral, it seemed if one could sour up one's face and wail convincingly enough, there were no questions asked.

"Community my ass. They're all pretenders. I fucking hate them."

"Has it occurred to you that your mother was well liked? That the community genuinely considered her family, or wanted to stand in for her family who couldn't make it?"

I snorted at the idea of Babbaye flying to Canada to attend Ema's funeral, or even see her grave. Babbaye, who had been so hostile to anything foreign since the resistance, then his exile from Ethiopia on the Sudanese side of Metemma, and finally his triumphal return to Ethiopia ahead of the emperor. *That* Babbaye coming out *here*!

I wondered if I should call him. I never had, only talked to him if I was with Ema or Aba when they did. I wouldn't know what to say. *Sorry for your loss? Sorry we buried your daughter out here? Believe me, I had nothing to do with it?*

I walked to Isak. "Fine, but I hate that now they can get to Ema any time they want, without an appointment. They don't have the right. Who knows what they'll do or say to her?"

Isak stood and hugged me. "You're paranoid, people have better things to do than travel across town to haunt your mother's grave."

"Oh yeah? Like what?"

I slid my hands down his back, under the waist of his pants, around to his front. I started unbuttoning his shirt from the bottom up. He pulled back, rebuttoned it. Back and forth we went, up and down, until he seized my hands.

"Dess!"

I got up on tiptoes and kissed him. He didn't flow to the next move. He never does.

"No," he said.

"I want you to hold me."

"I was holding you."

"Not just hold me."

I did want him to hold me, as Ema used to hold me at naptime. I wanted him to draw me into his chest, curve his body around mine so I could burrow deeper. I felt a clawing need to get pregnant.

"Touch my neck."

He massaged my neck. "Short hair suits you, unfortunately."

"Told you I'm a cutter. Kiss it."

While he did, I unzipped and pushed his pants down. "Your dick doesn't care who died either," I whispered, pulling at it until he was breathing in the way of all men inching up to the point of no return. I made him approach that peak, watched his hands frantic on my body. There it was. My Isak was gone, not in the room. He was just a hard heavy-breathing glassy-eyed male now. I was a hole to be entered.

I turned around, fell forward, spread open, bracing against the coffee table, and shoved him in, racing to replace an abiding memory with one as graphic, as scalding. Wanting to get and give it hard, fast, angry, mean. Rushing to be without my body, or to exchange it. Reaching to pass all shame and disgust. Wanting something slammed, clawed, wrenched, choked out. I thought of Ema. Of Aba. Of Le'ul. Of this body I carried around, these breasts I couldn't tear off. I was cold, in the room where Ema had lain, holding under her lifeless hands one desiccated rose.

Spent, Isak looked at me with the shame I wanted him to feel. I looked at him with sadness, not anger, at what he put me through. I couldn't imagine how I had ever found him attractive, how I had fantasized about our entwined, ecstatic bodies. We behaved cautiously toward each other the rest of the evening. We ordered in what I wanted for dinner, Thai. We got ready for bed without once touching each other.

He plunked down on the bed with a forced casualness and flipped on the TV. I lay next to him, my head on his pillow. I touched my belly as if it was swelling not with food but a child. "Don't worry, we'll raise her in Ethiopia."

He stared at the TV. I fell asleep, holding his arm tight. The next day, he said he had brought a lot of reading to do, having assumed I'd go to the residence for Ema's Seventh Day. I went out and wandered on the Danforth. When I returned late in the afternoon, he had changed his train ticket to an earlier time.

While he was still on the train, I sent him a text. *I need a break.* Immediately, I wanted to unwrite it, but I could see that it had been read. Days went by without a response. I ran the opal he'd given me for our first anniversary under hot then cold water, exposing it to sudden temperature change, exactly what he said not to do. It didn't crack. The opal was okay, so we were okay. I didn't have to try to remember the last thing we had said to each other.

EIGHT

On my third full day at Babbaye's, there is a new face in the living room, a cheerful man in a black suit, of medium height and build, with a head of dense, dyed black hair. When I enter from the porch after a routine trip to prop the gate open with the rock, he crosses the room toward me and blocks my path. I'm forced to stop.

He touches my shoulder with his fingertips. "To me, death is life," he says, by way of greeting.

I sit so I can separate myself from his touch. "Okay."

He takes a chair beside me and produces a business card, which he offers with both hands. *Tekalegn Sime, CEO of Gebre-Igziabher International Diaspora Funeral Services.*

"But please," he says, hand over heart, "know me as Teka."

"Do you want me to have the card?"

"Of course. Keep it, keep it."

If Babbaye came up with this next strategy after Emmahoy, the nun with the fetching dream, left yesterday, or if it is all part of the same play, who knows? Babbaye is not even looking our way. I fold the brand new card into four. Teka looks pained, as if I am folding him into four. I tuck it into the pocket of my grimy jeans. I have been wearing the same outfit every day, stuffing my dirty undies at the bottom of my suitcase, but if I'm smelly I can't tell because there are so many aromas flying around this house. Who knew grieving was so fragrant? If it's not the coffee, it's the fresh injera or bread, or the food constantly reheated, or spilled beer and soda, or the unmade-bed odour of the elderly. Right now, the predominant scent is the coffee Gela is roasting in the kitchen. Today might be the day I let my diaspora flag fly and ask for mine in a big mug.

"Who's my opposite in Canada?" Teka says.

"What?"

"Your funeral person there, who is he?"

"I don't think you'd know him."

"Try, try. I work with Toronto people, too."

"Stanley Chan?"

"Oh." Teka slaps his knee, as if I've mentioned a dear friend, with whom he came up mashing earth together. He wags his finger at me. "Because of that man, you know, I have seen countries where I never dreamed I would go. Stan hates flying. With the miles he earns from sending remains, he buys me airplane tickets for a small fee. So, you see, really because of death I have life."

According to Teka, the two have even met, on Skype, to discuss a partnership, a sort of one-stop shop for body repatriations. "Though of course the flow of remains sent home," Teka says, clearing his throat, "will always be greater from your end."

I focus on twirling pairs of cotton strands on the fringe of my netela. Since Teka's getting nowhere with me, he shuffles over several seats, to Babbaye, to introduce himself. Maybe Teka is the funeral director's version of an ambulance chaser, who scouts residential areas for signs of bereavement— the rental tents for the overflow of mourners, the inverted netelas, people dressed in black, coming and going, the wails. Oh, the wails.

It seems a genuine first meeting between Teka and Babbaye. But my suspicions return when Babbaye launches into questions too specific to have just occurred to him. Teka, to his credit, doesn't lose any of his verve. Using the formal plural to refer to Ema, he says, "After the accompanying person signs for their remains at Bole Special Customs, a representative from my shop will wait at the Customs Morgue to receive them."

"Who, exactly?" Babbaye says.

"I, gashe," Teka says, straightening up into *sir* mode.

"Are there special handlers?"

"Special handlers will remove them before any other cargo or luggage."

"What kind of vehicle do you drive?"

"A black Volkswagen van. We have removed the back seats. On the front and back we attach wreaths, with real roses of any colour of your choosing, at no charge."

"Your men are gentle, respectful?"

"What else would they do, gashe, peek?" Teka says, indignant. I am as impressed by Teka's daring as by Babbaye's self-delusion. He expects to contract this man's services one day.

"The coffin will not be opened?"

Teka shakes his head. "The same day, or next, we deliver to church, then to the resting grounds. We stay until the earth is sealed for the final time," Teka boasts, as if he has the power to ensure that. "We can recreate anything. The headstone, the flower arrangements. I only will need photographs of Stan's work." So Ema is *Stan's work* now. Soon she is supposed to be *Teka's work*. "Also of course a photo we can enlarge for the ceremony, or affix on the stone. Anything! I can create or recreate!" His eyes sparkle with a new thought. "Except life!" He chuckles. "I can't recreate life. Only Igziabher can!"

Babbaye sends me to his room to bring the pictures of Ema's grave that Aba mailed him, to show Teka the wreaths. I am to find the envelope in his dresser. In Babbaye's bedroom, I open the top dresser drawer, but it is full of the framed photos that used to be on the living room shelf, of my baptism and kindergarten graduation, my grandmother, and my six uncles who were scooped for questioning by the Terror on Christmas 1978. Each son had been a namesake of one of Babbaye's brothers who had been executed by the Talyans during the occupation. A kind of replacement. I wonder who Ema was supposed to have been a replacement for. Perhaps for Babbaye's runaway sisters, in case they, too, had perished at the hands of the Talyans?

I'm about to try a lower drawer when I spot the edge of a Canada Post Express envelope. The photos in it are Photoshopped. Le'ul, as promised, had integrated the photos of Ema's flowers, which I took on my bereavement leave days, onto the photos of the bare grave, which he made me take on the day I went with him and Aba to Scarborough Bluffs Cemetery. I had never meant to go. That day, I thought my time with them would be limited to the residence, where Aba had summoned me so we could pack Ema's belongings, as a family.

•••

For the ten days after Isak decided to ignore my breakup text, I worked non-stop, but only short trips in the Northeast. Aba called me several times a day, never leaving a voicemail. When I finally responded, he said, *All three of us have to pack her belongings together.* It seemed that Ema's death outranked what he knew of my childhood. March 14 was officially now the worst thing that had happened—a new, permanent grief, which we had in common, which cancelled out what happened only to me. Well, so be it, I thought. At least my terror had trained me to bear the unavoidable.

At the residence, I found Aba in the bedroom, between the walk-in closet and the bathroom, absent-mindedly testing the seams on a suitcase. Le'ul was in the walk-in closet. I claimed the bathroom. Even with the buffer of the bedroom, and Aba, between me and Le'ul, all my senses were alert to Le'ul. I sat on Ema's vanity chair, my grandmother's mesob full of Ema's hair rollers on the counter in front of me, taking as long as possible with my unnecessary task. I was extracting Ema's black and silver hairs from her rollers, one strand at a time, and collecting them on a white handkerchief dotted with tiny blue flowers which I had spread out on my lap. When I finished collecting the hairs, I folded the handkerchief and pressed it flat. Then I began to scrub the rollers, one by one, with an old toothbrush under running water.

I heard Le'ul walking to the bedroom. Aba spoke.

"The old man sent me more emails."

My instinct told me the messages must be about Ema's burial in Canada. I turned down the water flow so I could hear the conversation.

Le'ul said, "Email? I bet he bullied some kid into writing them for him."

Aba said, "He has not contacted me this many times in all the years he has known me. Now he is offended because he believes I am ignoring him, denying her body the company of her ancestors."

Before Aba gave up the professorial life to accompany Ema to Vienna, he had been a man close to his father-in-law's heart. Babbaye respected Aba's brand of patriotism, where the weapon of choice was the pen, not the bayonet. Babbaye hadn't anticipated how much Aba would disappoint him by supporting Ema as she accepted promotions abroad, instead of convincing her to return to Ethiopia at the end of each four year cycle. Babbaye had not changed his mind, even when Ema became a consul general, which Aba told him was as significant as the old royal title of Enderase.

"One ignores the Shaleqa at their peril," Le'ul said.

"You know the first thing he said when his old friends, my former professor and that group of men, told him the merdo? He wanted to know when we are bringing her home."

"Not *if*?"

I shut off the water. I knew it. Even after so much time had passed, and at such a distance, Babbaye and I once again wanted the same thing, for our separate reasons. I wanted Ema to leave me, so that I was not the one to leave her again.

I patted the hair rollers dry with a towel and replaced them in the mesob in neat concentric circles. Aba told Le'ul that he was concerned about the pointy heels of Ema's shoes breaking through the plastic bag Le'ul had stuffed them in. He ordered Le'ul to redo them, wrapping the heels in newspaper first. Le'ul went downstairs to get newspaper.

I edged into the bedroom, holding the mesob of clean-as-new rollers, and put it beside my purse. I was going to keep it. Aba was placing Ema's sandals side by side into a suitcase. I should have stayed out of this family complication regarding Babbaye's wish for Ema's body, but considering that I had no intention of calling Babbaye, I felt I should at least indirectly do something for the poor man, my hero as a child. He used to say openly what no one dared to say. He openly criticized Le'ul's adoption, wanted Ema and Aba to have a son of their own. Secretly, I wished for a sister.

"Aba, did you tell Babbaye what Ema wanted?"

Aba looked at me as if I had made an absurd suggestion. "How do you tell the Shaleqa his one remaining child didn't want to be buried in her country? How will that seem?"

I slipped the handkerchief containing Ema's hair into my purse. In Ema's jewellery box, I searched for my key. "That's not what she said. If you tell Babbaye exactly what she said, he would understand?"

"Perhaps," Aba said. "One day. When it is a better time."

"Then at least send him pictures of the gravesite. He'll appreciate it." I could have told Aba I already had pictures. But those were for Ema. "With pictures, Babbaye can see exactly where at least one of his children is." Nothing of my uncles was ever recovered at any of the sites outside Addis Ababa during the exhumations of mass graves. They were out there in unmarked ground, still answering for unspecified crimes.

"Don't you think a father deserves that, Aba?"

Aba said, "Yes, but when it's completed, with the stone, the engraving. We have to meet with Stanley about the stone."

"Or send pictures of the plot as it is now. With the wreaths," Le'ul said. I nearly jumped out of my skin. I hadn't heard him return.

"If they are still there," I said, to Aba.

Le'ul spoke for him. "When the headstone is installed, send more pictures. And when the roses bloom. We should plant a cutting from her garden. Continue what she started," he said. In every city she lived, Ema had grown generations of a cutting from the rosebush Aba had given her as a wedding present.

Suddenly, Aba became very worried that Ema's stone would not be ready for the dedication on her tezkar. "If you had answered my calls, we would not be so late in ordering it," he said, peeling newspaper sheets for Le'ul. He'd never spoken so harshly to me in my life.

"Don't worry about time, Aba."

To appease him, and be the better child, Le'ul insisted that we order the stone right then. So, we abandoned the packing and went to Stanley's funeral parlour. Le'ul and I sat on either side of Aba on a dark brown leather sofa in Stanley's office, browsing catalogues of headstones, statues, and fonts. Stanley sat opposite us. Neatly re-folded on the grand oak desk behind him, softly glowing in the light of his art-deco lamps, was a stack of snow-white cotton, the remainder of the netela and hager libs that I had given to Stanley to dress Ema in.

"She said to never bury her in Adisaba," Aba said, arguing with an unseen opponent, while he flipped through the catalogue of headstones.

That was a very different version of what Aba told me Ema wanted. So different as to not be the same, at all, as, *She wanted to be where all her children are.*

Aba paused, then responded to his adversary. "I refuse to have a permanent distance between me and Emwodish." Aba became more vehement, using his pet name for Ema, *you whom I love.* "I refuse to have to book a ticket, fly fourteen hours, stand in the visa line, pass through customs. Just to sit for hours by her, talk to her about this and that, hear her replies. To be harassed by a sour, underpaid guard for seeking this simple pleasure? To pay a lazy, unmannered watchman to retain the glow of her marble, the life in her roses, keep her unmolested? I refuse such affronts. For myself, and for her."

Stanley remained neutral. Aba tapped his finger on the catalogue at a picture of an irregularly shaped, dark grey marble boulder with thousands of beige flecks. It looked like the raw material that is sculpted, not the final product. "She made me promise to not buy her an elaborate tombstone," he said.

"Promises are like rules," Le'ul said, and gave Stanley a folded slip of paper on which was written the epitaph Aba had chosen for Ema.

I took up the stack of white cotton and showed myself out ahead of Le'ul and Aba. As they followed behind me, I heard Le'ul say that we should stop by Scarborough Bluffs now to take the photos for Babbaye. The light was perfect, apparently. It was ordinary light to me, but what did I know, I was no professional.

By then, I was queasy to the point of throwing up. I had prepared myself for a few hours, not a whole day, of being around Le'ul. I promised myself that going to the Scarborough Bluffs Cemetery with them would be the last obligation I forced myself to go through. When we arrived at the cemetery, we found the groundskeeper had removed Ema's wreaths. Aba got upset.

"By definition, cut flowers are dead. Who is he to decide they are too dead for a cemetery?" He sent Le'ul to find the man so he could complain to him personally.

I walked to the edge of the grounds. No blue butterfly today either. I sat on a bench overlooking the lake. Aba joined me. I took out the camera from my purse and clicked through the pictures of Ema's wreaths—going back in time, seeing them revive; going forward in time, seeing them shrink.

Aba watched the lake with fixed concentration, as if Ema might appear gliding on the water, like the biblical Queen of the South incarnate. Softly, he repeated the Bible verse that was to be her epitaph. Then he quieted. Then he started again, until I lost count. He mixed up the words. *Remain these three. Three these remain.* Over and over, until I couldn't bear it anymore.

"Aba, it's *these three remain.*"

"Faith, hope, love."

"Charity. The verse ends with charity."

"Is love not better?"

"We already ordered charity."

Sensing Le'ul nearby, I looked around. He had returned, alone, carrying a shopping bag. He kneeled by Ema's grave and began to arrange small objects and flowers on her soil.

I got up. "Let's go," I said to Aba. He needed to see what Le'ul was up to. But Aba had completely forgotten his earlier agitation about the wreaths. He was stuck on the difference between *love* and *charity.*

I made myself walk up to Le'ul, to stand on the other side of Ema's grave. He was tucking three heaven-gazing stone angel busts at the base of the simple wooden cross. There was more, from the cemetery gift shop: garish plastic flowers. He wrapped the wire stems around the cross, at the corner where the horizontal plank met the vertical.

"They didn't have real flowers?"

"The axis is the symbolic intersection of the earthly and heavenly," he said.

I wanted to stare, study him closely, his nest of uneven dreads, every shred of hemp he wore. To break him down to more manageable chunks. But I couldn't look at him for long without remembering pinpricks of daylight coming in through closed shutters. There in the cemetery, with him in front of me, my eyes wide open, I still felt blindfolded, disoriented. He was someone about whom I would always know too much, yet also about whom I would know nothing at all. I could turn him in my mind until the day I die. I will never find a satisfying answer to the first, lasting question of my life: *why?*

He got up, brushing soil off his knees. "Take the pictures."

"Me?"

"Is that not a camera in your hand?"

He went to the water tap. I aimed the camera and waited for my hands to stop shaking. The angels and plastic flowers looked even sillier on the small screen. I took pictures. On panoramic mode, I did a slow scan of the grounds, ending on the lake and the tiny figure of Aba on the bench. Le'ul returned with a full watering can.

"If you think the Shaleqa won't like these, how about I Photoshop your flowers on the photos?"

"My flowers?"

He grinned sheepishly. "I've come here with you all those afternoons. I kept my distance because I didn't want to disturb you."

The implication of what he said sank in slowly, like the ornaments in the fresh mud created by the stream of water he was pouring on the grave. My finger spasmed on the camera's on/off button.

"I came to be alone with her."

"You don't need to be alone as much as you think you do."

I knew exactly how alone I wanted to be.

Water dripped from the snout of the can, level with his hip. "Did you see the pictures I took for you?" he said. "Every day when I came here with you, and I saw you photograph the flowers, I kept hoping you would notice those pictures. That's why I wanted you to have the camera. Did you see them? I don't think you did; you would have said thank you. I was right to take the pictures for you. I know my sister. She wants to keep as much as she can of her mother. I preserved everything which was around Ema on her last day of life, and even after they took her away to the morgue."

I was paralyzed. What I deleted, on the first day I came back here to be with Ema, were not random mistake shots. They were the final moments of her life. The last places she went, the last things she saw: the last view she saw out the car window, the room she died in, last sheets she lay on, last pillow that cushioned her head.

Le'ul waited. If gratitude was what I felt, I resented it. This was the kindest, most bizarre thing he'd ever done for me. Not to. For.

"You deserved to have mementos. You were working non-stop. We don't embalm. Surely you know. So if you had been on a multi-leg trip, it would have been impossible to delay the funeral for you. But I would have taken pictures of her even in the coffin for you." He put his hand over his heart. "What a brother does for his sister."

He rested his hands on either side of the horizontal bar of the cross and kissed the wood very deliberately, first puckering his lips hard in preparation. He was there for several breaths before I understood that he was posing. I felt light-headed. I used to hate seeing him kiss my mother. And isn't kissing the dead inherently unfair, worse than kissing a sleeping person, who can at least wake up and refuse the intimacy?

I raised the camera and pretended to press the button. "Okay," I said, then I thought, he would find out that I did not take the shot, and even destroyed the pictures he took for me out of kindness. I shouldn't feel such girlish panic over such small deceptions and innocent mistakes, when what he had made of me was a thousand times worse. But I said, "Wait. Again."

He kissed Ema's cross again. Then he kneeled to cradle it from behind, pressing it with the length of his body. I took the shot.

I lowered myself to the earth, packed so tight even worms couldn't squeeze through. Ema didn't choose me. She chose us. *All her children.* Her final move in her forgiveness project was her very body, tethering her children together in this city forever.

Le'ul was waiting. I knew what for. "Thank you," I said. I wanted to scream at the lake, at the sky. Rake through this soil. Shake Ema out of her spell. Run to the cliff's edge and leap. Soar, over Aba, over them all. Fly, fly, fly.

•••

Before I take the pictures to Teka in the living room, I go through my phone calls and texts to see if I've missed anything. I refresh my browser window for news updates. Same old. Crickets from Barb. Ditto Isak. I scroll back through our texts from before the ferry ride. He is not communicating with me, nor I with him. We are in a holding pattern for a place that won't have us feeling robbed or manipulated.

I refresh my email. Another from Le'ul. *Dess, I am worried about Aba. He's unfocused, this life seems to hold no interest for him anymore. I've heard him mumbling "These three. These three." He means us, Dess. You must return fast.*

I shove my phone in my pocket and lean out of the window for air. The drying laundry on the clotheslines in the side alley is a multilayered rippling white wall. That roof-jumping tomcat is today curled into a crescent of sleep in the shade of a broken chair leaning against the clothes washstand. I envy his ease, and the confidence of a tiny green bird I see marching toward the edge of the corrugated tin roof of the service quarters, assured that when the tin ends its wings will take over.

From the kitchen comes the *thud-crack* of Gela pounding roasted coffee beans into powder, covering the mouth of the mortar with one hand, slamming the solid iron pestle through a gap between her index finger and thumb, grinding it against the bowl.

I hear the creak of the bedroom door and turn around, the photos in my hand. Babbaye enters. He sits on his bed. Avoiding the white glare of the laundry behind me, he addresses his words to the blue wooden chest at the foot of his bed.

"When you go, will you return with my Tobya?"

It has been thirty-eight days since Ema died, but I haven't given up expecting her to come around a corner or walk through every doorway. I wish she would come in now and convince him that she's fine where she is.

If I tell Babbaye how I wish Ema had been buried here too, he won't ask me why. He will assume it is for the same reason that he wishes it.

For all the good these photos did, Aba should have just sent the pictures of the grave as it really looked that day, before

Le'ul "decorated" it: an honest heap of crumbled brown earth stuck with an unadorned wood cross. Perhaps Babbaye detected there was something off about these touched-up pictures, and that was why he did not display them.

I consider showing Babbaye the headstone photo from my email, but decide against it. The last thing to do now is show him more evidence that what's done is done. I hold out the photos to him. He waves my hand away.

"If you will have me, I will return. Me only."

"Living long shows one much. The way of nature is, the parent punishes the child. I now see the child can punish the parent." He is speaking metaphorically, as people of his age love to do. Where's a translator when I need one?

"She will not allow me to bury her."

"Babbaye, no parent should bury his child. Her choice is a kindness to you."

"Tobya is punishing me."

"Why?"

"For Dessie."

"For sending her to live in Dessie? She survived the Terror because of being sent away to Dessie. You saved her life. She even named me after the city."

Behind his closed lips, he grinds with his front teeth on a strip of thought he wants to spit out. He regards me with pity, as an adorable, innocent lamb he must slaughter. "Tell her," he says as if Ema were alive, a petulant teen refusing to come out of her room. "Tell her it was for her own good."

"She has always known it was. Am I not named Dessie?"

"She waits until the end of life to punish me for Dessie? For Dessie, she refuses me, refuses her land the honour of her body? What did I withhold from her but a life of shame, as should any father?"

Never having witnessed, in real time, the unravelling of a mind, I don't know what to do. I feel as if I have blacked out and missed a chunk of this conversation. I steer as close as possible to what makes sense, things I know for sure about Ema's burial.

"Ema's plot is on the highest ground of a sloping clifftop over Lake Ontario." Aba had told me that Lake Ontario is as big as Tana, the biggest lake in Ethiopia, the source of the Blue Nile, itself once believed by scholars to be the biblical river Gihon. But I do not want to make a claim that I can't back up, so I cling to facts.

"Scarborough Bluffs Cemetery is in the southeast of Toronto, very beautiful. One can go by car or by the underground train. Line two. I just call it the Bloor. It's green on the map."

"I was not a merciless father who completely separates a girl from her mother."

We're not talking about Dessie the city. We're talking about me. Before I splintered off from the family to stay in Vienna and go to boarding school, I had wanted to come back to Ethiopia to live with him. He had refused me. I always doubted whether Ema had really asked him to take me in. I guess she had. I wonder if he also told her to tell me that it was for my own good. He thinks Ema has held a grudge about that all this time.

I sit on the blue chest. "Babbaye," I say. "That doesn't matter anymore. She was never upset with you over me."

"What you said, the day you came. She wanted to be where all her children are?"

"Yes!" I scoot over, and sit on the bed beside him.

He speaks each word distinctly. "There is no one such place."

"We travel, yes. All of us travel. But in the end we will always come back to Toronto, because she is there. She has been buried by an Ethiopian Orthodox priest. He did everything right, all the words, the movements. Three times."

Aba ensured that. I couldn't have interpreted the priest's motions, incantations, if my life had depended on it. And I did not care. We were about to leave my mother in a box deep in the ground, as if she wasn't a person anymore but shameful proof that I had failed to keep her alive.

"I allowed for so much. Other fathers would have been without mercy."

"Come visit. Her grave. We will send an invitation letter so you can apply for a visa. If the embassy of Canada here is made aware you are the father of a diplomat in their country, they can't deny you. For the one-year memorial maybe? Or come every year, if you wish. Why leave at all? Stay! Live with us!"

If he would only listen to me, it could be like those days we spent in the sun on the lawn of my old house, eating wild peaches, scraping our nails with thorns, brushing our teeth with twigs. All of High Park could be our lawn. We can buy our tooth-twigs from Noah's.

"Until then, well, she is still here in spirit, for forty days, right Babbaye?"

"I allowed for visits. I allowed for letters. Yet, when your mother came back to Ethiopia last time, two years ago, alone, under the shadow of death, she refused to stay in her old father's house. She chose to pay for a room in a hotel as do streetwalkers. That also was punishment. She saw me but once."

This is news to me. If Ema was making a personal trip, she always stayed here. Maybe by that last visit, it was impossible for her to hide her sickness from him. So she stayed at her home away from home, the Ghion, to spare him from having to look at her gaunt body every day. She began self-quarantining here. Babbaye must have been stung, though, not knowing why she really stayed at a hotel, so I exaggerate the truth to heal that hurt.

"She used to keep herself from us, too, to protect us from the harsh medicines in her body. In Toronto she had her own apartment. She never let us come in."

"For withholding from her a life of shame. For making her into someone with a name. For showing mercy by allowing her to see that girl, to write to that girl. For saying nothing when she visits longer with that girl than with me. For all the ways I forgave her shame, time and again, I am not in turn forgiven. I am punished."

"What girl?" But I babble on without waiting for an answer that terrifies me with its possibilities before I've even heard it, fills me in equal parts with the joy of anticipation and disbelief. "I can put earth from this garden on her grave. We can plant a mefakiya cutting?"

I offer him the pictures again. He slaps my hand. The photos go flying. I jump away as if he has smashed glass. Then I rush back in to collect and re-stack them. They are all out of order, like his mind, images of what occurred at different times juxtaposed as if they happened at the same time. I have to be careful. I have to take command. I did not realize what great lies great desires can birth.

Point by point, I re-establish order. "There is no other girl. She had me. I had her. She didn't keep herself from you on purpose. These photos are the best we can do for you."

"Bring my daughter to me."

"No."

"You do not wish to meet your sister."

"I don't have a sister."

"Bring me my daughter. I will give you your sister."

"Guests are waiting."

In the living room, I give the photos to Teka without a word and sit by the porch door. Teka flips through the photos, then hands them to the person next to him. They are passed around the room. The population of visitors has mushroomed. Everyone is keenly interested. More than interested, their faces brighten. The photos bring them relief. They needed this, proof of Ema's being gone, her actual resting place. Gela was right, the bereaved do need a physical place, some thing, to focus their grief on. Why had Babbaye denied them?

Gela is sitting by the back door. She covers her mouth with her netela, her hand supporting her chin. I can't read her expression at all, as if her mind were an unreachable country, the way all adults I knew had seemed to me when I was young. I'll be sad to leave her, when the time comes. I won't be back, soon or ever. I can't spit on the ground for her, like moms used to do when I was little, and promise she'll see me again before the spit dries.

If my mother wasn't home, I used to shadow the maids. For as long as each maid lasted, whether she wanted to play the part or not, she was to me a substitute for the big sister I didn't have. I would try to make myself as useful as I could, so that when Le'ul came to find me, she might refuse to let me go because she needed me. But she never did. She was glad to be rid of me. I was not her little sister. I was not her helper. I was a pest. She suspected me of being Ema's little spy, or she was just tired of me slowing her down. So she always told me to obey my big brother. She never asked him what he needed me for. He wouldn't have told her anyway. He thought maids were for pulling pranks on, not for talking to, definitely not for befriending. No matter how much I dragged my feet, I could not will any of my "sisters" to ask me to stay.

I go out to the porch, down the stairs, to the gate, stumbling on the uneven pathway. I remove the stone propping open the gate, step out, and let it close behind me.

NINE

On the rocky lane outside Babbaye's compound, I walk in a direction I've never gone, away from the main road, deeper into the neighbourhood. When we lived in Addis Ababa and came to visit Babbaye, Ema and Aba always parked outside the gate. They'd pick one of the eager neighbourhood kids to guard the car in exchange for some candy money. The next generation of those kids, playing soccer on the lane, stop to watch me pass. News about me has spread, I'm sure. Now here I am, their very own local diaspora. A few trickle over to keep pace with me. I smile. They do not scatter, but they do not return my smile either.

Here were little ones, Isak would say, enjoying an authentic Ethiopian childhood. I do what he would do in this scenario. I step up to a streetside kiosk and ask the shopkeeper for a bag of imported candy. From one of the yards on the other side of the lane, a girl, no more than twelve or thirteen, emerges. She scolds the kids for following me. She wears a drop waist dress, her week-old cornrows go down the side of her head from a centre part. She has tattoos, a small green cross on each side of her jaw and on her chin. In the middle of her forehead, there is a cross with a circle in its centre.

Touching my face, I ask her, "How long did that hurt?" She starts to herd the children away. "Your name is what?"

Before she opens her mouth, a spry little fellow who could have stepped out of one of Le'ul's urchin photos answers for her, struggling against her pull. "Senait! Name Senait!"

He breaks away and runs back to me. The other kids follow, all of a sudden animated like arcade Whac-a-Moles, in a hurry to have this get-to-know-you part over with so we can begin the important business of eating the foreign candy, which the shopkeeper has placed on the counter, his hand firmly on the bag.

"Henok Meron Selamawit Fasil Tsehai Enat Robel Nardos Abeba!" There isn't even one shy child keeping off to the side.

"I will bring you the money later. I'm right there," I say to the shopkeeper. I point to Babbaye's gate. In response, he points to a notice on the wall behind him. Written in bold, angry black marker, *NO CREDIT.*

"But I am of the Shaleqa's family."

He puts the bag back on the shelf. Out of pity, he plucks one piece of cheap local candy out of a plastic jar on the counter and drops it in front of me. No conversation on credit either, I guess. I unwrap the single piece of candy. Holding it in a pinch, I crush it between my back teeth. Gently, I release the shattered candy onto my palm. I offer the slivers, like the sections of a clementine, to the kids.

Each child steps up, plucks a piece. They get quiet, sucking on the candy probably lodged in the grooves of their tongues.

I could imagine these kids on Le'ul's web page. When he wasn't out on assignment for aid agencies, documenting their good deeds among the unfortunate all over the world, Le'ul's ongoing passion project was photographing street urchins, especially orphans, in developing countries. On his fancy web page, where he exhibits his photographs next to links for purchasing prints and making donations, he explains how he feels a special affinity with his subjects, being an adopted orphan himself. There go I but for the grace of God and all that crap.

"And me? Who am I?" I say, brushing my empty hand on my jeans. "Come on, I'm sure you know my name. No? Run to the Shaleqa and ask! It is the name of a city north of here, on very high ground. On posters it is the heart of Ethiopia. The kiremt chill there breaks bones." Cold heart, I think.

"Dessie?" Senait says. She scrunches up her face, surprised, distorting her sun-cross.

"Why?" Henok says. Senait smacks him on the back of the head, but he doesn't stop ogling me. She must want to know too, because she steps closer.

I had always accepted my name as Dessie because that is the city where Ema stayed during the Terror. But after what Babbaye has said, about Ema punishing him for Dessie, I wonder what else happened there, what it has to do with *that girl*. Everything feels suspect.

"Because my mother hid there from the Terror," I say. "Do you know the Terror?" They shake their heads. Maybe more exciting things have happened in the time since. Or maybe, their terror—like mine—is not the one in the history books.

"Well, sorry I don't have a better story for you."

I wave goodbye and walk away. Eventually, the lane joins up with the same main road that curves around the neighbourhood. I keep Babbaye's house behind me. The road rises steadily and meets a wide avenue. Across it is fencing so long I can't see where it ends. It must belong to a government building, maybe even the Palace, because on the stone pillars, at regular intervals in the fence, there are armed soldiers stationed in high booths, and signage forbidding photography.

For the first time in my life, I walk alone in Addis Ababa. I follow women walking with their arms around each other's shoulders, the sides of their bodies fused in a sisterly love, and smitten couples, the girl's arm hooked around the boy's, and young men loosely linking pinkies with their friends. We all have to step around maimed beggars, and destitute young mothers breastfeeding their babies, sitting on the ground behind tattered cloths laid out for receiving coins. I pass through parts of the city that feel familiar but soon dissolve into unfamiliar sights. When sidewalks crumble, then end, I walk a narrow strip between traffic and gutters.

I come to the entrance of the post office. I raise my arms for a pat-down by a female guard, then wander down to the basement. The numbers on the mailboxes extend into five digits now. As a girl, I loved being sent to get the mail while Ema waited in the car. Until the time both of us knew I wouldn't find any more of my pen pal's letters. I return upstairs, through the parcel section, and exit down the back outer staircase crowded with sleeping dogs.

Every time I see a woman my age, *that girl* sneaks up on me. No, if Ema had had a baby, it would have been years before me. *That girl* would be at least thirty. I search for resemblances between myself and the women I pass. I can't get any to make eye contact. I share with them all the features common to most Ethiopian women of highlands stock: red-brown skin, high forehead, huge almond-shaped eyes, narrow nose, plump lips, long neck. I don't see Ema in any of them. The only recurring trait among all the women I see is an air of melancholy.

My feet hurt. I sit at a café patio. The waiter floats by. I tell him I'm waiting for someone. I am. I just don't know if here, now, is how we're supposed to meet. Or even *if* we're supposed to meet. The men stare at me overtly, the women covertly. Are we all hoping to recognize somebody we used to know or feel we ought to know? The waiter takes away the three chairs around my table. Now the space around me is off-kilter. I had Ema sitting in one chair, my sister in the other, Aba in the fourth. Our waiter would be Le'ul. Aba would tip him well. Le'ul would be grateful. He would run after us to thank Aba personally. The end of this block would be as far as he would ever go with my family.

If I asked Aba about *that girl*, I don't know which answer would hurt less. Yes, it's true, I could have had a sister all along, become someone else altogether, led a different life, been happy. Or no, Babbaye lied, I never had a sister. How I am is how I am meant to be.

When Ema came to see me during Christmas holidays because I refused to come to Rome, she told me of a dream she'd had throughout her life, of falling from a great height. I thought that sounded terrifying, a nightmare. She said it wasn't a nightmare, because she always woke up before she hit the ground. It was just a dream. But to me, dreaming of falling night after night, never finding out if I got rescued or I shattered on the ground, was a nightmare. I feel that's what I am in, since finding out I might have a sister, a space between a dream and a nightmare.

I should wait until I am back in Toronto to ask Aba. I can't cause him more distress, when he is already in so much pain. *Did your wife have a child before she met you?* is a question one weighs the pros and cons of asking, then asks in person. For all the weighing, however, it is a question I have to ask.

The sooner the better. We're still in that raw phase where it is possible to ask anything. Not to mention, I suffered for him—going to the residence to pack Ema's belongings, then to Stanley's to choose her stone, then to the cemetery to take those pictures—all in Le'ul's shadow. Aba's turn now.

It's midday in Toronto. I dial Aba's number. I hope I will find the right words. He picks up. I get off to a mumbling start, asking what used to be a basic question.

"How are you?"

He makes general sounds that could mean he's all right, he's getting by, or he's pinned under by grief.

"Where are you?" he asks me, which he never used to do, since the answer, even when true, was only good for a day or so. But now he wants to know every city I'm in. Le'ul hasn't told him, then, about Sydney.

I would have lied to Aba too, but I have to come clean if I expect him to do the same. So I tell him where I really am, and why.

"Oh," he says. "How is the Shaleqa?"

"Only thinking and talking about the one thing." I don't have to say what. He knows.

"The pictures didn't satisfy him, as you had hoped," he says.

"They look so false."

"What can we do?"

"They've confused him more. Now he says things that make no sense."

"Well, his sense and other people's sense..."

"There's either a girl or there isn't."

"What girl?"

"Exactly. A sister he's convinced I have."

“What does Emwodish’s burial have to do with that?”

“Apparently I will want to meet her so much, I will make you return Ema.”

“What an arrangement!”

“I already said, his mind is confused.”

We are back to what is known. Babbaye is a very lonely, much bereaved man.

“Would you have wanted very badly to have a sister?”

I stand up, toppling the chair. I grip the phone tighter. “It’s true?”

Aba exhales more breath than he’s taken in.

“She was born.”

I walk away from the patio, and lean against a telephone pole.

“But, she didn’t live a moment. The child was a stillbirth. That’s what Emwodish said. Perhaps that was a blessing. She wasn’t ours,” he says, answering my next unspoken question. “It happened before, when she was young,” he concludes, as if that is all the explanation needed.

Before, and young. No long story.

I try to picture Ema with a man other than Aba. He must have been hurt to find out he wasn’t her first. Though there is no way, considering their age gap, that she would have been his first. She hadn’t broken his trust any more than I would be breaking Isak’s, if I had let some man buy me a drink at the café, and gone on for something more potent at his place without asking how many guests his house is designed to bed.

“Do you remember the verses I chanted from *Mezmure Dawit*, on the night you and I went to see her?”

“Yes.”

“Then you understand.”

"No."

"I spoke the verses of repentance," he says, as if I am fluent in Ge'ez and understood a word of the chant.

"Repentance for?"

"For denying her the family she wanted. To your mother, even though the child was never with us, this family always had three children. There should be three children."

"Should have been," I correct him. Could have been. I start to walk. Ema had a before, too. A secret grief she carried all her life. When her cancer first returned, shortly after she was posted to Toronto, she had said, *My body is a place of death.* I ignored her, thinking she was being melodramatic about a perfectly curable cancer. She must have meant that the body in which I had thrived had once before killed a baby. Maybe this is why she used to watch me so much. For all I know, she was trying to see if I was her first daughter reborn, or somebody new entirely.

"I saw pictures of Ema's stone."

"Will you be here for the tezkar dedication, day after tomorrow?"

"I don't know yet."

I tell Aba about my time here so far. To my joy, he chuckles a bit over the ways Babbaye has tried to ambush me, as if I had any say in the matter of where Ema is buried.

"I am surprised to hear Emmahoy is still alive and kicking," he says.

"Dreaming, rather," I quip.

"Remember," he says, "you are facing a man who used the Talyans' own weapons on them. No telling he won't lob something in your path still, to blow it apart just when you think you are making way. Speaking from experience. Keep your wits about you. Stay firm. Be polite."

"Yes gashe," I say, glad to have Aba to talk to about Babbaye. I let Aba go. I notice the depth of my anger at Babbaye in the moment it leaves me. I feel awful to have left him the way I did. Of course he has always known that the girl was only born. He just had to try everything to bring his daughter home. I can't judge him. We are both dealing with our loss of Ema in ways that make sense to us, make us feel as if we are keeping some part of her still. Do I not stick my face in her pack of Djarums for a sniff on the regular? Did I not almost go to the Ghion Hotel to lurk outside a stranger's room?

Suddenly, I can't wait to get back to Babbaye's. I call Wondu and describe where I am. I wait for him, pacing on the sidewalk, being ignored by shoeshine boys who take one look at my canvas slip-ons and conclude I'm no good to them.

Wondu arrives. I sit in the front. In preparation for merging into traffic, he crosses himself and kisses the wooden crucifix hanging from his neck by a thin, black thread. He is about the age of the men executed or disappeared in the Terror, and the men who were sent to the front to fight for Babbaye's enemy's enemy. I wonder if, despite his hard-knock life, he considers himself blessed to have avoided the fates of men like my uncles, or if he envies them their martyrdom.

Timid rain pitter-patters on the windshield. Wondu tells me the rain is the belg of April to May, before the deluges of kiremt from June to September. He cruises as slowly as the bluesy tizita playing on the CD player, a perfect complement to the orange-smeared sky, the emerging crescent moon poorly secreted behind thin clouds. The classic ballad for bygone love used to be the soundtrack of many of my parents' evenings, whether they were having their endless low-voiced conversations under the bottlebrush tree, or working quietly in the same room, but under their own pools of light.

"Whose tizita is this?"

"The only one worth listening to, of course," Wondu says. "Mahmoud's."

"My father would tell you no version compares to Bezawork's."

"Speaking of. Tell me about Gela. Where she is from, her family, relationship status."

"How is that speaking of?"

"She reminds me of Bezawork."

Gela looks nothing like Bezawork.

"I think she's getting over somebody."

"Oh, yes?"

"A guess, from her taste in music. Or she is fine being alone and just prefers sad love songs for entertainment."

"So," he says, "ripe for companionship, then."

What a beautiful expression, I think. In Amharic, that is. In English, in my translation anyway, it sounds lecherous. We reach the turnoff into Babbaye's neighbourhood. The trip was fast. I thought I had walked far, but I was only going in circles after all.

Wondu pulls over to the side of the road, shifts to neutral, and keeps his hand on the gear shift. "How old would you guess her to be? She would be your elder by ten years?"

"Outside-country air makes diaspora look younger than we are, don't you know? Wait here, I have to run in for money."

"Don't worry about it, you'll pay next time."

To reciprocate his trust, or his clever way of ensuring I'll call him again, I give him one more piece of information about Gela. "If you're going to make a move, better hurry. She won't be there long."

"Where is she going?"

"I don't know, but somewhere better. She carries herself with a certain . . . pride."

"For a maid, you mean?"

I feel that I've said too much. Oh hell, might as well finish what I've started. "Yes. As if she knows the indignity of this domestic work is temporary, you know? And her day will come. Or something."

"Her day will come," he says, grinning like he is the bringer of days. "She is happy working for your grandfather?"

"Well, you yourself saw, how she seemed happy enough to cry."

"Yes, forgive me. Of course, no one can show happiness in a house of mourning. But in her private moments, does she have cheer?"

"I don't enter her private moments."

I climb out of the car and pick my way over muddy rocks to Babbaye's gate. I find it open. I ignore the few guests in the living room and go straight to Ema's room. I close the door, and double over with silent, dry heaving sobs. For twenty-two years, I wanted a sister. For the duration of a couple of hours in Addis Ababa, walking, drinking in exhaust fumes, I had one, in my mind. Bit by bit, the swell of sorrow recedes. I undress to shower.

TEN

Hours before I was due to report for duty for my Toronto-Vienna-Johannesburg-Toronto trip, as I was coming out of the shower in my condo, I heard a key turning in my front door. I wrapped myself in a towel and cracked open the bathroom door. I saw the Shoppers plastic bag being placed on the breakfast bar first, then I recognized the hand. Le'ul's.

I slammed my bathroom door shut, but I felt as if the barrier wasn't there—so clearly could I still visualize him, as I stood with my palm flat against the door, staring at the floor tile, my heartbeat accelerating.

I added a bathrobe over my towel and triple tied it. My opal, sitting in the soap dish, gave me the courage to ask, through the door, "Who let you in?"

"Ema gave me her spare."

"When?"

"Last time she was admitted, she wanted me to have it," Le'ul said, in the same boyish tone he had used to convince Aba that he had not tried to turn a D into a B on his school report card. But I was not gullible Aba, willing to pardon all of an orphan boy's transgressions, with or without a confession. I dared not openly accuse Le'ul of lying, though, so I said nothing.

"I brought you the Ricola. You wanted to save them. There was an unopened bag, too. I brought all of it for you."

He sounded so proud of himself. Trying to impress, to woo, me?

He knocked on the door. "Don't you want it?"

He didn't have to stay out there. He was choosing to. In one continuous motion, I opened my door, stepped out, grabbed the bag from the breakfast bar and walked to the far end of the dining-living space, behind the coffee table. Only the floor-to-ceiling windows were between me and an eighteen-floor fall to the parking lot, wet from an April downpour.

"Thank you," I said, holding the bag against my chest.

"I'm sorry. I thought you would be out on a flight."

"I'm going out now."

"Where to?"

"Sydney." CanAir's farthest destination.

"Long trip. Let me give you a ride to Pearson. I came in the car."

It was an order, not an offer. I almost said that Isak was coming by, then I remembered I might never see him again. I hadn't heard from Aba either, since the "thinking drive" he took me on the previous week. Seemed he, too, had dropped me. I felt brutally alone.

"The shuttle will come," I said.

Isak stuck his hands in his pants pockets and frowned at the scuffed, pointy loafers on his sockless feet. I feared I'd upset him. But he started to sob, not covering his face. I could almost feel Ema at my back, nudging me toward doing what sisters are supposed to do. Comfort.

"What's happening to Aba?" Le'ul said, choking on his emotion. "I'm losing him."

Not *we*, but *I*. Ever since he was a boy he'd been possessive of his father. For the most part, Aba had reciprocated Le'ul's devotion. The one time Aba deprived Le'ul of his attention was when Ema first got sick. She and Aba had become newly inseparable.

"Help me. I don't know what to do for him."

The little boy whine in his voice touched my heart, despite everything. I couldn't help imagining the eight-year-old village boy I had heard about who had come to our gate clutching his shoeshine kit. I couldn't help seeing the thirteen-year-old adoptee who was bereft, thinking his new father had tired of him.

Seeing him crying, confused and afraid as he was back then, activated the five-year-old part of me, his little sister, who interrupted her big brother while he was doing his homework, wanting to make him feel better. But I hung back, not wanting to make the same mistake I made then. If I had just left him alone when he threw me out that first time, we wouldn't be where we are now.

Gulping his sobs, sucking back and swallowing his snot, Le'ul approached. I had no weapon, not so much as a thorn, only a word: *no*. But my voice would barely span the gap between us, much less carry any weight. So what was the point? I couldn't blame him for expecting comfort. I had fallen into his hug moments after I heard, *She didn't make it*. I left the basement unlocked. I shared Ema's Ricola with him. I discussed the Babbaye situation with him. I thanked him for his thoughtful photos. He wouldn't hear *no* from me now.

I let him hug me. I focused on the plastic bag in my hands, between us, containing the one unopened packet and loose pieces of Ricola.

"Please, Dess," he said. "I am only trying to be a brother to you again. You need one. For too long you have been without one. And I need my sister."

Why all this declaration? There was no one we had to play normal for. No mourners who needed to see two siblings being strong together for their grieving father. I didn't know what Le'ul meant by us needing each other. Brothers hug sisters, yes. I'd seen. In good times and bad. We must have hugged at some point in the before-time, the way children do—clumsy, spontaneous. But did a grown brother and sister hug when she was wearing only a towel? I had a robe on, too. Did that make it okay? I didn't know.

Still in his arms, I shifted my body left, toward my bedroom. "I can't be late."

He let me go. "When do you return?"

"Not for a while." I calculated how many days I would say, if he pressed me for specifics. I would need respite after I got back from Johannesburg, time enough to change my lock if not my address.

"Go get ready."

I wanted to shut my bedroom door, but I didn't want to be rude, so I left it ajar and dressed like I do in the change room at the pool, exposing only my legs and arms.

I heard him pull open the curtain of the shower where I'd been naked only moments earlier. He turned the water on, then off. "How long has your water pressure been so intense?" he called out. I heard the clink of him bothering the opal in the soap dish, setting me further on edge. Now I couldn't take the opal with me. He wandered through my condo. "Your walls need a new coat of paint, something other than this default eggshell. I love a sea blue for you."

I looked in the shopping bag. Le'ul had lied. The loose pieces of Ricola were Honey Lemon with Echinacea, but the unopened bag was not. He added that himself. Ema only bought Honey Lemon. I stashed the bag in the back of my closet's bottom drawer, with the camera.

When I came out fully dressed in my red uniform, Le'ul took my suitcase and tote for me. He locked my door with Ema's-my-his key and pocketed it. The keychain was a small, black leather pouch he had bought for Ema from Thailand. My key, on that pendant, was as close as Ema had managed to bring Le'ul and me to each other while she lived. Giving Le'ul this key was Ema's boldest, most desperate move in her forgiveness project, one whose outcome she wouldn't have to witness if it went sideways. I found her persistence maddening. But I couldn't walk out on her anymore. She had complete access to me. I felt myself more powerless to deny her now than when she was alive. If Ema wanted Le'ul to have my key, who was I to get in the way?

The whole ride to the airport, all I wanted was to reach between my blouse buttons to rub feeling back into the spot over my heart, where I was still numb from the tight twist of my towel. A simple enough gesture, no less innocent than reaching under my neckline to adjust my bra strap. I let my hands grow heavy on my lap. I looked out at Toronto, my eyes aching from suppressed tears. Toronto was never really my city, just as the residence where my parents lived was never my home. No matter where I went, there was always the risk of crossing paths with Le'ul. By sheer luck, I'd been spared that for five years; I had enjoyed a kind of freedom.

"How do buddy passes work?" he said.

"What?"

"I'd book top assignments if I had unlimited free access to any destination."

"Depends on where." What are "top assignments"? Where more photogenic people are suffering more picturesquely?

"I don't yet know where."

"It's not tax-free, and I can only get a few passes per year."

"Thanks, buddy." He winked at me. "I appreciate you."

I didn't know if this, too, was a ploy or a genuine need. He never had a problem charging trips on his credit card so he could nab assignments that didn't pay expenses. Letting our parents pay his bill. That was the final piece of information about Le'ul which Aba had offhandedly forced on me, in the early days after their move to Toronto. I never wanted to know anything about Le'ul, so I had tried changing the topic, and then stopped talking altogether. What finally worked was when I walked out on Aba from the coffee shop we were in at the time.

I reminded myself that I can do the same now. End this torture. I have had three conversations with Le'ul in the space of a little over four weeks. Enough. I am an adult. I don't have to do a single thing against my will.

I was on the verge of telling him to stop the car, but I said, "Will I get back my key?"

"You're not okay yet."

"I'm fine."

He didn't speak until he was pulling up to the drop-off area in front of Terminal 1.

"I love a sea blue for you," he said again.

I didn't know if that was what I would see on my walls when next I walked through my own door, or if he meant something else. What I left behind was not what I would return to. That much was a given. I could expect more expressions of his grief-stricken, new-found, brotherly love.

ELEVEN

When the last of the day's guests have left and I hear Babbaye's porch doors being latched, I go to his bedroom, resolved to be a better granddaughter from now on. He is in his nightclothes, his face wet, holding bundled up in his hand the clothes he wore today. I take them from him and throw them in the wicker basket. This would have been a nightly routine for us, had we lived together. I might even have improved on it, eliminated a step by tossing the dirty clothes out the window into the washstand outside.

He motions for me to come closer. "Have you been crying?" The pulsing vein on my forehead, the telltale sign I am about to cry or have been crying, must still be there.

"The way I left. I embarrassed you."

He pats my arm. "Don't cry." He opens the blue wooden chest and digs around. He knows that he, also, went too far. He must have spent the day coming to his senses, regretting the depths to which he sank just to gain control over a situation he was powerless in. He's pleased that I am saving face for both of us by not even mentioning *that girl.*

"You have accepted my Tobya will come. Rest with her own. Now, everything will be as it should."

I drop my head, suddenly bone-tired. I thought we were back to reality, but he can't even use Ema's proper name yet. "Nothing will ever be as it should. Please hear me." I lean to his ear and raise my voice over the clatter of the things he is moving around in the blue chest. "Tobya will not come. There is no girl. Aba told me there was, but she died as a baby, Aba said she never lived a day. Even if there was a girl, I still can't bring Ema to you. I have no power."

He finds what he had been rummaging for. An old, self-sealing plastic bag, protecting an overstuffed manila envelope inside. He tries to force it into my hand.

"Something to keep you, until you meet your sister. Didn't I say I was a more merciful father than all others? No other father would have allowed for all these. These are letters your mother wrote to that girl."

I hide my hands behind my back, horrified.

"To a dead girl?"

"They are not written to a dead girl."

He leans on the dresser and opens the bag, takes out a stack of yellowing papers folded in three. He unfolds the top page and shows it to me.

"Your sister is alive. She knows your life."

I recognize Ema's handwriting, all squat upper case, but I only read the first and last words, where she addresses Yene Abeba and where she has signed Tobya, her old name.

"If she is alive, why do you have these letters?"

"Your sister gave them for me to show you."

"Why she doesn't come find me?"

"She wants her mother first."

"I won't read this."

I refold the letter, return the stack of letters into the envelope, the envelope back into the bag, and the bag in the blue chest.

I close the chest.

I go back to Ema's room, where I drop on the mattress, hitting the ground of her nightmare.

I am transfixed by Yene Abeba. My Flower. An ordinary endearment of mothers for daughters. The longest, most complex phrase in the world.

Time to go to sleep, on a bed, not on the floor. I will not sleep on the floor for a mother who has betrayed me twice. Who destroyed my letter to the one friend I had, my pen pal, while sending letters to the daughter she preferred. Withholding my sister from me while forcing on me a brother she never wanted for a son. In the name of forgiveness and family, legacy. Because the quiet torment of a little girl who lives on, even while her body grows into a woman's, is secondary, at most.

I noisily dismantle Ras Dashen and re-pile it in a corner, where it looks less like a mountain, more like fragments of history the house has regurgitated. I drag the mattress onto the bed frame. *The Art of Forgiveness* slips out from under the pillow. I kick it to the corner where it sticks in the pile, back where I found it, and lie down on the bed, stiff as a doll.

A dog starts barking somewhere, the same dog that barks every-damn-where.

I get up, find the pack of Djarums from my purse. At the open window, I light one and balance the pack and matches on the windowsill. I cough, not from the smoke but the disgusting taste. All my life, I had assumed that Ema preferred Djarums because of their clove flavour. Turns out, she went around smelling sweet but had a bonfire taste in her mouth. My eyes water. The skin around my mouth itches. But I force myself to finish the nasty burning stick, spitting into Babbaye's garden throughout, and then flick the extinguished butt into the mefakiya bushes.

She didn't live a moment, Aba had said. *She was a stillbirth.*

How careless of him. Words can hurt people. Even thoughts can kill. What if my sister dies before I can get to her? Before I can say hello or goodbye.

Babbaye will be asleep by now. If I am very careful, I won't disturb him when I open the blue chest, for the letters. Soundlessly, I open my door. I don't have to go further. The letters are waiting outside on the floor. I take them in, and lock my door.

I need a new place to be. I hop up onto the windowsill and swing my feet out, dangling them over Babbaye's garden. I unfold the topmost one, light a second Djarum. The flame almost licks the edge of the letter. I read the letter in bits, as if taking it in all at once will hurt my eyes: the year it was written, 1980. Tobya to Yene Abeba in 1980. I smoke some more. Then, I brave the body of the letter.

Ema wants Yene Abeba to understand this when she is old enough to have the letter read to her: Ema had to leave Yene Abeba behind and return to her father's house because she was the only one of her siblings left, her mother was declining rapidly, and she now had not only her own life but all of her brothers' lives to live.

I drop 1980 behind me to the floor. Ema explains to Yene Abeba in 1991 why she must leave her again, this time going farther, to outside-country, a city called Vienna. Ema promises to be back in Ethiopia in four years.

I let 1991 fall to the floor. Their second year in Rome without me, in 1996: Ema says *she* was forced to leave me! That was the only solution she could think of for the curse Igziabher had burdened her with, two children who cannot get along, a third child who longs to be with her but cannot. As the adage says, the womb of a mother has many colours.

Ema hopes, with time and distance, Le'ul and I will relearn the value of family bonds. I will mature and understand, everyone has their pain. Pain shared among family is more bearable than the one inflicted by strangers. That letter is long, without any mention of the *why*. Dessie is just a girl of impossible, *catlike* anger, troubled from childhood.

I crumple 1996 and throw it to the floor. Ema reassures Yene Abeba in 1998 not to worry about "recent troubles." By then I was alone in Vienna, at boarding school, so I know it has nothing to do with me. I am not mentioned at all. Ema will come for Yene Abeba and find her a safe place to stay. She has as much right to stay in Ethiopia as any habesha. *I am not your mother if I cannot manage that for you.*

Ema writes in 2003 how she went halfway across the world to be with me in Canada, but *this daughter of mine would rather earn her bread as a maid of the sky, cleaning the leavings of others, than be on the ground with her sick mother. She shows no mercy for her mother's broken heart. She suckles at pain and refuses to forgive. Here I am, completely at her mercy, available to her utterly, yet she shuns me.* Ema promises Yene Abeba she will visit her more often, give her all the time she always deserved. The 2003 letter is the last of them, that my sister has permitted me to read anyway. I saw more letters in Babbaye's hand, I'm sure of it.

I want to tear 2003 in two. But I won't. I climb down from the window to reread—all the words this time—a sentence from 1980 that I had hurried over on the first read, because it hurt too much: *Please forgive that I had to leave you in Dessie and return to Addis Ababa.*

Dessie. My namesake is not the place Ema's life was saved, but where it was stolen. Dessie was where she bore, nursed, then left her Abeba. From Dessie, Tobya returned to Addis

Ababa, to the home where her father waited with her new name, a word that was both a lament for his lost sons and a command for her, the lone survivor: Zimita. *Silence.* The last seed of the Shaleqa was destined for excellence, not to be a single mother of an unplanned child. In silence, Ema resumed the studies she had been forced to interrupt because of the Terror. In silence, she carried her grief of denied motherhood. She graduated, began work, and married the other man who guided her in resuming her life—her tutor. On pain of disappointing the Commander of a Thousand, she excelled.

Now look how I turned out: not worth all that sacrifice.

I tear 1980 in two.

I tear the halves in two.

I stuff all the letters into my suitcase. I shouldn't have read them. But my grandfather said my sister wanted me to read them. Reading a letter not meant for you is only wrong if you don't then do something about what you learned from the letter. Yene Abeba is real. I've learned that. In Ema's letters to her, Ema has omitted the main thing, the complete truth of what happened to me. I've learned that also. What I'm going to do is track down this rare flower of Ema's, my sister, and fill in the missing parts of my story for her. Blood must know blood.

TWELVE

Yene Abeba, did you see earlier how I tapped our mother's cigarette with my index finger, but rubbed the ash into the windowsill with my ring finger? That was our mother's way. But you must know already. This habit comes so naturally to me because it is one of my earliest memories of Ema.

•••

I am four, sitting beside her at the edge of the deep end of the Sodere Resort pool. Our feet are in the water. She is on the side of the sun, her cigarette in her far hand, so that her shadow will shade me. I wear a pair of Le'ul's old swim shorts with the string double-tied around my scrawny waist, but I can't swim yet. Ema's swimsuit is bright swirling pinks and yellows and oranges.

Aba and Le'ul float near our feet, then swim away again. In the afternoons, they play cards in the poolside huts. One day, Ema and I are walking away hand in hand to find a hut to nap in when Le'ul shouts to her from the water about a dead leaf stuck to the back of her thigh. After we return to Addis Ababa, Ema goes to Tikur Anbessa. When she comes back, she has a scar where the "leaf" was.

Aba says, "The doctor removed it with a special eraser. From now on I must check your mother regularly for new leaves."

Ema says, "Can you believe it? Mister who didn't see the first one."

"I can check," I say. I don't want her to go back to the hospital.

"Bless you, my sweet," she says, her hands on my cheeks the same way she cups the first roses that bloom in her garden in the New Year. "You think I would trust your father's old man eyes with my life? I have a handsome young doctor to check me properly two times a year." She winks.

Aba laughs. "What did you say? I'll show you an old man!" He pretend chases her to their bedroom. More and more, Ema and Aba lock themselves in their bedroom to check her for new leaves. So more and more, it's just me and Le'ul, bored. Before, most of the time I had Ema all to myself. He had Aba all to himself.

Like I miss Ema, Le'ul misses Aba. He sits sadly at his study desk between our beds. To make him happy, I create a two-people game. I am good at drawing. I draw leaves on my skin with one of the Bics always sticking out of Aba's coat pocket. I go to Le'ul when he is doing math homework.

I pull on his sleeve and say, "I am getting leaves, too!"

Le'ul throws his ruler at me so that I will get out of the room. But it is my room, too. So I tiptoe back to the door. I sit in the hallway and watch him cry. Maybe because math is hard. But I think more because of Aba.

Another day, Le'ul throws his pencil case at me. The third time I try, I go to our room without my dress and undershirt, so he can see the leaves on my chest stomach upper legs.

"See, I am not lying," I say quickly before he picks up his compass. "Look at all my new leaves! See! I'm scared."

Le'ul's eyes open wide, like they did when he saw the three flavours of ice cream at Saiy's café. Ema and Aba took us there to celebrate after she got erasered. They bought us each one flavour but the man behind the counter gave Le'ul an extra scoop of a second flavour since he is twelve, almost a man.

Because I showed my leaves to Le'ul, I get him to play. He searches me like I search Ema's skin for new leaves. I do this when she naps with me because she is the one who falls asleep. I have not found new ones on her. But Le'ul finds the new leaves on my skin. I know he will, because I drew them. He cleans each leaf off my skin with an eraser, just like the doctor must have done on Ema.

"Will you help me if I find them again?"

"Get out."

I draw new leaves, so I can tell him I found new ones. Again, he erases them. I tell him he is a better doctor than Ema's, because his eraser doesn't make a scar. Aba and Ema don't know what we have found to do alone so often, but they are happy that even though Le'ul is so much older than me, we have a game we both want to play.

The next kiremt I am five. Ema and Aba room together at Sodere. They put me with Le'ul. The first night, Le'ul says he wants to check if I have new leaves. I am surprised. I want to go to the bathroom to quickly draw new leaves, but I don't have Aba's pen. I can't go to Ema and Aba's room because the resort people warned us that hyenas come out at night and even in the daytime I am scared of the monkeys that chase me on the terrace.

Le'ul says he must check right now, I will have new leaves by now. I don't want him to be disappointed and cry. But I have no choice. I take off my dress. He will find nothing to erase because there are no new leaves. I have to close my eyes he says, because his new eraser won't work if I'm looking. I close my eyes. His new eraser is softer, warm, damp. He only checks one place. I have never drawn any leaves there. In my triangle. But he finds leaves and erases. Maybe I do have real leaves in my triangle that I can't see myself; it is a hard place to see all of.

He stops quickly. There were leaves, but not many, he tells me. For every night in Sodere, he checks again. He takes longer each night, because he says he finds more of them each night. After we return home to Addis Ababa, he makes new rules about the checking. He slaps me when I make mistakes. I don't like the game anymore. It makes Le'ul frightening and mean. But I don't tell on him because it must be for my own good. I am afraid of the way his eyes look before he calls me in to check me, like when people fall asleep but their eyes are still open. He reminds me a lot that if I tell people he is checking my triangle, he will have to stop checking, and the new leaves he hasn't erased will kill me. Even his eyes say, *If you tell, I will kill you.*

Killing causes death. Death is a place people go to but can't return from. A person can also go to death if they have sickness. I haven't been killed. I am not sick. But I feel I have gone to the no-return place. Or I have left someone like myself there.

The me who is here, in the after, learns to escape even when she is blindfolded and locked in the bedroom, Le'ul pressed against her. To escape, the after-girl thinks of her doll. When Le'ul tells her to clean herself for checking-time she first lays her doll on her parents' bed to wait for her. Checking-time is always when Ema and Aba are not home. Checking-time is always when Babbaye has not come to sit in the garden with her. During checking-time, after-girl thinks of her doll. Sometimes she mixes up who is on her parents' bed, eyelids clicked down, and who is under Le'ul, eyelids pressed down. One day, after-girl stays on her parents' bed. The doll instead goes into the room where Le'ul is waiting. But he doesn't catch the trick. That the obedient girl is made of hollow, outside-country plastic, with a false face. When after-girl stays away, her skin doesn't feel his soft chilly fingertips; her nose doesn't smell his lunch breath; her eyes don't see his shining eraser; her ears don't hear, on the other side of the koshim, the sing-song refrains from the mop-hawkers and scrap collectors, cars honking to be let into their yards, dogs barking. Her smiling mouth doesn't open.

When after-girl turns six years old, she starts swimming lessons at the Ghion pool. She learns very quickly to float because she loves that nothing touches her. Her instructor says she is a natural. One day after her lesson, she sits alone on the edge of the children's pool, waiting for her mother to pick her up. Her instructor plays with his girlfriend in the grown-up pool. The grown-ups' pool is shaped like a fat cross. At the top of the cross there is a diving tower with three stone tongues.

After-girl sneaks carefully over the slippery cold stone from the children's pool to the grown-up pool and climbs the ladder of the tower. She stands on the edge of the highest tongue. She looks down. It is so far. If she jumps, she will be in the air, in another place where nothing will touch her.

From up there, her instructor and his girlfriend are as small as a boy and girl. The woman throws her head back, laughing. She sees after-girl's face, peeking over the edge of the platform. The woman shrieks, reaching up her hands. The instructor shouts at her to climb back down. But he doesn't come out of the water.

After-girl's warm pee flows down the inside of her legs. She pushes off. From that moment until the water slaps the back of her thighs, she is free. Then she is standing on the slippery cold stone again, her nose and eyes burning. Ema is shouting, crying. She turns and squeezes after-girl, like she has just been made and Ema wants to be sure all parts are in the right place, not in the wrong places like after-girl does to her doll when she rips out her arms and legs and head after checking-time.

"Do you want to die? Is that what you are trying to do? Who will I replace you with? Who? Did someone tell you Ema has another little girl somewhere?"

Ema wants an answer to all those questions but Ema doesn't ask why after-girl jumped. Aba doesn't find out she jumped. Her swim lessons stop. She is allowed in the water only once a year, at Sodere, where there are no diving towers. She promises herself that one day she will climb as high and fall as long as she wants.

She starts first grade. Checking-time changes to when the contract taxi brings her and Le'ul home at the end of the school day, while Aba and Ema are still at work. Le'ul always orders her to clean herself first. When he finishes with her, she is scum. She scrubs with a dry towel, until the skin he touched comes away in dark curls. In the garden, she breaks twigs from every plant and sucks the juice. She wants the poisonous one that will send her to the no-return place where there is no Le'ul.

Not a single one of the maids ever asks why a teenage boy needs to be alone with a little girl for so long, so quietly, in a locked bedroom, in the daytime, with the window shutters down. After-girl wills them to walk down the corridor, try the door, or go around to the front garden, tap on the window shutters. If just one of those women had cared to cup her ear against the door or the closed window shutters, she would have heard the boy's voice, commanding: *tie your eyes, clothes off, get down, legs open, wider, turn, sit on it, slowly, sway, kneel, mouth, no teeth, don't breathe on me.*

THIRTEEN

Early in the morning, a car honks outside my grandfather's gate. I roll out of bed, and over to the window. The Djarum pack with the remaining cigarettes is balanced on the edge of the windowsill. I toss it to the pile in the corner of the room. Gela runs out from the side alley to open both sides of the double gate. Outside, a pickup truck is backed up, loaded with stacks of white plastic chairs. Two labourers are perched on the edge of the truck bed. They hop down and carry the chairs into the yard, up the porch steps, into the living room.

From the clotheslines that extend into the courtyard from the side alley, Gela unhooks a black blouse and dress. "What's all this commotion?" I croak, picking out my eye boogers. My mouth tastes rotten. I feel and smell stale.

"The chairs are for tomorrow." She comes into the garden underneath my window and holds the clothes up for me. "I have washed these for you to wear. I think you didn't bring anything else black."

"I hate black. Black was Ema's colour. I'm red." Gela just keeps holding up the clothes. I take them. Even after reading Ema's letters, I am able to pretend as if wearing black, "celebrating" the Forty tomorrow if I am still here, all matter to me. Obviously Ema never meant for me to see those letters, not while she lived. Ema loves me. She does. She had to write the letters precisely so she could love me even in my worst moments. That is the only way I can accept them. She had to release all the resentment, anger, disappointment, and guilt about me somewhere, didn't she?

The clothes smell musty. Gela is lying. She didn't wash them. If anybody knows the difference between the dampness of washed clothes versus clothes hung outside overnight to give the illusion of freshness, it's me, the girl who lives out of a suitcase. But I am not a mean person of *catlike* anger, to quote Ema's letter. Today my face is as friendly as a clear summer sky. Nothing and no one is going to make me crack. So I let it go.

I say, "What needs to be done for tomorrow? Whatever it is, leave it to me. It is my duty. After Babbaye, I am Zimita's only blood here."

"Emmahoy too," Gela says, stone-faced. Four women I've never seen enter through the open gate alongside Lomi and Aberash. They greet Gela as they pass around the house to the service quarters at the back. As soon as they are out of sight, she drops her gracious smile for them and shoots me a blatant stink eye. "The new women are hired to make large quantities of food for special occasions. Should I tell them to go home, leave the tezkar cooking to you?"

I hear the chime of an incoming text message. "Is there a clothes iron? These things are still damp."

"You'll find it under the table in my room. The ironing board is in the kitchen," she says, walking away.

I open the message. Not Barb. Not Isak. Not Aba. Le'ul. *Aba is gone. He left his phone at the residence, didn't come back last night. What do you know about this?*

I know the same thing Le'ul should know. That Aba has

gone on one of his "thinking drives." When he does this, he rarely tells anyone he's going. But we know, because no one would have seen or heard from him for hours and he is not responding to calls or messages. Once he has had enough thinking, he always comes back. Ema never worried.

Last time Aba and I were together, we were in the car on the 401 West, heading back from the cemetery where Le'ul's plastic flowers were, of course, holding up against the elements. One angel bust had gotten decapitated though. I was driving. Aba sat with his body angled against the passenger door. With a month's growth of beard, he looked like a problem passenger who might try to shoulder the door open mid-trip.

As I approached the Don Valley ramp, he said, "Keep driving."

"Why?"

"Just keep driving."

My first thought was, Ema is not dead. There was a mistake, a big misunderstanding. She is alive. She just needed a new place where she could live where no one knew her and no one could ask anything of her, but she missed me, so Aba was guiding me to this incredible surprise. Finally, it would be just me, her, and Aba, only us three forever. I reached for the gearshift. By the time my hand was back on the steering wheel, the illusion had vanished. There was no mistake. Ema would always be under the headless angel.

That day, as I drove, I sensed Aba was on the verge of saying something. An hour later, outside Burlington, he did. "Let's go home." That was all. I realized I had just experienced one of Aba's "thinking drives."

I won't respond to Le'ul. Let him figure it out when he calms down. I throw my phone on the bed.

Aba never stays out for more than a day. He has never stayed out overnight. These tiny differences are the final pivot toward a truth I've already accepted: the girl, my sister, exists.

I hear again the verses of repentance Aba chanted the night before Ema's funeral, when we went to see her for the last time. I wonder now if his thinking drives were ever about his books, but instead about his guilt over the part he played in dissuading Ema from bringing her illegitimate daughter into their marriage, and over what he did, or said, to convince her to then be a mother to Le'ul. Such a burden has got to be worth a lifetime of thinking drives.

Inside Gela's room, I find the iron on the lower shelf of the coffee table. Rather than haul it into the house, I decide to iron the clothes here. They're Gela's own, after all. I set the boom box on the floor, press play on the CD player. "Hab Dahlak." I turn the volume to low. I wipe down the coffee table with the hem of my hager libs, and plug in the iron.

Underneath the coffee table, three small drawers beckon with all there is to know about this bossy Gela. I open them one by one. Each is full of fashion magazine cut-outs, dress patterns, snatches of fabric, sewing doodads. Thus animated by the spirit of inquiry—to borrow a line from Isak—I try the dresser drawers, but they stick, threatening noise.

I test the iron and press it to the skirt. I enjoy pretending to be Gela: in her room, ironing her clothes, listening to her CD. Would she dance? Yes, like me. Undulating her torso to the rhythm of the song, matching it to the rhythm of her ironing. The movement frees up some of the stiffness in my body from yesterday's long walk and troubled night.

I finish the dress and start on the blouse. The song repeats. The smell of spicy wot wafts in. When I finish ironing, I change into the clothes. Behind the door, there is something covered with an old bedsheet. I lift a corner. It's a rinky-dink sewing machine visibly in need of oil. Thinking of Gela trying to piece together something nice for herself, out of fabric swatches, breaks my heart. I roll up the hager libs I've been sleeping in and lodge it in the back of the wardrobe for Gela to find someday. It's not clean, she might have preferred my jeans or blouse, but the hager libs is good as new, and free.

On the porch, I nudge my grandfather's broken twig toothbrush from that morning with my shoe. I lean against the porch doorframe, not in or out of the living room, disrupting my grandfather's view of the courtyard and slice of the sky from his usual seat, his cane hooked on the armrest.

Before him is a small table on which Gela is placing his breakfast: a glass teacup brimming with cinnamon tea, a plate heavy with firfir, and plain injera in a basket. Steam escapes from the wot-drenched mound of torn-up injera. Gela samples a tiny bite of the food as if my grandfather is a king in danger of assassination.

He begins to eat. Gela pulls out chairs from the stacks in the middle of the room, and lines them in front of the existing chairs along the walls, creating a second row. The rental chairs are scratched, the grooves caked with dirt from innumerable gatherings, possibly including the farewell party here when we left Ethiopia. Back then they might have been spotless and perfect. What I wouldn't give to be lounging on one by the side of the Ghion pool, under the stars.

This is the first time since I arrived that I'm seeing my grandfather eat so heartily, feeding himself gursha that seem as gigantic to me as they did when I was little.

"You should have come back before dark," he says. "The time you returned last night was unbecoming for a girl."

"Night is not the danger. A girl can get pregnant as easily by day."

Gela drops a chair. I'm surprised at myself. I bet Gela thinks I should get a slap for my sass, two slaps that would turn my cheeks as hot as the strips of green chili peppers stuck in the Shaleqa's dark red breakfast.

I drag one of the house chairs near to my grandfather and sit.

"Where are my uncles today?"

Over the past days, I have remembered how I know the other three old men, like a developing Polaroid that captures the best parts of my girlhood in the before-time. They were frequent guests of my parents, three not-really-uncle uncles who only ever wanted to see me laugh, have fun, do mischief. Uncle Whiskey, a Dubai merchant who used to sneak me the dregs of his watered-down Scotch. Uncle Bug, an entomologist who would pin me high up against the wall like a specimen. Uncle Pilot, who brought me apples and other exotic fruits from outside-country.

"They know I will not be at home. There is a place you must see, and a task we must do together."

My heart skips. Just us two all day? My four-year-old self squeals and leaps with glee. Then I remember I'm hurt. I tear a piece of injera from the basket and stuff it in my mouth.

"Where are we going?"

"To arrange matters for Tobya's return."

Yes, I think, chewing the injera into a mush, let us arrange matters. I don't care about the interruption in the generations of our family's bones interred in this land, in marked and unmarked graves. I don't have such grand notions like my grandfather. I just want what I am due. Aba lied to me yesterday. My parents hid a sister from me all my life. They owe me a sister. Ema will have to come back to Ethiopia, if that's what it takes. Aba will have to make it happen. He will not refuse me when I confront him with the truth of what I have evidence of, a primary source, the highly valued type. I could have had a real sister all along, a protector from my pretend brother.

I wish I could cry until I get so exhausted that I either throw up or doze off. I should feel good. Soon, I'll get what I have wished for since I was five. So why do I feel ill? Maybe because none of them—not Aba, not Ema, not the Shaleqa—deserve my full loyalty, or even the greater part, but I wish one of them did, so that I wouldn't feel pulled in so many directions away from myself, even as I choose to do this one thing for the after-girl.

I swallow, suck the tangy aftertaste of the injera from my tongue.

My grandfather says, "We have to do all we can for Tobya's return while I have you. Who knows when you will leave?" *Again.* The unsaid last word hangs heavy in the air. Gela doesn't try to hide that she's listening to every word we're saying. If arranging the chairs slowly is her way of lingering, I don't mind. I need someone to be here to witness how I try to be good, agreeable. She's more family, in a way, than I will ever be. She's here for the day-to-day. She and my grandfather have shorthand, an unspoken understanding about everything, that I'm not a part of. My superior claim of blood is purely ceremonial.

"Save me those," I say to Gela, pointing at the final version of Ema's tezkar program pages snug in their open delivery boxes. They must have come at some point yesterday, while I was roaming the city in a way most unbecoming for a girl.

"As the daughter present, I should be the one to sort and fold them, no?" I say to my grandfather.

"All yours," she answers.

"Okay, we will go," I say.

My grandfather keeps his focus on scooping the firfir with injera. He's taken my obedience for granted. I find it painful to think of this cruel man sitting before me as Babbaye. Babbaye, who I missed, who I wanted to live with when I was a teenager, who I stood up for when Aba and Le'ul were so dismissive of his wishes. *That* Babbaye would not have let me find out about my sister this way. He would not make me jump through flaming hoops to meet her. My sister is not making me earn her love, either. She had nothing to do with this. I loved and wanted her before I even knew she existed. She feels the same about me. I'm sure our grandfather forced her to give up her letters, and stay away until Tobya was returned to him. My grandfather is powerful when it comes to ensuring mute compliance. Our mother should know.

A truck roars past on the neighbourhood road. The sound makes me long for the majestic, fuming beastliness of airplanes. My grandfather extends a gursha. I receive the bite from his hand, cupping my palm under my chin to catch the bits that fall so I can nibble them up. The breakfast is nothing special, just onions, tomatoes, garlic, oil, berbere, cardamom, but together with the pleasure of being fed, they mask my stale tongue. I feel like I have all of Ethiopia in my mouth.

FOURTEEN

I never imagined that when I finally did get my grandfather all to myself, I would invite someone else along. I hire Wondu to drive us for the day, figuring his entertaining banter would distract me from my churning thoughts. I sit in the front passenger seat for the long drive to the outskirts of Addis Ababa to our first stop, Kidus Yosef Cemetery, and try to get Wondu talking. In my grandfather's presence, he zips up. He responds to me in formal monosyllables, as though he has never met me. At Kidus Yosef, he even opens the door for my grandfather, bows to him as he gets out, and stands at attention until my grandfather reaches the entrance before getting back into the car to wait for us.

A watchman shows my grandfather a tattered notice posted on the gate. Large sections of the cemetery are being demolished to make space for a new highway to pass through, so families within the marked zone have one year to pay one thousand birr and remove the remains of their loved ones. My grandfather turns his back on him while he's mid-sentence. Meaning the expansion does not touch the graves of whoever we are here to see, or he is again refusing to accommodate reality—I am not sure.

We walk down a long asphalt road through the middle of the cemetery, past clumps of broken cement surrounding holes where remains have been exhumed. We turn onto a well-trodden path between intact graves. Occasionally, I stop to scan the area, one hand on my hip, the other shielding my eyes from the sun, for the boundaries of the cemetery. Not even in its earliest days could Kidus Yosef have been anything more than a place of absolute neglect, I think, as we march through loose rocks, mud, and underbrush.

He stops between a collection of raised graves protected by rusting cage enclosures, the marble netted by branches as dry as kindling.

"This is your family," he says touching the iron grille. "Your grandmother, her mother and father."

Behind ovals of cracked glass embedded in the marble of the headstones, there are black-and-white photos, so faded that they could be snapshots of ghosts. The engravings, long unpunctuated sentences in Amharic, describe of whom each was born, on what date, in which province, city, area, the reason for their rest, who has dedicated this monument.

My grandfather points out an empty, weed-infested space next to them and waits for me to understand its significance.

"For you?" I say.

"No."

"Who then? Emmahoy?"

"Nuns prefer to die in Debre Libanos monastery. Here is where my Tobya will be, encircled by her own."

I readjust my footing. I feel sharp pebbles, or dry clumps of mud as hard as pebbles, through the bottoms of my canvas slip-ons. The edge of Gela's long dress tickles my bare ankles. I will not be able to spend time with Ema here after she is reburied. I will never want to see again this dilapidated excuse for a resting place. I mean, there isn't even anywhere to sit nor a view to make the stay worthwhile. One step at a time,

I think. Get Ema here, then find a better cemetery in Addis Ababa.

"Where is your people's place?" I have never dreamed of asking my grandfather—or anyone—such a question. But there it is.

"They are in Ambassel. But for arbegna there is a special place in Selassie Cathedral."

Of course there is. "How about for little arbegna?"

"This land is for Tobya. I paid for it a long time ago."

I look at my watchless wrist as if I am expected somewhere. I've left my phone at the house. I sigh. "In this crowded wasteland, a space for Ema was available in this spot exactly? No one thought she would die."

"I have held this land for nineteen years."

"For your boys. You expected them to be found. That is why you bought this spot."

"For her."

"For your boys. Everything has always been for your boys."

"This land has never been for anyone but Tobya."

"Did she know you had it ready for her?"

He doesn't answer. I'm learning to distinguish which silences mean yes, no, or no comment. He walks past me, leading us out the way we came. What kind of parent buys a burial plot in advance for their child? Not even my grandfather, for whom death had long ceased to come as a surprise.

I follow him, talking to his back. "The land Ema is buried in, over there in Canada, is under Aba's name. By law, Aba owns it, same as you do this spot."

"No, not same. Only Ethiopian land is truly ours."

"I'm saying no one can move her or do anything to her grave without his signature."

He marches on. "I entrust your father to you."

"Someone else will be buried in that ground."

"They for their land. We for our land."

That is all my grandfather ever wanted, since the day after the farewell party. Habeshas should live and die in Ethiopia. Those who choose or are forced to stay away should be brought back. *Tell her it was for her own good.*

"What does the girl look like?" I will find out for myself, but I can't help asking.

"Her face shows little of Tobya," he says, unwilling to say *she resembles her father.* I doubt my grandfather has ever laid eyes on the fellow. I feel a chill. What if my grandfather killed him? This fragile old man using the headstones like a second cane is the Shaleqa, not squeamish about blood on his hands. Or maybe Yene Abeba's dad also went the way of the martyrs. How strange, I hadn't thought of a father until now. I imagined the girl as if she were an outgrowth of Ema.

•••

Yene Abeba, did you ever see our mother so scared, you could see her body tremble? I have, on the day she came to pick me up from school in the middle of one morning. I thought she was trembling because of my letter. I was eight, in second grade at school, the year my English teacher had paired each of us in class with a pen pal in outside-country. My girl was in Canada. Her name was Anja. We were to write the letters on our own, and seal them. We would then give them to our parents, to send them and pick up the replies for us from the post office.

In our first letters, Anja and I wrote about our schools, our friends, teachers, what we eat and drink, how we celebrate our holidays. Then, it was time to write about our families.

In her letter Anja wrote to me that if she doesn't make her bed in the morning before school, her mother does not put a cookie in her lunchbox. In my reply, I wrote to Anja about what Le'ul said never to tell anyone, or else he would kill me. He didn't say I couldn't write it down, in English, to a stranger who is far away in outside-country.

I forgot to seal the envelope when I gave it to my mother. He didn't say I couldn't do that either.

The day Ema picked me up from school in the middle of the morning and took me to her office, I thought she was going to talk to me about the letter. But she had to go to a meeting first. I walked around her desk, waiting. In the wastebasket I saw torn-up pieces of paper with my handwriting. I took out one piece. It was my last letter to Anja. For a long time I sat holding the little piece as small as a stamp. Ema came back to the office. I hid the stamp piece in my mouth. She sat down. I knew she was worried because she wouldn't look at me. I thought, now she will talk to me about the letter. But she didn't. I pretended I was looking out the window. I peeled the piece of paper from my tongue and stuck it to a corner of the glass.

At the end of the day, I was scared to go home. What if Ema talked to Le'ul first? I would die. She didn't know that part. But at home, nothing happened. That night, when she was tucking me in to sleep, I told Ema that I couldn't wait until Anja wrote me back. Ema said I might not get a letter back from Anja this time, because all the politics trouble in our country was disrupting the mail service. I would have believed her, if I had not seen what was in her wastebasket. Ema read my letter, tore it up, left the pieces in her trash. I felt Ema had torn me up and thrown me away.

There was one more month of school left before kiremt, but we didn't go back after the twentieth of Ginbot. Because, Aba said, Babbaye's enemy the dictator had run away, scared of Babbaye's enemy's enemy. They were three teams of freedom-fighters from the north who were entering Addis Ababa at last. Aba stopped teaching classes at the university. He stayed home. He started taking me and Le'ul with him when he picked up Ema from the ministry at the end of the workday.

The air in Addis Ababa was different. There were tanks in the street. At the ministry parking lot, mothers and children stayed in their cars, the motors humming. The mothers used to open their doors and drop their high heels outside to give their feet air. Boys used to run around yanking at the thin vine plant growing on the fence just to upset the old guard so he would chase them. When Ema came out of the revolving doors of the honeycomb building, Aba didn't walk out to meet her to stroll back to the car together. He leaned over from his seat and pushed the passenger door open for her.

Every day, from the car, I saw my little piece of letter on Ema's window. The curtains were white, so the paper was easier to see if they were open. Even when they were closed anybody could see it, if they knew it was there. But no one had reason to search. Anyway what was paper stuck on glass? Just one more thing the maid missed.

One of those afternoons was when Aba said that I would start third grade and Le'ul would start eleventh grade in outside-country. Ema had a new job in a place called Vienna Embassy. "Young, accomplished, brimming with promise—Emwodish is the quintessential face of this new Democratic Republic," he said.

I thought if Vienna was close to Canada, I would find Anja. I would tell her what was in my letter. On the morning after the farewell party at Babbaye's, we all went to the airport together but Aba and Le'ul got on a different plane from Ema and me. Suddenly, I had Ema all to myself. I was so happy, the happiest ever. That day, I finally went as fast as an airplane.

Up in the sky was like the bus to Sodere, but bigger, the engine hum was louder, and we had packed for four years not four days and outside the window were clouds not country girls and when clouds melted I saw all of Babbaye's Ethiopia like crumpled green and brown paper.

The hostesses were beautiful just like in the Ethiopian Airlines posters. They wore dark green uniforms, bright scarves around their necks, and red lipstick. They brought me extra pillows to sit on, extra peanuts, extra Sprite, extra crayons I could keep. I felt like a princess.

Ema put both our drinks on her little legless table. On my little legless table, I drew roses without leaves for her. A cutting from her wedding present rosebush was in her purse, rolled in wet paper.

"Your stems are empty," she said. I added thorns, badly, but I would improve because Le'ul was gone. I felt a little bit sad about that. I would miss the Le'ul who wasn't mean.

"Is Aba coming?"

Ema sipped her dark beer. "He will."

"Where is he now?"

"A place called Kulubi Gabriel." I looked out the airplane window. "We are going north, my sweet. Kulubi Gabriel is east. First you fly or ride a bus to Dire Dawa, but not as far as Harrar where Aba's people are. Then you walk seventy kilometres east again. You carry rocks on your back the entire way and don't wear your shoes or socks. You can drive, but you should make the journey in pain and difficulty if you earnestly need the archangel to grant your request."

Ever since I started full-day school, Ema's way of helping me to understand something new was to make it into a story but stop at the most curious part so I would have to ask a question. About Kulubi Gabriel, I only cared that it meant Le'ul was gone. But I felt her waiting for a question.

"Request?"

She caressed my hair. "For Le'ul to get better."

"He's sick."

"If the archangel listens, he will be healthy again. Aba should have gone with Le'ul to Kulubi sooner, but it wasn't safe for people to travel outside Adisaba. It wasn't safe for even letters to be sent. You know, they will be walking in the direction of Harrar." She had said that already. "Where Le'ul was sent from when he was a little boy."

"He didn't come from you and Aba?"

She ran my ponytail braid between her fingers. She finished her drink. She told the hostess to bring her a second one. She ordered only dark beer because it was the closest thing to tella. "Le'ul was found working as a listro boy by an old friend of his dead mother. The boy's father did not want him. That old friend asked around, until he discovered the boy's only remaining relative was Aba. He sent him to Adisaba. When the boy came to our door, he still had his shoeshine box with him."

"So Aba is not his father. You are not his mother."

"Not by blood."

"But he was my brother?"

"Is. He is your brother. Only you don't share flesh."

I drank my Sprite. It scratched my throat like tiny needles. "We do."

She kissed the top of my head. A hostess brought her a new dark beer and me a slice of sponge cake in a clear package, like Uncle Pilot brought me when he forgot the apple. Ema talked to me more, breaking a slice of sponge cake into one bite at a time, feeding me one, feeding herself the next. Crumbs fell to the line between her breasts.

"Your father named the boy after the title of the son of a king, Le'ul, because the meaning is the same as his own, Mesfin. But at first your father had wanted to rename him Alemayehu after a long ago Ethiopian orphan prince, who journeyed far from home and never returned."

I felt joyful. I understood the real story Ema wanted me to know. Aba took Le'ul to Kulubi to get him better, but then he was going to return him to the village. Then Aba would come to Vienna alone. At last, it would be just us three.

FIFTEEN

My grandfather and I come out of Wondu's taxi and walk up Churchill Avenue. I see Teka standing underneath his store sign, *Servant of God Funeral Service,* flanked by triangle wreaths propped on tall bamboo stalks. Corrugated cardboard rolls teeming with roses and carnations spill out from funeral home storefronts for many blocks, making the area look like a flower market.

Teka flirts loudly with a voluptuous woman jaywalking across the street. "Come in and look anyway, maybe you will need my services for your husband soon? Watch the road, lady! It's not a box I have plans to lay you in!"

When he sees us, he redirects his attention without missing a beat, like an azmari in a tavern who's spotted new subjects to satirize in song. "Shaleqa!" He gestures at the unoccupied doorways of his competition, knowing full well we've come for him. "They're dead! All dead, like your enemies! Sadly. So you must come to me."

The interior of the store smells like a combination of greenhouse and carpenter's workshop. Against one wall, narrow coffins lined with colourful fabric, embroidered with golden thread, are stacked all the way to the ceiling. On the floor, littered with rose leaves and stems, a circle of men sit making wreaths. Teka offers us plastic stools to rest on by the door but my grandfather declines for both of us.

Seeing the amazement on my face at all the roses, Teka says, loudly over the noise of traffic and passersby, which is amplified in this cramped space, "So many roses, I know! At Teka's we only use real flowers, not paper! Roses for premium wreath. Carnation for standard wreath. Now my supplier Highland Flora has so many roses she cannot ship out to the Amsterdam auction because of the flights to Europe being stopped. She is selling the backlog for very cheap. We can use roses for all the wreaths. But no extra cost to customer. Give thanks to Igziabher's weather."

The men on the floor carve the stems of the roses into sharp points with their stubby knives, twirling and slicing the bark off the ends of the stems in four quick strokes. They insert these beautiful daggers into a foil-covered triangle of foam on the floor between them, with a satisfyingly savage *pop*.

I want to stab the foam with the business end of a rose, too, instead of acting earnest while my grandfather negotiates a verbal contract over Teka's handling of Ema's body. I edge toward the carvers. One of them offers me a rose, I ask for his knife instead, causing laughter. I squat down, pick up a stem, and begin carving.

Next thing I know, Teka is coming at me with his cellphone held out. He has dialled his "opposite in Canada," Stanley Chan, who is on the line to talk to me.

I stand up slowly to hide my panic. "It's very late in Toronto."

"Oh, but death doesn't have office hours, so neither does Stan!"

Until I actually hear Stanley's voice on the speaker, I don't believe this is happening. I have no idea what I should say. I haven't thought that far ahead. Stanley sounds surprised. He is used to talking to Teka on the phone, but he didn't expect to hear from me again, especially all the way from Ethiopia.

"I'm calling about my mother," I stammer. All eyes, even those of the rose carvers, are on me. I sweep my hand up, away, and down in the motions of shifting an object. Teka carefully relieves me of the knife I still hold in my hand. He translates under his breath for my grandfather.

"Hello?" Stanley says.

"Sorry. It's about my mother."

"I understand that you want to disinter the body and relocate the burial site?"

"You said it."

"You've decided to repatriate after all, then." He's just as gung-ho as his opposite in Ethiopia about the prospect of new expensive business, but out of courtesy he feigns hesitation.

"Your father took such care with the selection of the stone, and the Ethiopic engraving. It is being delivered to Scarborough Bluffs tomorrow for the dedication."

"We're not asking for a refund. Just, you know, things happen."

"This being Toronto, there is plenty of repatriations," he says. Teka mutters in agreement. "Your people have had one kind of political tension or another back home since the seventies, so to bury your loved ones out here was the only way. Even the living didn't want to return. But for some time now, your people have been setting things right."

The man knows his customers. The carvers resume their repetitive motions, slower, listening. "That's the thing. It's about setting things right." Although my family must hold the record for how quickly we've changed our minds. "There was some misunderstanding."

"Because it hasn't been a year or even a season, it is unlikely the lid will be crushed in."

"What?"

"Your mother's was a wood casket. It has only been about a month since the interment," Stanley says. "Because of the weight of the earth, even a metal casket will eventually cave in. The more time, the more seasons, the more pressure. Snow, rain, it all accumulates. Regardless, we must incinerate the burial casket. A new casket will have to be purchased. I recommend you bring back the extra cloths I had returned to you."

All Ema's hager libs and netela are at my condo. I have a vision of blue-orange flames dissolving the last fragile handspun cotton Ema was ever supposed to have worn.

"You can leave it to us to deal with Justice and Health and the Bluffs and RCMP."

"What do you need the police for?"

"To ensure nothing untoward will happen. You never know. It takes all kinds to make a world."

"Doesn't it though?" I say, lamely.

I remember Sara and the others in university, talking in horrified tones about grave robbers in Ethiopia stealing coffins for resale on the black market, tossing aside bodies, prying crucifixes loose from mausoleums. Those tiny ovals of glass protecting the faded images of my grandmother and great-grandparents looked as though they had been deliberately smashed, just for spite, the cracks branching out from a single point of contact. The worst I can imagine happening in Canada is racist vandalism or graffiti. Maybe that angel's head in Scarborough Bluffs didn't fall off by itself.

"Your father will have to complete and sign the application and consent forms."

"No problem."

"Only his signature will be required. Whenever he decides to come is suitable. Then we arrange for the date of exhumation. Someone has to be present then because the cemeteries will do nothing but pull the casket out for you. If no one is there to pick it up, they assume no responsibility."

"Got it."

"I communicate with Teka directly. We know one another's procedures. We've done a lot of business together," Stanley says. Teka puffs up. Stan tells me about the rest of the process — resealing the body in a pouch, and purchasing a new hermetically sealed casket. Part of me finds it fascinating. "No rush, of course. Time is certainly not of the essence. The ground in Ethiopia doesn't freeze, and we have many months before winter here."

The magnitude of what I have set in motion weighs on me. "Thank you for all this."

"Glad to help."

I wait for him to hang up, as if we're sweethearts. Teka takes the phone off speaker, says goodbye to Stanley. As a token of further goodwill, Teka offers us free roses, insisting that even though his services are in great demand, the roses will spoil before he can use them all. I refuse, but my grandfather remembers Gela said to pick up roses for tomorrow, for Ema, so I pick two dozen, a mix of white and red.

•••

Yene Abeba, did our mother tell you that she grew her first outside-country roses on the balcony of our Vienna apartment? On Saturdays, she did my hair out there. It was while she did this on the first Saturday after Aba and Le'ul came to Vienna, that she said to me, "The water under your brother's bed is only for him. From Igziabher."

Aba did come to Vienna, but he brought Le'ul with him. Aba and Le'ul did not even go to Kulubi, I knew, because their feet didn't have bruises or even little stones stuck in the flesh of their soles from long walking without shoes or socks. The first night, before Le'ul went to bed on the bottom bunk, Aba did a ritual on him. I only pretended to be asleep, on the top bunk. Aba took a plastic water bottle from where he stored it under the bed. He made Le'ul drink one capful, like a medicine. He poured a second capful on Le'ul's head. He prayed over Le'ul's wet hair, calling him by a religious-sounding name: Kidane-Gabriel. I was curious about this water. The next morning, when I was alone in the room, I smelled and tasted it. It was just tap water.

My mother pushed the tooth of the comb into the top of my hairline and made a straight part down the middle of my head, then pushed the sections aside and gave me one section to hold. I wordlessly asked the lonely cutting from her rose plant, sticking out of the soil in the planter, why Le'ul got anything from God when he was so mean to me. God never answered my prayers to make the kiremt hail fall hard enough to break down the roof of the bedroom during checking-time. Ema parted the other half of my hair into two, this time from the top of my head to my ear, and gave me one of the sections to hold in my other hand.

"The water is holy because it is blessed to heal the sick," she said.

"Le'ul is sick?"

"He did things he didn't know a brother must never do." She swept the quarter section of my hair in her fist, the way our gardener gathered grass to slice it with his sickle.

"What will happen if I have some of the water?"

She twisted the quarter section of my hair until it was as tight as a snail without a shell, and secured it with elastic. "You are not sick so you don't need to be healed. You are perfect as you are. Look how well you do in school, my sweet, in English!"

She didn't know that I only spoke if what I had to say was something I remembered how to say in English from the five letters I wrote to Anja. "How easily you will make the best of friends, I can only imagine. How sorry I would be if you weren't mine."

She released my hand from the other small section of hair, and began to twist that. "Never touch the bottle again, hear?"

I nodded, loosening her painful grip. "The family Igziabher has brought together must love and forgive each other anything. We must be willing to do anything for each other. We must learn to love those whom our beloveds love. Remember with the holy water Le'ul is healed."

But he wasn't.

Ema and Aba were always telling me to reread passages for comprehension, but Ema read my letter maybe once only; Aba maybe didn't read it at all. Ema had probably told Aba what I had written, but in her words, making the checking-time sound not so bad. Why else would they have put me in the same bedroom with him, with the only protection of tap water?

I wished I had written a better letter. I could have. My English was good. I spoke new thoughts in the moment. Even my German was okay. And I took French on the weekends in a language academy. My parents were proud I talked to them in English, but I only did it to remind them of the letter. But I was too scared to write a second letter. I couldn't risk a second chance of Le'ul killing me. I decided that I would rather feel dead for two more years.

Only two more years. Then he would go away to university in a faraway place called America. So, whenever it was checking-time, I did what I used to do in our old house. I sent my doll to him in my place. I waited on my parents' bed, even though their bed was not there anymore, and the room was not theirs anymore.

SIXTEEN

In the side alley of my grandfather's house, a tarp spread over the clotheslines shields against possible rain. Under it, two of the new temporary-hire cooks who've come to make food for tomorrow stand beside giant pots of misir wot placed over two wood fires. They stir the stew with ladles long enough to lean on. I wade through the thick smoke and turn the corner from the side to the back alley. As I pass the first room of the service quarters, the mitad bet, I see Gela through the humid, yeasty steam wafting out, so I stop in.

In there, the other two new cooks have two mitads going. One woman makes the injera, pouring a high, thin stream of batter in a perfect circular pattern inwards from the outside edge of the hot flat clay of one mitad. The other opens the lid of the second standing oven and transfers the newest injera to a cooling rack, then into one of a pair of shallow, wide mesobs. Gela, her hands in the second full mesob, counts injera.

Recalling a bit of old superstition, I say, "Isn't that bad luck, to count injera? Or was it bad manners?" Either way it sounds like the kind of line invented by my grandmother's aristocratic relatives, who had more food than they knew what to do with.

Gela restarts counting. "I'm separating what will be for kurs at the church tomorrow."

"We have to serve breakfast?"

"Only for the dependents. In memory of Etye Zimita."

An insurance for her soul, I guess, a toll for the final passage of her spirit. I put the roses on the ground and insert myself into the bakers' work, attempting to pour injera batter in a perfect thin circle. I end up doing the same thing I did when I tried it as a little girl, standing on a chair. I dump the batter all in one gush in the middle of the mitad. When the oven lid is reopened, it reveals what looks like a thick white amoeba. The women tell me that is called ingocha. I made the mess, I have to eat it.

Gela finishes counting while I stuff my mouth with warm ingocha. "If we feed eighty dependents, it's enough," she says. She lifts the stack of injera, supporting the weight under her forearms, then stops at the door, remembering something. "A man calling himself your brother telephoned for you."

She walks the injera to the kitchen next door. I follow her down the alley, almost choking on my mouthful of goop. "Where from?"

She shrugs. "Is he to visit for the Forty, too?"

I rush to the house. In Ema's room, on my phone, multiple texts from Le'ul tumble out. *Over twenty-four hours Aba's been gone now!*

Did you get my message? Aba's gone missing?

Why aren't you saying anything? Is there something you know about this?

Should I notify the police? It's been 24h+

I need you right now.

I am alone in this world. I have no mother, no father. And now I have no sister.

Oh, fuck off. On top of these there are six missed calls from him. I delete the texts, I'll not have him next to Isak on my phone too. I respond by email.

Aba will come back. Just wait. Remember his thinking drives?

I fear that I am naïve to be so certain. Like a protective spell, I add a sentence.

He will come back, guaranteed.

Nothing from Barb.

I peek into my grandfather's room. He is taking a nap, so tired from his day out he still has his shoes on. Asleep, his wrinkles softened, he becomes Babbaye again. Gently, I undo his shoelaces and pull off his shoes. His socks are brand new, George's, the same brand Aba buys for himself in bulk from Walmart. I remove them too. I've never seen my grandfather's bare feet. He has the cracked soles of a man who has walked all his life. His veins are a map of rivers. I loosen his belt and cover him with a gabi from his dresser.

Through the partially open window, I overhear Gela telling the cooks in the alley that she's going to step out for an errand. I leave the house through the front porch and catch her halfway down the flagstone.

"Where are you going?"

"To Selassie to pay for Etye Zimita's prayer tomorrow."

"You were going to leave without telling me?"

She drapes on her netela and tugs it away from her mouth. "Are you police?"

"I'm coming with you," I say, descending the steps.

"I'm walking."

"I don't care."

On the way to Selassie Cathedral, I wish I'd stayed at the house. I see a phantom Le'ul in the dusk-obscured figure of every passing male. By the grand wrought-iron gates of

Selassie, Gela bows, crosses herself, and kisses one of the stone pillars blackened by the innumerable caresses of the faithful. I mimic her, except for the kiss. I don't want a nasty lip infection, Igziabher's holy healing spirit notwithstanding.

The cathedral sits as a high centrepiece surrounded by a lush compound of colossal eucalyptus trees. Stone angels and saints, from nooks in the building's walls, and along the grand staircase, dispassionately observe measly humans chasing salvation. Past the gates, Gela turns left toward a small brick bungalow, fronted by a colossal fig tree with a sign wired around its trunk, *Information and Ticket Office.*

Gela and I climb absurdly steep, rickety wooden steps to the one-room office. The clerk sitting at a desk inside has been thoroughly kneaded by life. He has rheumy eyes, and wears three layers of faded, frayed clothing. A flaccid baseball cap sits on his greying hair. None of this detracts from his officious persona. I sit on a chair by the door, under another sign. *People Without Business to Attend to Are Not Allowed In.*

"We are here for a name-giving," Gela says, taking a seat opposite the desk.

As soon as the clerk sees her, or rather the scars on her face, he turns hostile. I watch them like a tennis game. The clerk serves.

"You are not Orthodox."

"I am a Christian."

"Prayers are for Orthodox only."

"I'm here for the father."

"The father can come himself."

"You know my face," Gela says sharply. "Three times a year, I come here and pay the name-giving fee to have prayers said for members of this family. The Shaleqa is old. He suffers bone pain. In this damp season, he cannot travel from home."

That is news to me, or she's a quick thinker.

"Who is she?" he says, aiming his Bic at me like a dart.

"She's the granddaughter, but she's not from here."

I do my best to exude a granddaughter who's not from here.

"So why doesn't she do the asking?"

"We're cousins," I blurt out, in English.

Gela hands him a pocket-sized yellow booklet. He compares what's inside to Gela's face like a passport control officer. Catching himself, he compares it to my face instead. "Yes, this woman could be either of your grandmothers," he says. He picks up a calendar book, one of three notebooks next to his desktop flag. "For when?"

"Tomorrow."

He lifts and drops his cap on his head. "For late requests you pay extra." He flips to tomorrow's date. There is a long list of names on the page, in his indecipherable handwriting. Fifty-fifty shot that anybody's name will be said properly during their prayer.

He holds the golden tip of his Bic poised over the page. "The name?"

Gela turns to me.

"Zimita," I say.

"The name by which she was baptized," she says.

"I don't know any other name."

"How you don't know?"

"I never had reason to call her anything other than Ema."

"We need this name for the priest to call with those of other departeds in the mass."

"Igziabher knows her by her everyday name, I am sure." Then, I throw out a far-fetched possibility. "Tobya? She used to be Tobya. My grandfather has been calling her —"

Gela is irritated with me. "For your own private prayers to Igziabher, you can say any name you want, but not for the priest. I would think, if normally you don't know it, at this kind of time you would."

"Why should I?"

"Recently you would have heard it."

"I would?"

The clerk leans his elbows on the table and overlaps his hands, his pen sticking up between his fingers. He takes a moment, as though he's dealing with a child, then speaks to me in English.

"A compound name, often a joining of sibling names, as for example brother-of or sister-of, with angels' or saints' names, as for example Gabriel or Mikael. Ihite-Gabriel. Sister-of-Gabriel, do you see?"

There is one such name I do know well, having heard it every night long ago. Kidane-Gabriel.

"It is spoken at death, at the end of life just as at the beginning. The abbat didn't speak it at the funeral?" the clerk says.

"My father wasn't exactly all there."

"Abbat is priest, holy father," Gela says.

I switch to Amharic. "Oh, him. If he did, I don't remember. What use is a name you need exactly in moments when you are least likely to remember it?"

The clerk says, again in English, "At a baby's baptism, the parents tell their own baptism names to the priest. The baby receives his own."

"I don't have a baby. And for understandable reasons, I don't remember anybody's baptismal name from my own baptism, do you see?"

"This name is also used for brides and grooms." He looks at my left hand.

"Don't recollect my parents' Orthodox wedding either, I'm afraid."

Movement at the door distracts us. I turn, startled. Just a couple of white backpackers. I wish I was with them. Truly a stranger to this strangeness, not a stranger who everyone expects to know what the fuck is going on. I turn back to catch the tail end of an exchange of exasperated looks between Gela and the clerk. Gela whispers to him the name. "Welete-Mikael."

He writes in the calendar. "For full prayer or half prayer?"

"Full," Gela says.

"One hundred."

Gela gives him a hundred birr note. He sticks a carbon sheet between the pages of a receipt book and inscribes the purchase in triplicate, referring to the yellow booklet. He tears off a copy of the receipt, tucks it into the booklet, and returns it to Gela.

On our way out of the bungalow, I stop Gela partway down the steps. "Why did you let him do all that to me in there? You knew the name."

"Etye Zimita is your mother, right?"

"Let me see the book."

Gela gives me the booklet. She continues down the steps. On the cover is a sketch of the cathedral. The first page has a purple-stamped black-and-white photo of my grandmother. The star of Emmahoy's dream. The photo is a wallet-size of the portrait that used to be on the living-room shelf. Rows of plaits bloom out to loose black curls at the nape of her tattooed neck. The booklet is a cathedral membership ID, good for the owner and their immediate family—another perk of having royal blood.

When I look up, I catch a stunning view of a section of tombstones in the cemetery that, backlit by sunset, looks like a city skyline. Gela waits at the bottom of the steps. She follows the direction of my gaze. "That is the monument for the Ethiopian Airlines girls from the Beirut trip. Are you coming?"

"What does welete mean?" I say.

"Daughter of."

"So I would be Welete-Zimita?"

"Your mother is not a saint."

That she isn't.

"And kidane?"

"Promise. Or vow."

"I thought church names were for healing the sick," I say.

"The baptism name is used to approach Igziabher for any spiritual purpose."

"What else, for example? Beside sickness and prayers for the dead?"

"Please, let's go."

"What else, for example?"

She crosses herself. "For the casting-out of buda."

"Demons?"

"I'm not waiting for you." She hurries off, as if now demons will descend on us from the shadows, flapping and screeching.

"What if the wrong name is used?" I say, slowly descending the steps. Perhaps then the sickness stays. The demon doesn't go back to where he came from. When I was eight, I thought the holy water ritual didn't work on Le'ul because I had drank some of the water. Then, of course, I realized it was all nonsense. Or if not nonsense, not the kind of help he needed.

Maybe it was Aba's fault that the ritual didn't work. Because he had Le'ul's baptism name wrong. Maybe Le'ul never knew what it was, or maybe Aba changed it, or the man who sent Le'ul to us had it wrong, or Aba and Ema changed it. They did change his everyday name when they adopted him.

Despite her threat, I find Gela outside the gates. "What is the time in your city, maybe the man has called for you again," she says, moving fast again. "So late it is already."

Yes, I think. So late for so much: amends, new beginnings, for *if only*. If only Aba had used the right baptism name on Le'ul. If only that water had been holy. If only I had left Le'ul alone. If only he'd leave me alone.

•••

Yene Abeba, have you ever had an enemy you felt would never leave your life? When Le'ul went away to university, far in another outside-country place called America two years after Aba brought him to Vienna, I was ten years old, in fifth grade. I started to sleep all night, go anywhere in the apartment without thinking about it first. But after a month away, Le'ul quit. Aba brought him back from America. The returned Le'ul was quiet, walked around the apartment in his underwear. If he was not out all day, he was on the couch. He even slept on the couch at night because he couldn't stand to be near me. He ordered me to always keep a certain distance away from him. If he had to touch anything I had touched, he wiped it down first. If I annoyed him, he made me drink too-hot water.

There was no more checking-time. But Le'ul's touch stayed on my skin like the burn after a slap. My body angrily pushed out two aching bumps on my chest under my nipples and little hairs as ugly as black wires through the skin of my triangle, that stung when I pulled them out. I carved a daisy into my right wrist with my geometry compass, making my own bracelet like the one impressed on the arm of my old doll. I kept my daisy red by peeling the petals that turned brown. The girls at school avoided me. They were obsessed with boys anyway. There was a boy I had a crush on too, but I couldn't have him find out how disgusting I was so I didn't talk to him. The day-students were always jealous of the boarding students because the girls and boys could secretly meet in each other's dorms. I wished I was a boarding student, too, but so I could be away from Le'ul and living in a house full of sisters.

After I turned eleven, Ema and Aba let me go out by myself, so I roamed Vienna on foot for hours after school, after swim club, or French class. I stood too near the edge of the U-Bahn platform. On the train, men stared or stood too close and rubbed their knuckles against my triangle or sat across from me and petted their thick red veiny flesh outside their open zippers. I went up to Kahlenberg, where Ema and I had taken the bus on our first weekend in Vienna. *We can see all of Vienna from here,* Ema had said. *Equal to seeing all of Adisaba from Entoto,* Aba had said, when all four of us went up there later that month because he wanted to celebrate our reunion.

I was twelve, at the end of our last year in Vienna after which all four of us would return to Ethiopia, when I realized that I could never get rid of Le'ul, but I could get rid of me. I didn't plan it; I let it happen. I disappeared. On a Sunday when Ema and I went to Prater amusement park, I took a different path on my way back from the toilet. I wandered into a thin scatter of trees which gradually became dense. The trail ended. I walked on, alone. I knew I was lost, but I didn't feel anything. I was watching an uninteresting film about me.

"Brown Venus, why do you look so sad?" said an Austrian man in German, weaving out from between the trees on a bicycle. He was thin, with a thick blond ponytail, watery eyes. He walked his bike alongside me. I wasn't surprised or frightened.

"Where do you walk?"

I shrugged.

"Would you eat a Magnum?"

I stopped walking.

"I have one."

I looked at the bike.

"You only have to hold on. I will not let you fall." He remounted his bicycle, one foot on the ground. "Sit in front."

I did. He would speed off with me to another nowhere, which would be better than our apartment, than our house in Addis Ababa, than any place with Le'ul. Pedalling fast, the man threaded his way through the trees. I thought he sniffed my ear, or my hair.

By a tree with long drooping branches, we got off his bike. He guided me behind the curtain of branches, into a space around the tree trunk. I remembered the signs that meant checking-time. I closed my eyes to undress. The man said stop. Only watch. I pretended to, but really I was swaying with the leaves.

Afterwards, we left the park through a wide gap forced in the chain-link fence and came out many blocks up from the main gates of the park. At a pedestrian light, we had to stand waiting even when it was our right of way, because there was a police siren. The man became nervous. He sped away from the crossing, back into the forest through the forced-open fence.

I went the long way around to the park entrance. There, Ema wept. The Austrians ignored her. She grabbed and patted me all over like she did the day I jumped from the highest diving platform at the Ghion. She pinched the underside of my upper arm, where it used to hurt.

"Don't you know what can happen to a girl out there?" she said through her teeth.

I unstuck her nails from my flesh. "Out where, Grinzing?" I said, the name of our neighbourhood. She didn't speak to me the rest of the day.

Late at night, after Le'ul was asleep on the couch in the living room, and Aba had turned in, she came to the room Le'ul and I used to share. She stood by the top bunk in the dark, eye to eye with me. The light from the hallway spilled in. The top of her breasts showed through the black lace trim of her green silk slip. Her head wrap slipped off her head partway, so I knew she had slept some, or at least tried to.

"You don't say good night to your mother. Have you no love?"

"It's almost morning."

"What do you want me to do?"

I turned over and pulled the covers over my head.

One night later in the year, as Ema and Aba ate dinner from the same plate, chatting in low tones, I heard them say how Babbaye would react when he found out his daughter would be serving in the capital city of the Talyans next. That was how I found out, when we went back to Ethiopia at the end of the year, it would be only for a visit. Ema had been promoted. The ministry was sending her to a new post. We would leave Ethiopia again, for four more years, to go to Rome. I knew of Rome. Babbaye had picked a fight with the people there for many years, about a stolen rock.

I didn't wonder if Le'ul planned to go with us to Rome, too. I accepted he would always go where Aba went. Aba said that Le'ul was fragile because he had fallen into a depression. The only depression I knew of was Danakil, in Ethiopia, the hottest place on earth. For every thing I learned in school, Aba always taught me the Ethiopian version or equivalent. But Le'ul was not in any faraway geography. He was in my life still. If he was burning up as much as I did when he forced me to drink hot water, I could not see it. All I knew was that if he could, he would peel my skin and feed it to dogs.

I went to Ema in her bedroom late at night. Aba was in the kitchen, transcribing notes for his manuscript. I knelt beside Ema's bed and waited until she felt my presence. She woke up. She turned on the bedside lamp. I turned it off. I said, "I can't do this anymore. I can't be in this anymore." I began to shiver like I do after I've thrown up. She leaned over, raised me to the bed, and rested my head on her belly until I settled down.

"Ask Babbaye if he'll take me? I can live with him. You three go to Rome. Let me stay back." I began to rise but she pushed me back down. She combed my scalp with her nails for a long time. It was so soothing I almost fell asleep, but I fought it, determined to fix my eyes on her upside down face until I heard a yes.

"If he wants you. I'll ask."

What a silly thing to say. There was no question he would leap at the chance to have me stay. She moved to the middle of the bed, pulling back the covers. I climbed in and tucked into her side. We lay down front to back. No words needed. She drifted off to sleep. Out of old habit, I counted the kisses on her back.

Only two days later, Ema told me Babbaye said no. She asked him to take me in, to let me live with him. He said no. Of course he would say no, I told myself. Why would he agree without knowing the true reason? He shouldn't need a reason, if he really loved me, but I pushed the thought away. I went to her room another night, my eyes stinging even before I spoke.

"You didn't tell him why."

"When your grandfather says no about something, that's it! No," Ema said angrily.

"He wouldn't say no if you told him why I can't, I can't..." Hiccups and sobs stole everything else I meant to say.

"What is the *why* you would have me tell an old man who has grieved so much in his life that people tell him to his face they wish him the blessing of death? What is the *why*?"

Since the day she explained the holy water to me, this was the most we had not talked about *it* while still talking about *it*.

"Say I gave him the *why*, penetrated the knife into his soul. He will kill Le'ul. The life of an enemy is nothing to him. He has killed men with his hands. He's the Shaleqa. He will walk right here to where we are and kill the boy. Can you be sure he won't? Do you know how far that man has walked for revenge? What then? Of your father? Of me? Will you smear the lineage with the stain of shame?"

I was silent. All this talk of her and Aba and shame and murder was confusing.

"No one, but no one, lives life without a burden. Don't think other families don't have their secret pain. Other families, you think they are as happy as they look? Believe your mother, their joy is for show."

"Can't just you and me go to Rome?" I said, speaking for the first time of my deepest wish of having her all to myself again.

"Go tell your father his wife is leaving him. Turn off his light. Shatter his peace so he can't continue the passion book he has waited his whole life to pursue, that Ethiopia will never be able to claim, that generations of her scholars will never get to hold, because one girl had to be happy."

Aba had said his latest book would be his masterpiece, his ultimate legacy, a book about the *Mezmure Dawit*, the psalter he learned by heart when he was a boy in the seminary in Harrar, training to become a priest, following in his father's footsteps. By the time he rebelled and left the seminary to go to secular school—leaving religion to the monks, he said— he was a deacon. Once, washing his hands bloodied by a leaked red pen, he'd told me that in the neighbourhood where he grew up, he was the go-to boy for the women when they needed a male to bless a chicken or sheep and cut its throat.

Ema shoved me. "Why aren't you moving? Go tell him. Go, make your mother and father gossip for the community to chew on."

I went, but to the place Ema knew I would end up, my bed.

Stupid, I should have kept my mouth shut, gone to Ethiopia for vacation, then refused to leave Babbaye's house when it was time to go to Rome. Four years too late, I could have finally answered his question, and said, *I don't want to leave this land.*

SEVENTEEN

Hail crashes onto the corrugated tin roof of my grandfather's house. I snap awake on the bed in Ema's room. Hail, so early in the season? I get out of bed, freezing, and add a second hager libs to the one I'm wearing over my slip. I open the inner window and push the outer shutters, just an inch, but I get pelted by dozens of tiny pearls of ice all the same. I close the shutters. From the floor, I pick up a few pieces of hail, and eat their refreshing coolness. There is no going back to sleep with all this racket. Warily, I look at my phone, which I have avoided since Le'ul's messages. All the screen has to tell me is the time, almost midnight.

The rest of the ice that I let in dissolves on the floor, leaving a wet trail as if someone walked by with a dripping cloth. The hail tapers off, replaced by a steady belg rain. A mouth-watering smell of wet earth seeps through the gaps between the wall and the window frame. I open the shutters. The courtyard appears sprinkled with clusters of softly glowing Styrofoam balls. In the aftershock of the icy torrent, the plants in the courtyard tremble. I too shiver from the cold hug of the night.

I hear water dripping. The sound is not coming from the drainpipes, nor the tap in my bathroom. I open my door and look into the living room. The white chairs glisten.

Gela enters from the back door, wringing out a washcloth into a small bucket. That was the sound I heard. She wipes more white chairs clean of grime. I knock on my door softly so as not to frighten her. She turns, sees me. I wave, wait for her to speak. She waits for me to speak. In the end neither of us says anything. It's too late, or too early, for human voices.

I notice the boxes of loose pages of Ema's memorial programs. Sticking to her word, Gela hasn't let anyone touch them. I'd forgotten all about them. I sit by the boxes and lift out a stack of cover pages from one box. I flip them like an animation flip-book, but Ema's image doesn't move. She's fixed as Tobya or Zimita, depending on the direction I start from. From each box, I take a page of the program, arrange them in order, and fold them as cleanly as Ema would fold her newspapers after she finished reading, so precisely they looked unread. I run my nails hard along the edge. I tuck the folded program under my thigh. One down. I allow myself to look at the family photo on one of the booklet pages, taken on Ema's birthday on the lawn of our Vienna apartment building.

•••

Yene Abeba, would you agree, some birthdays are more special than others? On my thirteenth birthday, I got the best gift of a sad realization that approached me like a new friend. The perfect solution had been in front of me those four years. I had no pen pal. I had no sister. I had no parents, no grandfather. I turned one precious thought in my head—I only had me.

"If I can't stay with Babbaye then let me stay here alone," I said to Ema, in the bright light of morning, one month before the move to Rome, while we were at breakfast. Le'ul and Aba were still in Ethiopia on vacation. The three of them had gone together. Ema returned earlier. I hadn't gone at all. She didn't trust me to come back from Ethiopia with them, so she had—accidentally she said—enrolled me in an expensive, non-refundable, after school German intensive.

Having Ema to myself didn't bring me the same joy as it once did, because I knew the feeling wouldn't last. She was reading her crisp *International Herald Tribune*. She started to do this every morning after her double promotion from Third to First Secretary, because Aba said it's clear they now consider her ambassador material, though as far as he's concerned she has always been Her Excellency.

Ema contemplated what I'd said without taking her eyes off the newspaper. Then she imitated me like a noteworthy headline she was reading aloud. "*I will stay back,* she says."

"Why do you always change my words? I said let me stay *here*. I want to become a boarding student. You'll always know where I am." She lowered the newspaper, letting it crumple. I sensed my advantage. "If you make me go to Rome, I could go missing again."

"You think you can handle being alone in the country of strangers?"

"I was fine the last two weeks you all left me alone. You lived alone in Dessie, when it was bad for you to be in Adisaba. Staying away was how you survived."

She blew on her cold coffee. "We'll see if your father agrees."

Aba and Ema did not say anything to Le'ul about my staying in Vienna. We were all packing, so he did not guess that this was where I would split from them. On departure day, they three got on a plane. I stayed on land. Maybe Le'ul felt happy for the first time in a long time when he realized

I wasn't coming with them, as I had felt on my first airplane ride four years ago, thinking he was out of my life forever.

•••

Gela and I work quietly, she cleaning her chairs, I folding Ema's programs, under Tobya's photo over the mantelpiece. The phone rings. I jump. Gela picks it up before the second ring. She doesn't say anything after *hello.* She holds out the receiver to me. "It's him again. The one who calls himself your —"

I don't hear the last word, because my mind has skipped over the now, to another year, another hushed moment ruptured by the ringing of this same phone. It was a kiremt afternoon, the hail drumming on the roof, Le'ul guiding me to the bed for checking-time.

He pauses, I pause. Through a thin part of my blindfold, I see the light change his naked brown shoulders to gold as he turns toward the sound within the sound. We wait for the ringing to stop. But the phone insists, its noise breaking through the hammering of the falling ice. It must be Ema, calling from the office. Le'ul throws a bathrobe on me, unlocks the door, pushes me out to the hallway still blindfolded. I stand disoriented. I feel a hard shove, Le'ul's foot on my back. I hit the wall. I push my arms into the sleeves of the robe, tie it, and pat my way down the hall toward the nook, to the phone that has saved me like a screaming mouth.

Gela holds her arm extended toward me as if it's too dark for her to see that I am waving her away with both hands, refusing. Why this phone? Why didn't my parents sell this phone as they had everything else we owned? She puts the receiver on the floor and goes back to her chairs. I approach the phone. I raise it to my ear. I hear my name.

"Dessie." In my ear is the pillow of Ema's voice. "My sweet, you ate your snack and lunch?" Before me, I see only black. Under my feet is cool tile. At my back, I feel Le'ul's eyes. Words that could save me spill from my mouth, but they are soundless. Ema is not here but through the phone I can smell the burning clove of her cigarettes. So my mother should smell my stink. Ema and Aba know all, how do they not know what is happening to me in their own house?

"Dessie?"

"Yes Ema, I did."

"And your penmanship exercises?"

"I did."

This kiremt I am practising writing the English alphabet letters without lifting my pencil. I am between first and second grade. Ema and Aba make us study ahead. Our reward is the same each year, a weekend trip to Sodere. Ema starts to say goodbye.

"The afternoon is long, Ema."

"Do something else then, my sweet. Paint me the roses in the vase."

I try not to breathe on Le'ul, but I do.

"Dessie," he says.

Gela moves to the back door. I yank her shirt to make her stay. I turn in a slow half circle, to keep her in my sight. The telephone cord wraps around me.

Le'ul says, "I called Stanley when they didn't deliver the stone. Why is he saying you cancelled the order when we are supposed to dedicate Ema's gravestone tomorrow?"

I don't remember all I said on the phone call from Teka's shop, with Teka echoing my every word to my grandfather and the rose carvers. But I am sure I did not say anything about the gravestone.

"Did Aba come back?"

"I told you the car was always here." He had not. "He was upstairs," he says impatiently, as if that was never an issue, as if yesterday he hadn't been losing his mind about it like a bitch.

"Where're you calling me from?" I want to lock Le'ul into a specific location I can visualize, so as not to have all of him in my ear.

"I told you. The residence. Aba is upstairs praying."

Chanting, probably. His rediscovered hobby. Of course he is upstairs. Now it seems obvious that after Ema was gone he would seek her out in the one place she didn't admit anyone.

I can see Ema so clearly: pen poised over a paper on her desk; gesturing to her assistant through the glass separating her office from the secretaries' area; crossing her legs under the desk so she can massage the scar on the back of her thigh, through the fabric of her slacks, with the ring finger she uses to rub away her cigarette ash when it misses the ashtray. But she can't see me to ask me, Why are you wearing nothing but a bathrobe in the middle of the afternoon? Why is your hand shaking? Who tied your eyes?

"Aba says he made no such call telling Stanley we wanted to cancel the stone. I didn't either. You're the only person that misdirect could have come from. He's very disturbed."

"I didn't cancel the stone."

"Then what did you tell Stanley to do?"

"Nothing."

"Or not do."

"Nothing."

Le'ul knows. *Disturbed* is too strong a word to describe how Aba would feel over a delayed stone. But Le'ul is going to make me suffer. He wants me to confess. Or he is going to let me go now, so he can use the information he has, to force me to do something for him later. Something that will cost me more than a couple of buddy passes.

"Did you or did you not talk to Stanley," he says.

"Yes."

"What are you even doing in Ethiopia?"

I seek eye contact with Gela. She's obviously eavesdropping, as much as she can understand. I push my fist against the wall.

"I'm stranded here."

"Of all places?"

"Haven't you watched the news? The volcano?"

"I know the news. I don't know if I can trust you."

"Ask Aba."

"You told me you were going to Sydney."

Ten days that feel like ten years ago, I lied to Le'ul about where I was flying to, only so I would have some extra days of peace after I returned from Johannesburg. Not to ensnare myself. "The volcano..."

"Which took place on the other side of the globe from your flight path?"

"I wasn't going to Sydney."

"Please. Stop it. Stop your lying. If you and I are going to have a relationship, trust and honesty are paramount. Tell the truth."

"It's late here..." I'm scared to hang up.

Ema she has to go, she has work to do. Even if I could keep her on the phone, I will have to let her go in the end, so she can drive home. In that time, I will be alone again with Le'ul. I don't want to live even that short time.

"Dessie. The best thing you can do for yourself is tell the truth, now. What did you do? Why did you do it?"

"I was only pretending, at first."

"What you're up to, what you've done, is not right."

"I didn't do anything."

My head hurts, I don't know which side is up, which down. I feel I am wading through versions of a nightmare I have been having since Ema called from her office that loud afternoon. Sometimes in my nightmare, there is an emergency. I must make a phone call, shout out something important. But I always dial the wrong number. I know it is the wrong number, but my fingers will only press the wrong numbers. Other times, I dial the right number. Someone answers, but no matter how much air I push out through my throat, even until my stomach cramps, I can get no sound out. My mouth is clogged by a stringy glob. I use my fingers to pull at it. I only make it more viscous. Other times, I get sound out, but just a hollow wheeze, or the wrong words, or the right words jumbled out of order.

Ema says goodbye. I don't. I can't. My mouth is numb like after the dentist's needle. There is only the busy tone, but I hold the phone for a long time.

Many years too late, the blindfolded girl naked under the bathrobe, spills the saving words, the right words in the right order.

She is gone. She can't hear me anymore. I tell her.

"I'm cold."

Le'ul's voice. "What did you say?"

"I'm not wearing enough."

"Shut up."

"You forced me."

"Do not accuse me of something you started."

"*Legs open, mouth, if I feel teeth I will end you.*"

I listen to the husky dial tone for a long time. I turn to Gela. She is still pretending to not care about me. Ema, in the big photo, is as usual: there, but not.

I move to Gela, until the phone cord tightens around my

hips. I drop the receiver to the floor and continue toward her, gripping the tops of the chair backrests, dragging the phone on the floor behind me. I let go of the last chair before I reach her. In that moment, Gela coming to catch me with open arms, everything goes black.

When I come to, I am retching, gagging over the bathroom sink, scraping my nails down my tongue, pulling out something invisible. Gela wets the face towel she had been cleaning the chairs with in cold water. She pastes it to my forehead. She fights me for my hand and rinses it under the tap in hers, not disgusted by my saliva. Clear water swirls down the drain. Because I am not sick. Ema said so.

How sorry I would be if you weren't mine. Did she say that to you, Yene Abeba?

"For you to cry is good," Gela says. "It's good."

She drapes the towel over the edge of the sink and walks me to Ema's room. She pushes me to lie back on the bed and sits on the edge. Our bodies are as close as they were on the day she threw her weeping self at me.

"From when I opened the gate until now, you never cry, about anything. Here your grief is, expressed. From now on, I don't worry for you. There. Only a delay in feeling. Was it something the man said?"

"Will I ever know the *why*?"

She strokes my face. "Princess, you are unwell." She shuts the door and comes back to the bed. She lies down facing me, but upside down, like a playing card.

"The programs. I didn't finish Ema's books."

"Sleep now. Tomorrow comes with a lot of work. Before sunrise I must make food packets to give to the dependents at Selassie."

"The charity? Let's prepare it now."

"Who told you Gela does not sleep?"

"You were awake to wash the chairs."

"Now I want to be asleep."

"Oh."

"Sleep, little flower."

From this angle, Gela has a different face. To have her body so near but her voice coming from so far away is strange, like speaking to her shadow, her nighttime self, instead of the one I know by day. She turns on her other side. Her attention, which has been a balm to me, is gone in an instant. I close my eyes.

A few minutes later, the door handle clicks.

He *is* here. Paralyzed with fear, I peek through my lashes.

My grandfather stands in the open doorway. I almost get up, thinking something has happened to him and he needs help. But he is still.

I count my breaths, willing the apparition gone. He retreats quietly. I sit up. On Gela's face are telltale signs of deep sleep: dropped jaw, softly parted lips. I turn myself upside down and curve my body behind hers, mirroring her position without touching. When people spoon, they can't see each other, yet it is the most tender embrace. Sometimes that is the best kind of comfort, like a child in the mother's womb.

EIGHTEEN

"It will wash," Gela says, shaking me awake. The air smells metallic. I scoot away from a huge leak of blood that has spread on the bedsheet, from my side. I am mortified.

"I am so sorry."

"It's only blood."

What could be worse than blood? We get out of bed. She gathers the stained sheets and goes out. The mattress hasn't fared any better. The stain will never come out completely. What will we do, flip it over? This will be the house's souvenir of me?

Faint dawn light filters in through the window shutters. I am standing over my open suitcase, tearing at a new travel-size box of tampons, my thighs sticky under my two ruined hager libs and slip, when Gela returns with a blue plastic bag of Modess. I haven't worn pads since junior high, but I accept her offer. In the bathroom I roll up what I'd slept in and stuff it into a plastic bag. I wash and change into a clean pair of underwear and yesterday's black clothes. The pad feels as cozy against my triangle, just like the first time.

•••

Yene Abeba, isn't it funny how so many phrases have abeba in them? Ema was making a cutting from her rosebush on the balcony. I was with her, to be close for the last hours we had before they flew to Rome, memorizing the outline of her body that I could see through her hager libs.

She closed her hand around a red rose and pulled out the petals. "You'll need to know what to do with these," she said, opening her palm. I thought she was going to give me a cutting from the plant too. "Soon, you will see yewer abeba, messy red like this."

In the bathroom, she wrapped her cutting in wet toilet paper. She took out a pad from a blue box of square white cottons labeled Modess. Sitting on the edge of the bathtub, she demonstrated how to catch my monthly flowers with the cottons.

She gave me a pad. "Show me you know what to do now." I showed her, washing my hands before and after. "And change it no less than every three hours," she said. I waited for the part about babies, but Ema didn't mention that, as if these blossoms were just poorly healing cuts that broke open every month. She played with the adhesive strip of the pad, folding one corner to the opposite long side, then over to the other long side, until at the end a small strip was left, which she tucked into one side of the triangle.

"This will continue until you are an old woman."

"Like you?"

She pressed the tip of the paper triangle down the centre of my face. "Take it off."

"Later?" I liked having a tiny, snug pillow between my triangle and the world's harm.

"You have to bleed to wear it."

"Why waste it?"

"Well, you might as well get used to the feel." She packed six boxes of Modess in my suitcases. "Never leave your blood behind. Always check you don't leave petals on your clothes or bedsheets. People will laugh at you before they tell you what's wrong," she said, as if that was the worst thing that could happen to a girl.

•••

From memory, I fold the waxy adhesive strip of the pad Gela gave me, in a repeating sharp triangle the way Ema had—the way, as I would later learn, the flags used to cover the coffins of fallen soldiers are folded. I tuck it into the mirror frame. I wash my stained underwear, squeeze out every last drop of pink water, and roll it up in the cleaning towel Gela had draped over the sink last night.

On my way to the clotheslines outside, I pass Gela returning to the house with a fresh bedsheet folded in a triangle. In the cold dawn air, I hang my underwear, hidden within the folded towel, at the farthest end of the clotheslines, almost under the eaves of the service quarters roof. Below, the sheets soak in the washtub, making a mockery of my attempt to be discreet.

I re-enter the living room. In the moment when I have a sightline into Ema's room, I see Gela standing over my open suitcase. I pause. The bedsheet triangle that she holds against her chest is still. She is not breathing. Slowly, reverently, she lowers her hand into the suitcase. If I moved a little bit to the right, I could see what she's reaching for, but even the softest creak would risk breaking the spell of this moment. I know, already, what she is reaching for. I hear the crinkle of paper. The only papers in my suitcase are my mother's letters.

Gela's hand trembles as she picks up a piece of 1980.

What girl? Her.

She is the hidden image in an optical illusion, astonishing for how invisible it had been while in such plain view, and impossible to un-see. All our moments together coalesce into a simple truth. She is that girl. How she welcomed me; her stares; how she lacks the self-effacing quality of maids; her overbearing, big-sisterly inability to mind her own business. Even her testy moments. My sister.

Fearing she will vanish, I try not to blink. But I do. The floor creaks. Gela swiftly drops the torn letter and unravels the bedsheet. I enter the room.

"My mother used to fold her gabi that way too," I say.

"It's a common style."

She snaps the sheet open like a clap of thunder, her fury at the torn letter. The sheet refuses to land evenly over the mattress. The fabric furls back to her, desiring its original, imperfectly contained form. She snaps it away from her. It hurries back. The corners of her mouth go up. She has my fake smile. The next time she tosses the sheet out, I catch the opposite side. Together we position it evenly over the mattress, covering the stain she has scrubbed as best she could.

"Don't stretch it too tight," she says. "It will soak up the wet."

I want to sweep her up in a hug. That's how this moment should go. Haven't I imagined it? But I'm blocked because she has known who I am all along, who Dessie and Gela are to each other, yet she has said nothing. I remind myself her silence can only be my grandfather's doing. He must hold so much power over her. He has told her to keep her mouth shut, until he says when. She has obeyed. Even Wondu, who has nothing to lose, took one look at our grandfather and clammed up. I don't have to. She is close enough to touch. We can start being sisters right now, just us two.

But I can't speak. I am afraid Gela is mad at me about the crumpled and torn letters. Their dishevelment is proof that I am *the lifelong pain* Ema told her I am. I won't reinforce that impression by stealing our mother's special day too, and making it all about me. No, today is your day, Ema. I may not owe you my reconciliation with Le'ul, but I am not stingy enough to deny your spirit a drama-free release. I can be generous now. Let today be about marking off the past from the future. I want to wait for a proper time to tell Gela I now know who she is. For now, I have a new memory—the time I saw my sister—to add to my imaginary box of precious odds and ends, except this memory is fresh and whole.

We watch the loosely laid sheet. The moisture doesn't seep through.

Our reasons are different, but at our core Gela and I are the same. We are waiting for the perfect moment to speak, to acknowledge, while causing the least collateral damage. It would have been hard enough to meet each other had it been planned, had Ema brought us together herself. But we have been thrown together without warning. I was not supposed to be here. Ema was not supposed to die. I almost laugh with relief that I can now stop the ghoulish process of bringing her here.

"That's how it will stay?" I say to Gela.

"For now. We will take care of it properly later. Go back to sleep on the dry side."

"No."

"Or should I prepare the sofa cushions on the floor for you?"

"I am going to Selassie with you."

"Mass begins later. You attend with the Shaleqa then."

"Are you going to stop me from giving charity on behalf of my mother?"

"Who am I to do that? Do what you like. Only, it might displease the Shaleqa."

"God forbid." I jokingly flutter my fingers. But Gela doesn't crack even a pretend smile.

NINETEEN

The clink of china on marble as the Shaleqa places a saucer on the mantelpiece under Tobya's portrait seems to gently announce the official start of the Forty Day. Still in his nightclothes, he lights a tall white candle for Ema, melts the base, and presses the candle on the saucer. I am beside him, where he wants me to be today for this daily ceremony. He puts my hand over his until the candle is fixed in place. He closes his eyes, to pray, I presume.

My hand is on top of his, but I'm his captive. I grew up hearing of the feats of poorly equipped arbegna who exhausted a modern adversary, but only now do I feel that I have grasped what the Shaleqa is capable of. He allowed for so much between his daughter and granddaughters—letters, visits, being under one roof—not out of mercy but because he knew we lacked his caliber of baffling nerve.

Gela tiptoes in from the back alley, with a vase of water and Teka's roses in their cardboard chokehold. She puts both on a chair and leaves. I remove my hand from my grandfather's. He opens his eyes. I free the roses from the cardboard and arrange them in the vase. I put them in the fireplace. They fan out and glow against the sooty brick.

"I am going to do the charity food giving," I say, tearing up the cardboard.

"That is well."

He returns to his room through the two-row deep amphitheatre of clean-as-new chairs. In the kitchen, I wedge the pieces of cardboard between the coals in the coffee brazier. Gela presses a knife deep into the stack of injera she had separated into a mesob yesterday, cutting the pile in half. Onto the topmost half, she scoops out one ladleful of misir wot from a bowl, which she must have portioned out from the giant pot of the stew the cooks made. She folds the top injera over the misir wot, making a loose samosa shape, which she puts in a baggie. She ties the baggie, with extra air for cushioning, and lays it in a deep, stiff canvas bag on the ground. She repeats the process. I take over holding the baggies open and packing them.

"Where did you say you grew up?" I say, fully expecting her to lie.

"What does it matter where a nothing like me grew up?" she deflects.

"It's a simple question."

"Simply, I grew up in Ethiopia."

I wish I could tell her that if she'll just acknowledge me first, I will move us through the Shaleqa's anger and the rest.

"Do you dream of her?" I say.

"Who?"

"Etye Zimita."

"Why should I?"

"Anybody can dream of anybody. I wish I dreamed of her."

"If we don't dream of the departed, it means they are truly at rest."

"Rest? I thought she is still travelling everywhere where there are people who love and miss her, until after today."

"Besmea'b wold mefes kidus," she whispers, crossing herself to cast out my blasphemy. "At least you remember about the reason for the Forty."

"There are many questions she left behind." All beginning with why. Why, for a woman with so much power and independence later in her life, did she continue to be ruled by her father and husband?

"The questions we would ask of the departed, our soul already knows the answers."

She is full of convenient theories. Eighty injera-samosas later, the canvas bag is full of baggies, the mesob is empty, and there's not a drop of misir wot left in the bowl. Gela's portioning was exact. She takes a yellow jerry can with a rope looped around its handle, and a small jug, to the storage room next door. I follow, avoiding the stream of rainwater coursing down the alley. She breaks the mud seal on the blue barrel of tella, releasing a sour ale smell, and dips in the jug, from which she fills the jerry can. I follow her back to the kitchen. From a cupboard she passes me a roll of one birr notes.

"Hold this."

"We have to pay them to eat, too?"

"It's symbolic. Not even a hundred gets you anything these days."

She shoulders the jerry can of tella by the rope. We each grip one handle of the canvas bag, and set off under an umbrella she holds over us against the day's first belg rain. At the gate, on impulse, I kick off my flip-flops and wiggle my toes. The flagstones are slippery, the dewy grass chilly from last night's melted ice.

"Today is my Kulubi Gabriel," I say, in response to Gela's bewildered look.

She tilts her head up to the umbrella, beseeching divine forbearance. The light filtering through the blue polyester gives her face a greenish hue. "What are you requesting from the archangel? Common sense?"

"I am thanking him, for a gift I received this morning."

"You call blood a gift?"

"The greatest."

"Princess, you are walking in the city, not in the open countryside. Wear your shoes."

I lay my flip-flops on the food packets in the canvas bag and drag her out through the open gate with me.

On the main road, we catch a minibus taxi. From my window seat at the back, the cushion springs digging into my legs, I refold each birr note individually. Gela extracts two birr for the fare collector who is perched on the rear wheel arch of the van's interior. He is a strikingly hot teenager with toffee eyes, razor-sharp chin, and gabi lint in his curls, dressed in threadbare Western castoffs. He's organized his bills lengthwise by colour and tucked them in the groove of his thumb. He plucks our change from the cylinder of coins in the middle of his palm.

The taxi drops us across from the roundabout circling the resistance monument, a grey five-sided pillar spotted black by the morning drizzle. As soon as we start the walk to Selassie, a beggar woman, wearing plastic shoes, with a baby slung on her back, comes up beside us. She opens her food sack full of leftovers from many households. It smells like a compost bin.

"What is the name?" she asks, keeping pace.

I stop, forcing Gela to do the same. She glares at the beggar. "Selassie is where we are giving." The woman glares right back, shoving her sack at her.

"What's the difference between here and there?" I say.

Gela snatches the topmost baggie of food from the pile and picks one birr from my bundle. She slaps the money in the woman's hand and throws the baggie in her sack. She slams the jerry can on the ground. With each sudden noise the baby twitches in its sleep. The woman pats its bum with one hand, holding out a wrinkled empty water bottle to Gela with her other hand. Gela fills it halfway with tella, without touching the mouth of the jerry can to the bottle.

"Welete-Mikael," Gela says.

The woman bows to me, tosses a nasty look to Gela, and walks toward Selassie. Even with the child on her back, she is nimble, one shoe barely touching the ground before the other leaves it. I imagine her prayer for Ema will be just as efficient. *Igziabher hoy, please look after the soul of Welete-Mikael, daughter of your archangel Mikael. Amen.*

Gela closes and re-shoulders the jerry can. We have almost reached the south branch of the roundabout when another pair of beggars, a blind man with his hand on the shoulder of a guide a step ahead of him, make a beeline for us. I tug the handle.

Gela snaps at me. "Don't you mistake me for your pack animal! There is a system to this. The difference between here and there is I have made enough for the dependents there, not for every beggar your heart jumps for on the way."

I grab two baggies and let go of my handle. She snatches up the second handle and waddles on under the weight of the bag in one hand, the tella on her other shoulder. I realize I've left her umbrella in the taxi. I'll wait for a better time to tell her that.

I grip my toes on the asphalt, waiting for the blind beggar and his guide to reach me. Breathing through my mouth to not smell them, I give them the bunch of baggies and money.

"What is the name?" the guide says.

I remember the look the Selassie clerk exchanged with Gela in the office yesterday, making me feel stupid.

"Zimita," I say. Ema's everyday name for her everyday soul.

"What is the name?" the guide says again.

"Zimita," I shout, wondering if he is deaf.

They hesitate. "What is the name?" the blind one says.

"Zimita Tessema! Tobya Tessema if you want. Or Emwodish. Or Ema. How about Her Excellency? You want your breakfast or not?" I reach for the bag of food in the guide's hand. He dodges, and leads his friend away.

I catch up to Gela at the cathedral gates. She places the plastic baggies firmly into the hands of the blind, mouths Ema's baptismal name for the deaf, and aims her jerry can very carefully at the plastic water bottles, not wasting a drop of tella. I leave her half the remaining roll of birr in the canvas bag, and wander off to continue my mischief of telling Ema's true name. When the dependents go over to Gela for tella and food, she'll tell them the fancy one. They can take their pick, or pray twice. It's all a sham transaction anyway, so the dependents can get food and the independents can get peace.

Case in point, the mother we first gave alms to brazenly comes back for seconds.

Finished, Gela and I sit on a stone bench so I can brush my feet clean. Gela falls into a contemplative mood, her netela draped softly around her head. I search for any other inheritance I might have missed on her face.

"Staring is rude," she says.

"You could be a tourism postcard." She gets up, compacting the canvas bag. "What are you thinking of?"

"The things postcards must think of."

"How wrong it is to be sent out into the world without the privacy of an envelope?"

"That's why the space for writing is small," she says, indulging me. "So people don't say too much."

•••

At the house, Gela rinses and hangs my bedsheets. I collate the rest of the memorial programs and distribute them on the chairs. Mid-morning, I return to Selassie for mass with the Shaleqa, his friends, their families, his neighbours and compatriots, and my grand-aunt, Emmahoy. Gela stays behind to oversee lunch preparations and set up the coffee.

I usher Emmahoy into the women's section of the cathedral's cavernous interior, down a side colonnade of white mosaic pillars. Wall-to-wall red carpeting absorbs the sound of our footsteps. We settle in the first of a dozen rows of wood pews. The altar area is layered with Persian rugs. The back half of it is hidden behind an opulent green velvet curtain hanging off an arch. Above the arch is a mural of brown angels in Afros, against a soft yellow backdrop, flanking a haloed trio of red-robed elders on a platform of clouds.

A microphone crackles. Then, the voice of an unseen male, seeming to come from behind the curtain, releases the first drawn-out syllable of chant. The sea of worshippers covered in white netela swells to standing. The clergy emerge, a vision of beards, head wraps, jewelled crowns, gilded umbrellas, flowing satin robes and capes. Their cryptic motions don't resemble what the priests at Ema's funeral had done, motions I was told were very important for her soul.

The four hours–long loop of standing, sitting, bowing, prostrating, preaching, and chanting puts me in a trance. I snap out of it only when Emmahoy tugs me down.

"Now, the baptism names of the departed are called," she whispers in my ear.

The disembodied male voice that started the show tears through dozens of names in one breath. I miss hearing Ema's. Gela was right. Even a hundred birr gets you nothing these days.

After mass, we exit at a snail's pace, through throngs of worshippers pushing containers at a deacon wielding a giant kettle of holy water. By the entrance, dependents have been replaced by trader women, propping up steeples of freshly cut grass and refusing to haggle. With Emmahoy's money, I buy three thick bundles for Gela's coffee service.

TWENTY

The chairs in my grandfather's living room are askew. Guests who've reached the house ahead of us have already ruined Gela's two perfect rows so they can sit in clusters, chatting in cliques. The relaxation is palpable. The living are finished keeping Ema's soul company in this realm for forty days. Her being truly gone is now just another fact, a rock, around which the river of life—food eaten, news shared, plans made or revised—will flow on.

As she requests, I seat Emmahoy close to the coffee service, which Gela has set up beside the fireplace and the vase of roses, so that she'll be warmed by the heat from the brazier later. I undo the knot around the bundles of grass from Selassie, and spread it around on the floor in front of the coffee service with my hands, creating a thick carpet. There's a soft, fetid smell to the roses, sweet but on its way to repulsive. I yank out petals and sprinkle them on the grass. The conversations become subdued. I turn around. The guests raise their eyebrows at each other, look to the Shaleqa, *Who's going to be the one to tell her?*

"What, it's a celebration today, right?" I say. I know damn well it's not that kind of celebration. "A farewell. Today my mother departed to the heavenly realm."

Gela enters from the alley, carrying an urn, bowl, and towel to begin the hand-washing rounds for lunch. She stops dead when she sees what I've done. "Didn't you say so, Gela?"

Uncle Whiskey speaks. "The child of Zimita is not wrong."

Gela is so thrown off that she begins the hand-washing rounds with him instead of the Shaleqa. Uncle Whiskey soaps his hand. "Zimita bid us farewell today." He plonks the soap into the water and rinses his hand, turning the water murky with his dirt.

Uncle A B Z, next in line for the water, chimes in. "Yes. This room has seen many a farewell for Zimita. The last was nineteen years ago."

Uncles Pilot and Bug contribute in turn, reminding all about the celebration for Ema's university graduation, which she accomplished on time. The uncles' wives pick up the subtle reference to the Terror and address me in chorus.

"We raised Tobya, after."

"We women were also at Zimita's wedding, the farewell to her girlhood."

"We who cooked her feast then are eating Welete-Mikael's tsebel meal today."

I listen, shucking the thorns from the rose stems with the edge of my thumb and throwing them on the grass. Tizita about that grand day, their most cherished recollections of Zimita and Mesfin's wedding, are tossed from mouth to mouth, a lazy game of catch, as people clean themselves by fishing the doughy soap out of the increasingly filthy water. They direct their words to me, but I know they are really speaking to Ema. Their kindness is meant to reach her, just like their joy so long ago was not for the new graduate or bride but for her father, and for the dead on whose behalf she would live well.

"Soon," the Shaleqa says, "we will celebrate her final welcome, her rest with her own."

The plates, the injera, the wot, are trotted out. The feasting commences. That's it. Between mentions of what are agreed to be Ema's milestones, dutifully reflected in the memorial programs — the unstapled pages of which are half falling out of the pockets and purses they've been haphazardly stuffed into — Ema's whole life is deemed honoured. Her first love, teen pregnancy, the daughter she had to leave behind in Dessie — never happened. Whether the omission is intentional or the guests truly don't know that Ema's time in Dessie wasn't only about survival, this enormous fact which so deeply affected me, her, and Gela, goes unacknowledged.

Shaleqa radiates contentment. I should sit to eat beside him, but I have no appetite. From the kitchen I bring around bowls of food for seconds. No one objects to my working on this day, perhaps because the food today is tsebel, eaten in honour of the departed's spirit. Therefore they think it appropriate that her daughter serve it. I spoon out generous additional helpings of wot on the guests' plates, heap on the bread and injera. I want them to eat until they hurt, so they will feel some pain, even if it is the temporary, physical kind, not permanent like mine and Gela's. And boy do they eat. Their megderder doesn't have the typical false note of a pretend refusal. They genuinely welcome being overfed, as if they are eating for two, themselves and Ema, to prove how much they loved her.

I try to fill in the missing part of her life story, get them to see that Gela and I are both Ema's daughters, by smiling every time Gela does, imitating her gestures and phrases. I fail. Other than our height, we have nothing visibly in common. She resembles her father, I our mother.

Gela doesn't get recognition even for the tella, which flows before, during, and after lunch. No compliments to the brewer on the polished, creamy aftertaste of the bitter fizzy ale. Claiming good tella never runs out, Gela frequently dispatches Lomi and Aberash to the living room with brimming pitchers from the kitchen, where she keeps two backup pitchers full from the barrel in the storage room.

On one of my trips down the alley from the storage room, where I prefer to top up my glass in private, filtering through my teeth the bits of what I assume is gesho, I misjudge the lowered step into the kitchen and stumble, spilling half of it on my blouse.

"Like mother, like daughter," Lomi says, giggling, clearly tipsy.

"What?" I say.

Aberash reprimands her with a hard push. The women slink out around me, carrying full pitchers. "Don't mind them," Gela says, heading out to the storage room with an empty pitcher.

I follow, suddenly intoxicated. "I mind." Gela lifts the barrel lid. The ladle that was on it slides and falls. She looks down at the ladle, sighs, then plunges the pitcher in the barrel. The tella swooshes in.

"Well?"

"When the Terror..." She lifts out the full, dripping pitcher, wipes the sides with her hand. "When the Terror came, the Shaleqa hid Tobya."

"I know."

"You don't know where he hid her."

"In Dessie."

"Before Dessie."

I had never considered before Dessie. I had assumed the

squads simply didn't consider a wisp of a girl like my mother worth taking up space in their truck.

Gela dries her hands on her dress. "He hid her in one of these barrels."

"She never told me that part."

"Often all a woman needs is for someone to ask."

I want to slap the smug out of her. "The barrel happened to be empty?"

"On Genna day? What do you think? It had tella."

"She would have drowned."

"If she had, you wouldn't be here. Aren't you her child?"

"Aren't you?"

She quickly picks up the ladle from the floor, as if it fell that instant, and dashes out. I mean to go after her—it's what I do, I trail after maids—but my body moves in the direction it is facing, to the open barrel. The tella reflects my face. I look aghast, like the angels in church art, whose wings seem to grow out of their cheeks. Could it have been this one Ema was hidden in?

I break the surface of the tella with my right hand, sending my arm in up to my shoulder. I sweep my fingers along the inside of the barrel, feeling for bumps, grooves Ema scratched out with her nails until they broke, while she held her breath so that she could live. I pull my arm out. I imagine her being pulled out of the barrel. Dripping, gasping, drunk, fingernails bloody. Stinking, as I do. She vomited what she had to swallow. Her smell washed off. What stuck was the silence, after. After Dessie. She suffocated for life anyway.

I walk down the alley with new caution. From the back entrance to the living room, I watch Gela. All I have to do is wait out here. She has to come out eventually. She has settled behind the brazier, and is about to roast the coffee beans on the pan. Her eyes dart quickly to me, then down to the flames leaping out of the brazier. She balances the pan on the flaming coals. I'll wait. She fans the coals. She will roast the beans with a long flat iron rod for about ten minutes, wrap a cloth around the wire handle to remove the pan, and then set the kettle of water to boil on the brazier. While the water heats, she will take the pan to the alley and crouch, skirt tucked behind her knees, slide the glistening hot beans into the mortar, and pound them into powder—*thud, crack, thud*—covering the mouth of the mortar with one hand, aiming the iron pestle in the gap between her thumb and forefinger, never missing, never tearing that delicate web of flesh. The coffee powder she doesn't use up today, she will save for later. Always later, always when it is a better time. Always how will it seem?

I enter the living room, which vibrates with the murmurs of the sated. The guests and the Shaleqa are too involved in their clusters of conversation to pay me or my tella-soaked clothes any mind as I squeeze around the chairs and go to my room. One by one, I smooth out the crumpled letters on the bed. I refold each neatly. And tap the stack until the edges are perfectly aligned.

They come with me to the living room, weighing my hand like a live grenade. They jump on Gela's lap. She springs back, her arms up, away.

"I'm done with these," I say.

"No," she says, barely above a whisper.

"You didn't want me to read them?" I raise my voice. "The Shaleqa said different."

We've captured some attention. Most know what this scene

seems like at first glance, the lady of the house confronting the maid with a charge of theft.

The coffee beans release an earthy steam. Gela nudges them around the pan with the rod, as if there's nothing in her lap. I can't see her expression, but her shoulders have collapsed. I avoid looking at our grandfather. I don't want to go back to being a coward. I sense no gesture from him. Maybe he doesn't believe I will speak on, even after having come as far as bringing the secret out of the bedroom.

I point at Gela, like an accused saving her skin by exposing another's, and say a simple phrase I've always fantasized saying.

"That's my sister."

As if I've inflicted a curse on her, Gela drops the iron rod and covers her face. She stumbles out, blindly, her body bouncing off chairs and the frame of the back door. The letters sail off her lap and land on the moist grass. All breath and motion in the room cease. I am out of words. I thought there would be more to say, volumes, but the rest of the words fell behind in Ema's room.

I startle back as from the edge of sleep. From where I stand, I can see the porch, the courtyard, Gela's little house, the open gate. I should run after her, and beg her to believe me when I say I didn't mean for our reunion to be this way. All the way from the storage room to the living room to the bedroom and back, I wanted to stop. But something said *now.*

A sip, a rearranged limb, a cough later, the hum returns. The guests shake off the spell and resume their enjoyment where they left off, tucking this incident away to dissect later. For now, though the letters are on the floor, the thing to do is behave as though nothing has happened. This is the generation that, even in private moments, does not react, whom Terror has killed with fear. I don't know why I expected that speaking would bring about change, when I've had warnings all along that those present, those living, are often no better than the dead when it comes to acting on what they know.

Finally, I look at the Shaleqa. He watches me from a distance wider than the room, as if I am already only a tizita. His gaze is as unreadable as the framed Tobya's; what made her laugh, who captured her smile, will remain a mystery. She cares nothing for tears, rituals, programs, candles, or stale roses in the black chasm of the fireplace. All that is for us, the living. None of it is what we need to live: the truth, spoken and heard. Wrongs corrected.

The coffee beans crackle and burn. I grab the wire handle of the pan, burning my hand. I yell in pain and drop the pan. I suck my fingers. My chin crumbles at the taste of myself, the rest of my face follows. I cave into a cry. Finally, I am wailing excellently. But my grief has no dance. I am fused to the parquet, a freakish growth that should be sanded off. I hide my face behind my hands too. No one rescues me either. Gela and I are like enchanted girls. We have bodies but no one can see us.

At last, tenderness. A paper-soft hand pulls me into a deep embrace. Prayer beads caress my cheek. Emmahoy. She shuffles me to Ema's bedroom, onto the bed, my face buried in her unsuckled breasts. Finally, I am held as I've craved to be, since I grew too big to nap with Ema. She coos in time to my sobbing. "Beka beka," she says. Enough.

TWENTY-ONE

I awake to the sensation of being pushed away. Emmahoy, having protected me as long as she could, is rising to leave. In the disordered living room, only her angelic escort, the novice, waits.

My grandfather's door is closed. Tobya's candle is flickering its last.

I guide Emmahoy down the porch steps and over the flagstone pathway, keeping ahead of her, holding out my arms as if I am teaching the old woman to swim the air. We part without words. She has had no dreams. I am out of questions.

Gela's door is closed.

From the side alley, I hear the *tinkle, splash,* and *clang* of Lomi and Aberash washing dishes in the washstand outside, with hardened feminine hands that have wed, birthed, buried plenty. I find a straw broom among the hydrangea bushes. I sweep the flagstones. I sweep the Shaleqa's steps. I sweep his porch. I sweep the parquet twice. It's hard to get around the chairs and the letters. Using a stray booklet page as a pan, I collect grass, rose petals, crumbs, and dried mud in a corner and lean the broom over it. Daylight fades, but I don't turn on the overhead lamp. I'd rather not see how much I've missed.

I scrape the melted candlewax from the saucer and light a new candle. While I flatten, knead, and mould the old warm wax into a ball, the rising flame from the new candle brings Tobya's image back to life. I tuck the ball of wax into the base of the new candle.

I reorganize Gela's letters and put them outside her door, under the rock that I'd been using to prop the gate open.

I stoop to the soil under the mefakiya bushes to search for the two cigarette butts I threw out last night. I find them, and push them deep into the soil, which is still soft from last night's downpour, easy for me to dig up a fistful. I squeeze it. When I open my hand the oval has the impression of my fingers, like besso, the food of soldiers on the march back in the Shaleqa's day.

I feel watched. The Shaleqa is looking down at me from the window of Ema's room. I brace myself for hard words. I can survive a hit. I am a Little Patriot after all. But in this dense quiet between me and my grandfather now—he studying me, me worrying a leaf—I feel something I doubt the real Patriots felt. Regret. That I didn't wait to see if Gela would claim me herself. That I gave in to a righteous impulse at the worst possible time. That I didn't heed Ema's advice to *never rush*.

Tentatively, I reach back further in time, to my second grade pen pal letter. Was that worth all the pain that followed? Would I, and those I love, have been better off if I'd just kept my story to myself and learned to deal? Couldn't I have just pushed on alone?

There is a wall of regret that will always be inches from my nose. I think maybe, the wall won't be so dense if I say I am sorry. The three short words collect in my chest, they move up sluggishly to my mouth, teeter on the tip of my tongue.

But Babbaye speaks first.

"My wife," he says, resting his elbows on the windowsill, "my wife willed her womb to first make six boys. To replace my martyred brothers. Kidist Mariam granted my wife six boys. Then, my wife travelled to Gishen to pray to the Virgin: close my womb, firmly and permanently, as the door to a room a woman never wants to re-enter. The Virgin granted once more. But after five years I wished for new fatherhood. 'Wife,' I said, 'I desire a damp child, as we say in the old way.' She said, 'Husband, dip your youngest in a tub of water.'" He smiles at the memory of grandma's wit. "But by the Virgin's grace, we received one more child, a girl, a gift covered in her kisses."

"Not a replacement for anyone."

"No. Simply herself. Tobya."

I look across the courtyard at Gela's closed door. "Babbaye, please believe Gela did not tell me she is my sister." At Tobya's letters to her under the rock. "She wants her mother first," I say, admitting that that's why she had kept quiet, not because she was afraid of Babbaye sending her back to Dessie or wherever.

"She will still want her mother," he says.

"Do you want your daughter still? Now that her full story is known?"

"Tobya wanted to be where all her children are," he says, and repeats the phrase, lingering on each word, his face brightening by an almost childlike wonder of new understanding. "But for me, she would have been. She wanted to see her daughters asleep side by side every night of their youth, as I saw you with Gela yesterday night. She wanted to see the younger grow up trailing the older everywhere she went, helping her, learning from her, irritating her, as I saw you with Gela these five days. All I have seen, my eyes did not deserve. It was for a mother's eyes to have beheld. Your mother spoke the wish of her life, not of her death."

Right. Because in the end, it doesn't matter where one is buried. So much doesn't matter. "She won't mind coming home to you now, Babbaye. I can still bring her. Aba will protest, but he answers to me now. He has much to atone for. And if he followed Ema all over the world for love, he can follow her one last time to where they began their love."

"Leave things be. I have earned my punishment."

"Babbaye, Ema wasn't punishing you. I want you to know, she tried so very hard to find out how a person forgives, so she could forgive you."

Ema pushed me so hard toward forgiveness not because she thought what happened to me wasn't bad enough to hold on to, but because she knew the cost of a life lived without having forgiven. She knew the body will eat away at itself. She wanted to spare mine that worse misery, not deny the misery that had already happened to it. I had been unable to imagine anything worse, but then thinking about the lifetime of pain she and her father caused each other, and themselves, I can.

I look at my fist, clutched tight the way nurses tell you to make your hand when giving blood. Flesh becomes soil. Where Ema is, one day it will become Ethiopia. I step nearer to the window, to Babbaye, and raise my arm.

"Bless this for her then. I will mix it with the earth where she rests."

Almost shyly, he drapes his hand over mine, briefly closes his eyes. I lower my arm. In Ema's room, I roll the soil in the handkerchief where I had collected her hairs from the rollers.

The labourers return in their pickup truck for the chairs.

When they have loaded their truck, Babbaye tells them to move the smaller furniture and décor from Ema's room, and the larger furniture from the two maids' rooms, back into the living room. He gives me their pay and puts me in charge of directing them. I don't know where everything is supposed to go. Babbaye says it's my home. I decide. So I do.

I arrange the room the way I had wanted to find it when I first arrived, full of things older than me: Babbaye's long sofa, three single seaters, coffee table, dining table for eight, television and stand, sideboard, and shelves. I give one of the men Ema's leftover Djarums. He asks me where *The Art of Forgiveness* should go. With you, I tell him, it's brand new.

After the men have gone, Babbaye prepares for bed. I wait for him in his room and receive from him the shirt he wore that day. I toss it from his window, aiming for the clothes washstand in the side alley. It lands on the ground, nowhere near it.

"With more practice," Babbaye says, getting into bed.

Yes, if I had lived with him, this would have been our ritual. I spread a gabi over his bedcover. "Babbaye? When we were leaving Ethiopia, would you have let me stay with you, if I had said I don't want to leave this land?"

"To that there is no answer outside of *yes.*"

"Would you have taken me in if I had wanted to come back?"

"Child, must a tired old man repeat himself?"

I laugh. I take from his dresser drawer the last things missing from the living room, the framed photos of my child self, my grandmother, and my uncles. I line us all on the top row of the living-room shelf. I nudge Ema's photo from above the porch door, stretching up on my tippy toes. I wipe away the water spots and dust and place her at the end of the row.

TWENTY-TWO

In the morning, after Babbaye and I say our goodbyes, I clatter my suitcase and tote down the flagstone path. The noise does not draw Gela out of her house, as I had hoped. The letters are gone. I knock. She opens, holding the letters in one hand, and in the other hand the ends of the shawl she has wrapped around her shoulders. Her black clothes are in my suitcase. I've decided to keep them. That's what sisters do.

"I'm going to stay at Ghion Hotel. Where I wanted to go in the first place." I intend it as an invitation. "I want to spend some time where Ema was, last time she was here."

Without a word, she walks with me to the main road and gets in Wondu's waiting taxi. Wondu perks up, excited to see Gela. I can practically see his brain spinning for something impressive to say in the short time he has with us. He makes the most of it, of course, by driving exceedingly slow, letting many cars nudge into his lane, steering with his palm, resting his other arm on the open window.

We ride alongside a lorry piled high with hundreds of yellow jerry cans strung together. "All that is going to be for water collecting, you know," he blurts, building his ideas as he talks. "I go on field work for Highland Flora—a flower company that exports to Europe." I recognize the name of

Teka's supplier. So I know Wondu is not bullshitting. He looks for Gela's eyes in the rear-view as he talks. "Highland Flora has their rose farm in Oromia, out by Sebeta, just off the road to Jimma. I drive a Rover for them. I can show you a tour."

He pauses to let us be impressed. He shifts to sit straighter in his seat, energized by a new idea. "On the road I see rural girls carrying water in these yellow jerry cans. Their foremothers fetched water in traditional insira. So many tales of love from their time begin with a girl weeping over her broken clay water jar. But now, with unbreakable plastic containers to draw their water in, what love stories can our generation possibly create?"

He shakes his head, regretting this great loss of culture. I think, How about romance which doesn't begin with a girl weeping? Gela, watching the streets go by, ignores him spectacularly. Already, my big sister is teaching me a lesson. Sometimes the best response you can give a man is to just be silent, so he can hear himself.

When Wondu pulls up at Ghion, Gela follows me in. In the incense-cigarette-cologne-perfume-coffee-infused lobby, many people glance at us—one local woman in black dress and netela, one diaspora in flimsy floral sundress and sandals—but no one's gaze stays on us. If Gela was carrying a baby, their eyes might linger, assuming her to be the nanny, wondering if they know, or should know, the rich man whose girl I am.

At the reception desk, Gela finds her voice. "We want 521."

With those words, she finally acknowledges our sisterhood. But 521 is occupied.

"Yes I know," she says. For a split second, I, too, believe Ema is in the room. She would be smoking on the balcony, the TV volume turned up on Al Jazeera so she can hear it, wondering what is taking us so long, rubbing her ash into the stone railing.

"The guest is expecting you?" the receptionist says.

"Remember me?" Gela says, as if she were here two days, not two years, ago.

"What's the name of the guest, please?"

I wait for Gela, Gela waits for me, to say the name. But neither of us want to spoil the illusion. This could have been real, if Ema hadn't hid Gela, if Ema had let me stay with Babbaye when I wanted to. Gela and I could have been two regular sisters going up to see their mom who is visiting from abroad, bringing us fresh supplies of the toiletries and junk food we've developed a taste for. The three of us could have been so happy.

I slide over my global discount card. "Give us whatever you have."

•••

Gela unlatches the balcony door of room 421, one level directly below Ema's, and steps out of view through the curtains. I turn Al Jazeera on and sit on the bed. Banners across the bottom of the screen say that all flights are expected to resume in a day. I will hear from Barb soon. Almost a week has passed since Eyjafjallajökull erupted. Still, no news anchor has learned to pronounce its name, which reads as if it were made by a tomcat skipping across a keyboard.

Through netela-thin white curtains, I spy on Gela, in plain sight, as from day one. There are two wicker chairs on the balcony, but she crouches on the cement ground, fidgeting with her letters. I go out to the balcony.

From up here, Addis's ugly spill of metal, wood, and glass is almost scenic.

Gela stares vacantly through the gaps shaped like the Axum Obelisk in the balcony railing. I say, "My father claims the obelisks were the pagan Axumites' grave markers."

Gela is as responsive as a statue. Maybe I shouldn't have mentioned fathers.

"Symbolizing doorways to the afterlife." Shut up, D. No one cares. Faint pop music wafts up from the patio restaurant. The nebulous clouds of steam on the thermal pool are mesmerizing.

"You can see better from up here."

In the pool, children splash and dive, their wet, black hair pasted on their gleaming brown skin. They shout up to me, making silly faces. I tap my chest. *Me?* They flop around in the water, slapping their butts. *Yes you.* I blow them kisses. They mime choking. I ball up my fists under my eyes in a pretend cry. I stick my tongue out at them. They bellow *ahhh* while slapping their palms against their open mouths.

I look up. Sure enough, there is a plane passing overhead. "When you were little did you also yell at the airplanes in the sky?"

Gela looks up. Thank God, a sign of life. "When I wished they brought my mother."

I turn and lean on the railing. "How was it when you were upstairs with her, when you had her all to yourself?"

She puts the letters down, unfolds herself from the corner and stands in front of me.

"I should ask you to tell me about having her all to yourself. What are my rare few days, my two weeks, when you have had her for twenty-seven years?"

"And yet, you were a better daughter than me. Good, loving, forgiving."

She opens her arms in supplication. "Please, my sister,"

she says, hopelessly, knowing she will be rejected. "Still bring my mother. Don't deny that I, too, can bury her." A breeze nudges the unbound letters toward the edges of the balcony and the gaps. "Give her to me now. Even after the end. I will take her. Because such is my fortune."

When she welcomed me on the first day, falling, weeping, it had seemed part performance, but now her hoarse voice, the hiccups she suppresses, the vein tracing a path down her temple, are all true. The way she says *sister* has blood in it. One by one, the letters flutter through the gaps in the railing and land on the branches of trees, the surface of the pool, the lower balconies, the thatched roof of the patio restaurant. On the wet children. As if the papers have an innate wisdom, not one piece glides on the wind back to where we stand, from where they have been released.

"Please, my sister. Our mother is gone. Aren't I, your living sister, enough for you?" I say. But I sound hopeless, too. I know I'm not enough for her any more than she is enough for me. There are angular spaces in us only a mother as sharp-edged as Ema can fill. Gela grabs and tries to kiss my hand. I pull away. "It's her you want? So go to her. In letters, in visits, she has always been the one to come to you. Now is your turn to go to her."

Gela looks pained. "How? I am a dog leashed to this land."

Now I'm the one making up my ideas as I go. "I will help you. You are my sister. I am allowed to bring my sister into my country." With those scars on her face, we could claim she's a veteran. No one would doubt us. "Ema should have brought you when we all left. That day, I cried very hard, you know. Do you think my soul sensed you were being left behind?"

Why not, I think. What if the problem all along hasn't been those of us who left failing to return, but that there has been one who should have flown away with us, whose departure has been too long delayed? Our future can belong just as much in the outside-country where we have already committed the first, the best of us, to its equally welcoming earth.

"My father says you are dead. I will bring you to life." Gela gasps and begins to cross herself. I stop her hands. "No. No more rituals. *I* am your deliverer. I know you have dreams. I dream, too. I was always good at drawing. I want to help people paint their stories if words in any language won't do. What do you want to be?"

This idea of leaving here is already growing on her, I can tell, because she tells me the truth that I know. "A dressmaker?"

"Say it like a statement! I talked to Babbaye about coming too. Four days ago, he didn't want to hear of going to outside-country to see Ema's grave. But this morning, he didn't say no. You will accompany him. I will show you everything about Ema in Toronto, in Vienna. Now, please, show me how you spent your time here with her. This room is identical to hers, I'm sure. Let's pretend she was here. I want to share in her time here through you. I want to know where she sat, which side of the bed she slept on. Where she kept her things. Even from which cup she drank her coffee." I pull her inside. "Come on sister, let's play."

Gela satisfies my demand. She remembers everything. Every inch of a room our mother never entered becomes crowded with her, Tobya, Zimita, Ema, Welete-Mikael—the teenager who was ordered to start over, the mother who wanted still to have her child know her, the woman who loved the man but not his son, the woman who could help the son but not rescue the daughter, the woman who had to lose both daughters so she could keep them, the woman who believed her body was poison. Our mother becomes numberless, more than the sum of all her names.

We end up back in the lobby, where an entire corner is a stage set of a large, permanent coffee service. Gela sits on one of the three-legged duka arranged in a semicircle around the server. I ease myself into the low scalloped seat of the stool next to hers, praying the inward curving legs do not give out under me. Focusing on one muscle group at a time, I cross my ankles and tuck them in, trying to imitate Gela's demure elegance, which matches the server's.

The server is a poster-worthy brown Venus, hair plaited back in shurruba like our grandmother, wearing a blue hager libs decadently embroidered in gold, green, and purple on the wrists, neckline, down the centre, and around the hem fanned out at her feet. She sits on a platform behind a brazier of hot coals that sear a jumbo jebena even I couldn't drink all of in one go.

For once, Gela and I are going to be served. The other customers gathered for this mid-morning coffee are a mix of tourists, locals, expats, and in-betweens—the kind who live abroad half the year and sport at least one patriotic tattoo. There are also the latest generation of business-class dads I know so well from work, who after a few drinks always lament to me how with their frequent absences they've already repeatedly broken their children's hearts long before their children are old enough to break theirs.

The jebena spouts steam like a freight train. The server lifts it off the coals and sets it at an angle on a woven ring to settle. She holds out a bowl of kolo to the customer to her immediate right. The roasted grains are passed around, each person taking a token pinch. With a pair of tongs, she removes a few lumps of red-hot coal from the brazier and drops them into an incense holder. She heaps a spoonful of loose, rocky incense from a mesob, a mini version of grandma's mesob, and sprinkles it on the coals. A cloud of smoke curls up into a thin hypnotic line.

"Sign of a good day to come," the server says, pouring the coffee high and thin.

"You have bigger cups?" Gela asks her.

"It is okay," I say. "For this round let's be the same."

The server stands and walks around the circle with the tray of sini brimming with scalding black coffee. I lift one carefully by the rim, not wanting to burn myself but aware also that her dress is dangerously close to the fire while she waits for us to help ourselves. We drink our hot-as-love buna, lost in our separate thoughts—what Wondu would call "private moments."

"He was so curious about you," I say.

"Who?"

I give her a look. She knows who. She has known, from the way he held her body when she cried on the ground on the morning of my arrival, from the way he pretended to be confused by a simple gate latch, from his earlier attempts at smooth talk. But I don't press the point. Our sisterhood is too new for frank boy talk. We return our empty sini to the server, and wait for the second round, watching loopy incense smoke merge with loopy cigarette smoke.

I ask something I feel I do have a right to know. "What's Dessie like?"

"Nothing special."

"I would love to visit."

"It's a rest stop on the way to better places."

"You have people there?"

"Not anymore."

"They died?"

"Could have, by now."

"Is it fair you know everything about me?"

"No one can know everything about anyone."

"But let us balance our stories a little bit. Who raised you in Dessie?"

She sighs, exhausted with her little sister. She wets her fingertips on her tongue and twists the strands of the fringe of her netela in pairs. "My father's parents. The year I was born, 1978, the government sent my father to the Eritrean front to fight for Ethiopia, knowing his parents were immigrants from Eritrea. They had lived in Dessie since the time of the emperor. Whether he defected to his ancestral side, or died, we don't know. He never returned."

Like mother like daughter indeed. Of all the boys Ema could have hooked up with when she was out of her parents' house, she had to pick an Eritrean. And now look at me, with Isak, my Talyan boy.

"So... your grandparents?"

"Seventeen years ago, they voted for Eritrean independence in the referendum, never thinking that a war would come and they would be deported to an Eritrea they had not seen in forty years."

My mouth hangs open. What has been merely the background noise of my life—Babbaye's grumblings about his enemy's enemy, Ema's constant trips for mediations—has been Gela's real life, not in the least abstract. The most I'd thought about it was if Ema happened to have "Hab Dahlak" playing, and even then only brief ruminations on how it seemed all the Eritreans ever wanted, from the British, the Talyans, the Ethiopians, was to be left alone. And was that too much to ask? Why should one be bound to a family one never chose?

"How did you escape being deported?"

"Escaping is what criminals do."

"Sorry."

"Our Ethiopian mother saved me." I remember one of Ema's letters, about "recent troubles" Ema swore she would keep Gela safe from. "That was when I came to live with the Shaleqa."

"So long ago."

"I told you, I have been there some years."

"Eleven years is more than some years. I thought you came last month."

The server hands out the second round of coffee. "When I look at our map," Gela says, sipping her drink, "I see the borders as they used to be. I try to un-see it, look at the shapes of Ethiopia and Eritrea separately, but I can't. I know the new border is there, clearly drawn in black. They will kill each other over one millimetre of it. All the same, my eyes refuse. I must force myself to not see the whole, what used to be."

I feel terrible for her. Almost everyone she loves—mother, father, grandparents, maybe even me—has always been on the other side of a border she can't cross.

Haltingly, I say, "Maybe, because borders are what you make of them? What the heart knows is stronger than what they tell you is real."

"Maybe."

"Stay with me. I have to go, but you can stay here as long as you want. Switch to 521 when it becomes available."

"The Shaleqa's is my only home."

"At least let me call Wondu to drive you back."

"That hustler?" she sneers.

"Can you blame him?"

She shrugs. "Our grandfather has been by himself all morning. God knows what you gave him for breakfast. I have to return soon. Call who you want."

I decide this is progress enough for now. When Wondu texts to let me know he has arrived, I walk her to the parking lot. His eyes sparkle with delight when she opens the front passenger seat.

She pauses before climbing in. "So, am I to wait until you send for me?"

"I'll return for you."

"When?"

I spit on the ground. "Before that dries."

She shoves me playfully. I catch her hand and draw her into a hug. We hold for many breaths, our chests rising and falling in time.

"I'm sorry I mishandled your letters," I say.

"I have others."

"Is . . ." I don't know how to ask her if the rest of my story is in any of them. But she feels my question somehow, and steps back so I can see the answer in her eyes. *Yes.*

"You, little flower, are a miracle," she says. I feel newly created. "Don't be a grinning tree out here. Go back inside."

Those were the first words she said to me when I arrived, if I don't count the wailing. My stomach feels sloshy with tears as Wondu takes her away from me, but I manage to keep myself together until I get back to our room.

TWENTY-THREE

I'm awakened by a whisper. The balcony door is closed and the curtains hang still. I hear footsteps upstairs. I put a bathrobe over my sundress and pad along the hallway in the anonymous nighttime hush. I take the stairs to the fifth floor, and approach the *Do Not Disturb* sign on the door handle of room 521. No light under the door. I press my ear against it. No sound. From a tray of leftovers on the carpet, I collect slices of tomato, strawberries, and honeydew. I return to the stairwell, eating my findings, bypass my floor, and come out at the far end of the lobby. I push enormous, wood-framed glass doors open onto the landing overlooking the garden, patio, and pool area. I go down two stone staircases, past chairs upturned on the patio restaurant tables. There is a low, feeble metal fence around the pool. I hop over it, crushing young blooms into the soft earth under my heels.

I climb to the highest diving platform and walk to the edge. Steam rolls off the water below, like wind-chased clouds, obscuring the cross-shaped water. The greenery is pulsing globs of oil paint. I look up at the hotel building. The dim glow from my bedside lamp is a setting sun in the dark, looming mass of the hotel. Ema is not watching me from the unlit balcony above. She won't rush down to scold me, to make sure that nothing on me is broken. She knows I won't jump again.

This silence, save for the gossipy leaves and smacking water, is the best conversation between Ema and I.

I sit on the edge of the platform, swinging my feet, creating invisible ripples in the air with my toes. The turnstile squeaks as someone comes into the pool area. I pull up my feet, expecting hotel staff. It's a guest. A man, the leathery-tanned, lithe, ponytailed Aryan species endemic to Africa. Of course he'd enter in the civilized way, past the ticket booth, and even leave money at the counter. He dives into the pool and swims vigorously, causing a minor tsunami in his wake, slapping the water with his oar-like arms as if it has offended him.

So much for companionable peace. I walk back down the platform to the ladder. That's when I see Ema's room is ablaze, every light is on, when just moments ago the room was dark. I descend the ladder, and sit on the edge of the pool, the hem of my robe lapping the water. The man makes contact with my legs. He rears up from the water, pasting back his hair on his head.

"The fuck! I didn't know anyone else was here."

"Why not? You're here."

He blinks at me. He's forgotten English, or thinks I'm a hallucination. I point behind me at the hotel building. "That's you?"

"My wife is forever on my case about lights," he says to my chest.

When *my wife* is among the first words a man says to me, I know he already wants to sleep with me and is reminding himself why he shouldn't.

"What's your room like?" I say, reaching under my robe to adjust my perfectly secure dress strap.

"What's my room like?"

"Show me? When you're done here."

Hey presto, he's done. He heaves his long, toned person out of the water, throws his robe on, and leads the way. "I'm Braam."

We're doing names? "Beza."

While the Scandinavian gets ice, I stalk room 521, wary as a cat, willing there to be something, anything, Ema might have left behind and that was miraculously never found by two years of guests or housekeeping staff.

"You look as if you are searching for evidence of another woman. No forgotten earring, alas. I'm alone," he says when he comes back. His words sound as if he has spoken them before, to another woman, perhaps in another language, when she surprised him in a hotel. He scoops up ice with the glasses and cracks open mini bottles of Rémy.

"My mother stayed in this room once. She died."

He blushes so hard it shows through his tan. "In here?"

"No. I mean recently."

"My condolences." He pours the drinks, gives me a glass. "To...?"

I toss back the stinging cognac. Our hands touch again when I return the glass. I point at some papers with the logo of Highland Flora on the coffee table.

"This from your job?"

"You know the company?"

"My mother grew roses all her life, the same plant, many gardens."

"I'm a breeder. I come up with new cultivars. My latest, seven years I spent in the lab, maximizing her vase life, bud size, hip width, stem length."

"Her colour must not be a selling point."

He approaches me. I stand my ground. "She's the colour of every woman's rose." He picks up the papers, charts with thumbnails of different roses. "My latest is this one."

Some tight, pink number. "Heidi? Doesn't sound very Ethiopian."

"I named her after my daughter."

"Perks of being a breeder, eh?"

"You could say."

I see photos of the red and white roses Teka had given me, also known as Gloria and Athena. I brush his fingertips with mine. "You're pruning."

"Sorry?"

"When you've been in the water too long, see the ridges? It's called pruning."

He puts the papers on the coffee table, coils his arms around my lower back, pulls me in to feel his erection. "I also do grafting," he says suggestively. He talks while kissing me. His mouth tastes of ash. I feel the honeydew come up the back of my throat. "After all my hard work, plus three years spent getting her ready for market, I come to Addis Ababa to shepherd the first batch of ten thousand to the auction, and what happens?"

"Something big and hard erupts."

"All the way up to the sky. Ten thousand Heidi rot on a Cairo tarmac for a week."

"Wouldn't want to be there when they open that cargo door."

"That's exactly my fate, tomorrow."

As in, we'll never see each other again. As in, are we doing this or not? The night is old.

"Why don't you go freshen up?" I say.

"We can freshen up together."

"Darling I was born clean." I slap his ass. He jogs to the bathroom, pulling down his shorts. The minute I hear the shower start, I grab a teacup from the breakfast bar, the closest thing to a memento of Ema I will have from 521, and scram.

TWENTY-FOUR

When Ema took up her first of two postings in Rome, Babbaye had started going to our old house. He would walk across Addis Ababa and sit all day on a boulder across the road from our gate, sometimes helping himself to a koshim fruit from the hedge. This went on for weeks. The expat tenants' watchman left the old man in peace, but the unnerved tenants contacted the district authorities, who in turn contacted the real estate broker, who in turn contacted Aba, who in turn passed the problem to Ema. She called Babbaye to ask him what he was doing there, as if there might be a valid explanation. His response was, *I have come for mine.*

So have I. I have come back to my childhood home, for me. It is my last stop before the airport. Barb did call finally, after I went back to bed for a few more hours' sleep last night, to tell me to report for duty this morning. I said to wait for me, I had stuff to do.

She thought I'd lost my mind. "You want the flight to wait for you?"

"What can I say, Barb. Sometimes you *can't* take the girl out of Ethiopia."

My new, as yet nameless, taxi driver wanders in my old neighbourhood, which has become a mishmash of new shops and eateries. Granted, my directions were less than specific, but Wondu would have found it, if he didn't already have a date with Gela at Effoi pizzeria.

The driver passes a new high-rise hotel several times. He holds no hope of finding the house because everything in this area has been redeveloped. Then I see that the hotel occupies the land of the house which used to stand behind ours, the cats' shortcut from our place to the main road. We drive around the hotel and into what is now a paved, gated zone. Perhaps because it's daytime, the road barrier is up and the guard booth unmanned.

The dense koshim hedge concealing our house is the only bit of nature in the row of new brick boundary walls topped by electrical barbed wire, protecting a mountain range of mansions that have risen around our compound. Our rooftop, visible over the top of our gate, looks so pitifully small in comparison to the grandiose villas that it could be mistaken for the service quarters. I order the taxi driver to wait for me, no matter how long I stay. I intend to go into my garden, into the room where I lost my childhood, to cast out forever the demons in the walls of my bedroom and lurking behind the door.

Most of the baby blue paint on our gate has peeled, exposing metallic grey underneath. The outer doorbell hangs like a popped eyeball. I press it. The house next door has been turned into a bar. Drinkers on the patio upstairs, birds of prey attracted by my red uniform, watch me from above. A watchman half-opens the small door in our gate. He's bundled up in a knit scarf and army surplus style trench coat. After a period of mutual staring, I accept he can't just tell by looking at me that I am the first inhabitant of this place.

"I know this house."

"No one is living here," he says, suspicious.

I was too young when we left to have been issued a district ID card with the house number, which would identify me as connected to here. Impersonating Babbaye's powerful tone, which tells and does not ask, I say, "This is my childhood home. I am looking in."

The guard pulls out a flip phone from the folds of his coat and dials uncertainly, as if the keypad is a Ouija board. Barely two rings later, he hangs up.

"No answer. I have not been told to let anyone in."

I sigh heavily and go through the motions of the powerless. I've picked them up from Lomi and Aberash. I set my face in a broken, resigned expression and step back, eyes downcast, adding a deferential bow, mumbling, "Igziabher repay you." Just as he begins to shut the door, I flip the script. I hold out two hundred birr. "For your troubles."

He is unimpressed, never mind the birr are crisp from the Ghion ATM. I stuff them in my purse. I pull out a Canadian ten dollar bill instead. He looks at me fiercely, as if I am taking him for a fool. He's about to slam the door in my face when I produce an American ten dollar bill.

He takes it and swings the door wide. "As you want."

I step over the threshold. The hibiscus, bougainvillea, yewef zer, bottlebrush of my childhood bob their heads in the breeze, seeming to say, yes we remember you too, little flower. I trek through the front garden. The mefakiya has been trimmed down to knee height, or perhaps it was only ever that high. The lawn seems minuscule now, as if it has shrunk away from the expanding stone tile.

"What happened to the roses? Here were yellows, there were pinks."

The watchman pats the diagonal tips of bunches of short stems sticking out of the ground between the mefakiya. "The gardener makes cuts at this time."

I squat to one such drastically pruned rosebush, pressing one hand on the moist earth for balance. The watchman squats, feet flat, legs folding easy. He crumbles the loose soil like so many lumps of soft gold.

"It is good earth," he says.

"Good enough to eat."

"Isn't it so?"

"I used to make people. Their dusty-wet aroma, so irresistible, a mother's scent."

The bedroom window on the right side of the house is shuttered. I feel a flash of panic, then remember. I am outside, safe, and all of the windows are shuttered, not just the one.

I adjust my purse strap. "I am going inside the house."

He nods, smartly interpreting my casual gesture to mean more American dollars are in it for him if he complies. He walks back to the gate to shut the door. He is short but thick, with arms sculpted by labour, or perhaps violence. But I don't feel even a twinge of fear that I am going to be alone with a strong man in an empty house and not a soul, save for the taxi driver, knows I'm here. And he may abscond, figuring he'll get more value out of whatever is in my bags than what's in my wallet.

The watchman and I walk down the driveway, past the cinderblock wall and the car shed, to the backyard. He unlocks the back door and leads the way, turning on the lights as we walk through the small family dining room, then the formal one, and the living room. Unfurnished spaces should feel bigger, but this is a dollhouse. The watchman blabbers about how well the house has held up for being over thirty years old, too bad it will be demolished sooner or later, how the person who bought it has patiently waited as the land value skyrocketed year after year, waiting for the perfect time to sell for a maximum return on his investment. The last phrase, perhaps having heard it often, he says in English.

I am trying to feel something beyond language. In the dining rooms, bathrooms, hallway, the nook where the phone used to be: nothing. I can't believe I feel nothing now, when I endured such vivid terror here for three years. I walk more quickly than I want to, trying to lose the man for even a precious half minute, so that the past might creep forward with the shakiness of a traumatized puppy. At the end of the dark hallway, much shorter than I remember, where there's nowhere left to go but to the bedrooms, my legs won't budge. I sift through my store of Amharic for a tactful way to tell the guard to let me have a moment alone.

"Wait outside."

His wariness comes back. "Why?"

"I need personal time in here."

He regards me with a look that says, not kindly, who can ever understand why diaspora do what they do?

"What is in here but walls, windows, floor?"

"Brother, don't you have a special place, where you grew up and wish to go back to, so you can go forward?"

"My lady, I grew up on Kazanchis road. I go back to it every evening," he boasts in the way of sufferers.

"This place has tizita for me."

"You are too young. From what I am told, the first owners left for outside-country with their children twenty years ago."

"Nineteen. They had one child only. I won't stay long. Please work with me."

I adjust my purse.

On cue, he obliges, walking out the way he came, through the living and dining rooms, to the back door. I hear him switch off all the lights, and the shriek of metal on concrete as he pushes the back entrance closed.

I reach the end of the hallway in three strides. Then, the bedroom. I enter the dark and stand in the middle. I lock the door. It's pitch black now, save for pinpricks of light coming through the lowered shutters.

I unfurl my neckerchief and let it fall. I unbutton my shirt and remove it with my blazer. I take off my skirt, slip, nylons, shoes, underwear, bra. I walk naked to the bed. I don't bump into the past, into the body of Le'ul. I wait to hear his commands. There is no sound. No cool, soft hands. No scrape of a withered fingernail on my skin. My inner thighs touch only each other. Only tingling air outlines my body.

I lift my hand out to my side to feel for the shutter ribbon. I find it. I wonder if I could have reached it then from the bed; if I could have exposed us; if I could have saved myself so easily. I pull the ribbon. Sunlight leaps in. Illuminated, the room is still nothing more than the facts of it. Built-in closets. Aged hardwood floor. Dirty white walls. I drop the shutter. I dress, unlock the door, pull out the skeleton key. A flimsy thing. I bury it in my pocket. I look through the keyhole. There is the bedroom where my mother and father slept through my terror.

I open the door and cross the gap between the bedrooms. No doll in my parents' room.

I retrace my steps back down the hall. I crouch in the dim phone nook and breathe, little by little, until I fill out from girl to woman and beyond, too big for the walls to contain me. I have to go outside. Dry-faced, calm, I walk out to the front yard.

In a far corner of the lawn, there is a boulder as big as Ema's headstone. I guess that must be what Babbaye used to sit on. The tenants probably rolled it in here from outside, to pre-empt any more visits from the strange father of their distant landlady. But when I get close to it, I realize it's a giant tortoise, soft parts retracted, but alive with the quiet self-importance of a paperweight.

The koshim is so thick it has swallowed its thorns. The bottlebrush tree in the centre of the lawn, on its own circular patch of soil, has grown so much the drooping branches touch the grass, hiding the trunk. Back when the tree was young, Ema and Aba, their passion ignited by her first surgery and believing the worst had passed, used to sit underneath it every evening, leaning against each other to spare the tender trunk their combined weight. They would stay there until the moon joined them. If it was the warm season, my bedroom window was left open. I would fall asleep to the soft bubbling stream of their murmurs. Tizita. Remembered pain, remembered pleasure, a sweet melancholy for a lost place and time, for a love, for a mood your soul revisits endlessly.

I missed happiness here by such a narrow margin. It was as close as the hibiscus under the bedroom window, where, on the odd days when I felt brave, I would hide in a crowd of leaves, to delay the inevitable.

Such memories aside, it is a beautiful house. Deep red brick, plenty of space to park cars, to play. French windows which open to a generous porch, cream-coloured iron grille railing, a lawn with enough space for a pan fry of the string-cut, marinated meat of a whole sheep. A lawn dripping pink and yellow and burgundy from plants looming like gentle elders. A house you should pass down. But I have all the inheritance I want from here. My key. He will never lock me in again.

TWENTY-FIVE

At Bole airport, the telltale red of my CanAir flock is nowhere to be seen in the parking lot or the terminal. Barb's phone is off. They didn't wait for me. I'm glad. At the ticket office, I join a lineup of stranded travellers all trying to get out of Addis Ababa at the same time. I have no choice but to buy a ticket for a labyrinthine journey with multiple stopovers. No rush. I will get home.

I text Isak. *On the move! Will reach Boston in 2 days. Meet at Peet's?*

I email him a picture of my itinerary. It settles in for the long wait in my Outbox, like the passengers at my gate, a separate glass-enclosed area with its own entrance, bordered by other gates, the security screening area, and the walkway to and from planes. We're all early to resume interrupted journeys, our faces dazed like people who've awoken from a long, disturbing dream when we hadn't meant to fall asleep in the first place.

One row down from me, a little cross-eyed habesha boy plays with a puzzle. He is so small his feet stick straight out from his seat. He is like a tiny professor, with Coke-bottle glasses too big for his face, a sweater with elbow patches, and corduroy pants. I instinctively love this boy. I feel a primal concern that when he messes up in life, there will always be someone who will remember his once innocence.

The boy completes the puzzle and looks up, proud of himself, at a middle-aged white woman in a yoga outfit, who I think is his adoptive mother. I look to her, to make sure she is not wasting this moment. She is looking at me, as are a lot of the people at the gate, collectively willing for me to turn toward the gangway.

There, beyond the glass, like a fixed pillar around which arriving passengers flow, is Le'ul.

I am stunned. A memory of the after-time crashes through. I am coming around the side of my house. I feel Le'ul's glassy, hungry stare. I turn and see him at the window. I hear the summon of his eyes, *Go clean yourself.*

My phone rings in my purse. Le'ul has his phone to his ear. I stand up and walk to him, slowly at first, then suddenly I charge the glass and slam it with my palm. Le'ul leaps away, startled, as if I'm a tame zoo creature that's suddenly gone wild.

Of course he would come all the way here. Hadn't I been braced for it since he called for me at the house yesterday? A couple of annoyed airport security staff get him to move along with inviting gestures that are really strict orders. They follow him close until he reaches and disappears down the escalator.

"Who was he?" a nearby passenger says to me.

"Nobody." But Le'ul is not nobody, no matter how much I wish it so. I pick up my purse and walk to the security check. I prowl for Le'ul from security through passport control, customs, baggage claim, and in the expectant crowd gathered behind the barriers in front of the sliding doors discharging passengers.

At the Arrivals café, a lone patio island in a sea of black-and-white marble, I sit at a table for four. The waiter comes. I tell him to first take away two chairs. I don't need a mother and father any more. Twenty-one years ago, Ema and Aba could have made a real difference by talking to Le'ul and me openly, instead of doing roundabout hocus pocus on Le'ul, convincing themselves that I was all right. But now, the reckoning can only be between Le'ul, the brother I never asked for, and me, the sister he never deserved.

The waiter brings my order, bombolino and a tea. And one large mineral water, which I tell him to open, but leave the cap. Then Le'ul comes, composed, stern again. But fear peeks through his mask. He drapes his jacket on the back of the other chair, brushes the seat, tosses his phone, wallet, and keyring—my condo key included—on the table.

I gnaw an enormous bite of my sugar-coated lump of deep-fried dough. I blow on my tea, replace the cup on the saucer.

"I'm going to let this cool."

He interlocks his hands on the table. I lick my sugar moustache.

"What you started to say on the phone. Don't say any more."

I'm cold. That is all I remember.

I take a second bite. "Or else what?" I say, spraying crumbs out of my mouth.

"Aba will find out what you're really doing here."

Savour my pastry. Sip my tea. I put up my finger, channelling Isak. I laugh. I feel a little kooky. "Firstly, there's no law which says buried once, buried forever. Secondly, do you think Aba will be more *disturbed* by what I almost did to a dead body than what you did many times over to mine?"

Le'ul's mask dissolves completely. He looks terrified. All this time I was scared of him, he was actually the one scared of me. He had admitted as much, inadvertently, by threatening to kill me if I told.

He fidgets with the bottle cap, scrapes the bottle label with it. I wipe my hands clean of oil and sugar. Easy as that, I can kill this so-called grown man. To this day, Le'ul has had no idea, or he has been in denial, that his parents have known what he did to their daughter. Not everything, but enough to drag him on pilgrimage to an exorcist. But there is no demon here. Only an avenging angel. I will rob him of his life. He has robbed me of mine. There has always been the skin-crawling intimacy of a murderer and his victim between us. It's high time we reversed roles. Who wouldn't rather kill?

I gulp my tea, savouring the lead-up to his annihilation. The warm syrup glides down my throat. I slam down the cup. Le'ul jumps. *He* jumps! I speak too loud too fast like a kid hyper over a brand new toy.

"Why do you think Aba took you on pilgrimage to Kulubi in '91, before Vienna, and whatever rituals they did on you while you were there? It was what, more spiritual tourism? And after you came to Vienna, with the holy water, the prayer on your head every night? Was Aba initiating you into the priestly life he himself abandoned, oh, Kidane-Gabriel?"

He scrapes his hand with the bottle cap. "That was father-son time."

"Oh like your annual vacations for two?" Maybe that was Aba's way of giving me some respite from Le'ul.

"Yes."

He looks so boyishly happy with the memories that something stays my tongue. A new feeling where my fear used to be. I don't know what it is. *Is love not better?* Aba had asked me by the lake. Yes, Aba. But it's still too late for love. The closest I can come to love, much less forgiveness, for Le'ul—this lost soul who'll spend his life evading the magnitude of his wrongs, clamouring for shreds of peace—is pity.

"Love was all I was offering you, when we were little, in the form of an innocent game meant to make you smile. Why did you respond with terror? A brother protects."

"I don't know why. I'm sorry."

"Did you ever stop to think what kind of damage you were doing? Or you did, but didn't care? Why was I just flesh to be used?"

"I wasn't thinking. I'm sorry."

"You didn't always hate me. Tell me the *why*."

"I never hated you."

"Why did you come into my family?"

"I didn't. I was sent."

"So leave. You should have, long ago. Go back to shoe-shining. You still have your listro box? Maybe some mediocre photographer will snap arty pictures of you, too."

I brace for him to lunge across the table and attack me. He bends the bottle cap, blinking away tears. "So long I've wanted to beg your forgiveness."

"For? Name *it*."

"What I made you do."

"*Name it.* You do something so horrible, for so long, but can't speak the name once?"

"Erasing you."

I grab the bottle, wanting to smash it on his skull, drag the edge across his neck. He flinches. "Don't flatter yourself, you failed." I sit back, clutching my weapon. "So what now? Confess to Aba yourself. Let him know who he has for a son, what kind of brother he gave me."

"He is suffering already. The blame, the responsibility, the guilt, the shame should only be mine, always has been mine."

"This better not be your grief talking."

"Something was wrong with me."

"Something is. So, what now?"

He extracts my key from his keychain, too slowly, what with his shrivelled index fingernail. He offers the key to me, his hand spasming, as if he's scared I'll stab him with it. But the thrill of thinking up ways to torment him is already old. I blink fast, to banish the speck blurring my vision.

"Keep the damn key. I don't live there anymore. I am going to be where and with whom I want. You, stay away from me. I used to wish so much that you would find wherever the dead go and recognize it enough to stay. Make my wish come true now, be dead to me. Trouble me again, Aba will hear about every detail of checking-time from me. You will become again some feral little thing, wandering the streets, starved for love. Whatever scraps you ever got, will ever get, from your borrowed father is thanks to me. Never forget. That's the *or else.*"

I pour water from the bottle on my palm, and toss it in his face. "From holy springs. Full of healing minerals."

Then, I stand up and leave him, really leave him, behind.

As I journey to Departures, I feel I'm catching up to the before-girl who races speeding planes. One day, I will fall in perfect time with her. As one, she and I will sprint down the observation deck until, at the edge, freed from gravity's jealous grip, we soar. We will rise and keep rising, flapping our blue butterfly wings to the rhythm of a little phrase that once began a broken child's letter.

No body know one thing about me.

ACKNOWLEDGEMENTS

Thank you to my parents for steadfast love, and initiating me to the wonder of books!

Much misgana to my tribe of sisters, repeat readers, commentators, advisors: Meseret Mekonnen, Serkalem Mekonnen, Elsa Haile, Djamila Ibrahim, Heran Tsedeke, Adey Kidanu, Rehaset Yohanes. Thank you to the best cheerleaders Haimanot Kidanu, Milka Khattar, Colin Knight, Omar Khattar. Betam ewedachualehu! And Biggie, you're all right too.

My agent Marilyn Biderman, thank you for tenaciously championing my work and patiently addressing my million concerns. The Goose Lane Editions team, thank you for bringing this novel to the world. Paula Sarson, thank you for insightful, exquisite copyediting.

A special thank you to my golden editor Bethany Gibson, for going above and beyond, trusting my impulses, and making me a better writer.

Karen Connelly and Janice Zawerbny, thank you for multiple reads, edits, and your mentoring and friendship. Pauline Holdstock, Helen Walsh, Erika Westman, thank you for your kindness and support. Thank you to editor Erin Parker for substantive and stylistic edits on an early draft. Sarah Curley, via Becky Blake, thank you for telling me about flight attendant life.

I am grateful for the support of the Writers' Trust Scholarship through the Humber School for Writers, and the funding of the Ontario Arts Council, the Toronto Arts Council, and through the OAC Recommender Program: Diaspora Dialogues, Mawenzi House Publishers, Dundurn Press, Inanna Publications.

Finally, thank you, dear reader.

Rebecca Fisseha explores the universal and unique aspects of the Ethiopian diaspora in her writing. She was born in Addis Ababa and now lives in Toronto.

A graduate of York University, the Vancouver Film School, and the Humber School for Writers, Rebecca Fisseha is the author of *wise.woman*, a play that reimagines the legend of King Solomon and the Queen of Sheba, produced by b current in Toronto. Her articles and short fiction have appeared in *Selamta: the in-flight magazine of Ethiopian Airlines*, the *Maple Tree Literary Supplement*, *Room Magazine*, the *Aesthetica Magazine Creative Writing Anthology*, and *Joyland Magazine*. *Daughters of Silence* is her first novel.

photo: Chris Frampton